Love's Winning Plays

ALSO BY INMAN MAJORS

The Millionaires
Wonderdog
Swimming in Sky

Love's Winning Plays

INMAN MAJORS

W. W. NORTON & COMPANY

New York   London

For information about permission to reproduce selections from this book,
write to Permissions, W. W. Norton & Company, Inc.,
500 Fifth Avenue, New York, NY 10110

For information about special discounts for bulk purchases, please contact
W. W. Norton Special Sales at specialsales@wwnorton.com or 800-233-4830

Manufacturing by RR Donnelley Harrisonburg
Book design by Helene Berinsky
Production manager: Julia Druskin

Library of Congress Cataloging-in-Publication Data

Majors, Inman.
Love's winning plays / Inman Majors. — 1st ed.
p. cm.
ISBN 978-0-393-06280-9 (hardcover)
1. Football coaches—Fiction. 2. School sports—Fiction. I. Title.
PS3563.A3927L68 2012
813'.54—dc23

2012020171

W. W. Norton & Company, Inc.
500 Fifth Avenue, New York, N.Y. 10110
www.wwnorton.com

W. W. Norton & Company Ltd.
Castle House, 75/76 Wells Street, London W1T 3QT

1 2 3 4 5 6 7 8 9 0

For Nancy and Nina,
Two great ladies who love to laugh

What it was, was football.

ANDY GRIFFITH

CVD

In the locker room after practice one of the quarterbacks had coined a new song and was performing it to the clapping delight of the others. It went like this:

> *Coach Love rollin down the street*
> *Got that Mack Daddy grin*
> *Gal so fine, she got to be kin*
> *He stepping high, stepping low*
> *Like a Playa above*
> *But do he know, do he know*
> *How to coach that love?*

Unfortunately for Love, the balladeer had a good voice and a capacity for endurance. The lyrics, unsurprisingly in a locker room full of dressing and undressing college men, focused primarily on the juxtaposition between Love's looks and physical endowments and the attractiveness of the woman the players had seen him walking with over the weekend.

During the lion's share of this Love had tried to maintain a certain professional decorum. He'd yet to shower and typically didn't

linger in the players' section of the locker room, but one of the quarterbacks had experienced a tough day and Love was trying to buck
him up a bit, walking him through the three-step drop right there
in the main dressing area. By now, however, the discouraged player
was laughing at the troubadour's lyrics as well as the dance steps
he'd incorporated into the number, and Love saw it was time to give
up the ghost. They'd listen to a graduate assistant coach out on the
field, but in the locker room, their side of the locker room especially,
he was more than fair game.

So with a wave of acknowledgment both to the singer and to
the spirit of the song, namely that Love was in over his head with
Brooke, he passed through the door and into the coaches' dressing
area. Behind him now was call and response:

CALLER: *Coach Love*
RESPONSE: *Badass love machine!*

CALLER: *Say what?*
RESPONSE: *He so bad, he so mean!*

Love had showered and was now dressing on a bench in front
of a number of empty lockers, grabbing his clothes out of a bag
he'd neatly tucked in the corner while out on the field. Though he
was referred to as *Coach Love* by the players and coaches, he wasn't
technically a coach. Instead, his official position was that of an *off
the field graduate assistant*, meaning he did all sorts of things for the
football team, but wasn't allowed to coach during practice or official
player gatherings. The coaching he'd done today was just a volun-
tary workout, one attended exclusively by quarterbacks well down
the depth chart—the walk-ons, the scrubs.

While he dressed, he eyed the empty lockers before him. One
in particular held his attention, for it was the dressing space of the

coaching graduate assistant who had left last week for Clemson. It was his position that Love coveted, for it would mean actual on-the-field coaching and an end to round-the-clock errand running. Of course there'd still be errands to run as one of the low men on the totem pole, but Love would also be on the field during practice and games, instructing players, running drills, a real member of an SEC staff.

How he wanted to be on the field and actually coaching. How he wanted that dressing space. So big it was. So plush. He could fit three changes of clothes in there, an aquarium, a moped. He sat half-dressed on the bench, trying to imagine his name over such a locker.

His name. It really wasn't the greatest to be paired with the word *coach*. His name, when preceded by the standard appellation for one who instructs athletes, sounded like a New Age sex therapist. Or the title of a nasty rap song. He thought Mr. Love sounded okay. As did his given name: Raymond Love. But Coach Love? It was a name to inspire clever athletes, a name to keep the muse on high alert.

Now that same silly name was being called. Or one that sounded a little like it. He turned toward Coach Driver's private dressing area. There it went again. *Lowe! Coach Lowe!*

Love looked around. He was alone in the empty locker room. Slipping on a T-shirt and sandals, he made an uncertain march toward the head coach's quarters.

Coach Von Driver. Now that was a name for a college football coach. Snappy, aggressive, unique.

Coach Von Driver took the SEC by storm, winning a conference championship in his first year at the helm. He followed up that initial success with consecutive top twenty finishes in the polls and back-to-back New Year's Day bowl appearances.

Love stopped just outside the head coach's dressing room, being sure not to intrude in any way, and called out in a hesitant manner: *Coach Driver?*

Yes, Coach Lowe, come in. I've been calling you for five minutes.

Love entered to find a naked fifty-year-old man, hirsute about the shoulders and back, with one equally hairy leg propped up on a chair. This same man was sawing a towel back and forth between his hindquarters and that part of his anatomy that Love least cared to witness au naturel. A fog of antifungal foot spray hung heavy in the air, but not quite as heavy as Love might have liked. He could see clearly.

Now Coach Von Driver went flat-footed, seemingly lost in thought. The towel was limp in his hand, then flung casually over his shoulder, as a matador does his cape. He reached for the sports drink on his desk and drank heartily. Love wasn't sure if he had been summoned simply to bear witness to this or if there was actual business at hand. He stayed where he was, just inside the doorway, trying to look attentive without actually looking anywhere specific.

When the head coach reached for the volume button on the stereo and turned up the music, Love breathed a sigh of relief. Surely this would signal the dressing portion of the performance, a mood enhancer if you will. But no. Apparently the sports drink was only the halftime break, for Coach Driver now hiked his other leg and resumed the two-man-saw action of before.

In his efforts at not watching, Love found himself staring at one of the coaching maxims framed on the far wall. It read:

Every man to the ball!

Love wished he'd picked a different one. He'd just noticed that Coach Driver was not completely nude, but wearing shower shoes. He thought things would have been better without those plastic gizmos.

You like Bon Jovi?

Coach Driver had spoken and Love felt compelled to turn in his direction. He knew it was only his imagination and sense of discomfort that made him think coaches could find more ways to highlight that part of themselves—the part you really and truly didn't want to see—than anyone else on the planet. At this moment that high-lighting was being accomplished by: whipsawing, leg lifting, and a potpourri of flapping, flopping, and flipping.

Love recalled a school field trip to the mountains and an old-timer who could make a little wooden man dance upon a board by jiggling his leg and tapping the board. The wooden doll was loose-limbed and jigged every which way and in the most unpredictable and ramshackle fashion. Love wished this image hadn't popped into his mind just now.

All the while Coach Driver swayed a bit to the music. At a par-ticularly rousing portion of the song, something about cowboys and horses, Love was sure the coach was heading for the dreaded hurdler's pose, but the heartfelt chorus made him reconsider. He stayed as he was, riding the towel like an outlaw on a mustang. He gave the impres-sion of having the wind at his back and a sizable lead on the posse.

Love assumed the question about Bon Jovi was rhetorical and hadn't bothered to answer. But then Coach Driver asked again: so, do you like Bon Jovi?

Love did not. He most assuredly did not. He wondered, not for the first or last time, how Coach Driver had ever ended up coaching down south.

They're all right, he said.

All right? said Coach Driver with mock incredulity. He flung his towel in Love's direction. You country boys don't like anything without a fiddle and a steel guitar, do you? Shit, you wouldn't know rock and roll if it bit you on the ass.

Love didn't consider himself a country boy, but this was the first time the head coach and he had talked about anything remotely casual and he thought he'd best make the most of it. It was rare to see Coach Driver so jovial. He was usually the epitome of the new breed of corporate businessman as head coach, deadly serious and speaking in punchy sound bites like someone practicing to be a motivational speaker. Granted, Love would've preferred slightly more formal attire for the conversation. The head coach was now sitting naked at his desk and rummaging through a travel kit for a chest-hair comb or thigh gel or god only knew what.

Love would draw the line at any nude flossing of teeth.

Suddenly Coach Driver turned around to the marker board behind him where a series of X's and O's were scattered about in offensive and defensive positions. He looked at Love and said: how would you attack a two deep zone?

Love looked at the board as if studying it. He knew his response already, had known it for as long as he could remember. He and his father, a longtime high school coach, had spent hours discussing ways to attack this very alignment.

I don't think the two deep zone can stop a tight end running deep down the middle of the field, said Love, staring intently at the board and not at the nude coach beside it. You send your wideouts on fade patterns or a deep flag and those safeties have to go to them. So that leaves a linebacker, usually, to cover your tight end. If you have a tight end who can run and catch, it's one of the best, and easiest, long plays there is.

Coach Driver went to the board and began drawing the different receiver patterns. For a moment he looked at a stack of clean towels on the leather chair beside him. Love held his breath. A quick towel to the waist would solve a lot of problems. But the head coach was now lost in the moment of diagramming plays. It was a kind of reverie that all serious football men found themselves in. Love had pulled himself out of bed many a night to jot down plays that came to him after a day of studying film. He'd compiled his many notes and diagrams into twenty or so spiral notebooks. This accumulation of football knowledge and philosophy was called *Love's Win-*

ning Plays, and with a mixture of pride and self-consciousness, he labeled each notebook as such.

Coach Driver was making a long stripe across the board to indicate the tight end's progress downfield. When'd he'd finished the diagram, he said: the trouble is finding a tight end who can run deep and then catch it.

Love nodded in an agreeing fashion. He thought now might be the time to venture an opinion to show his football acumen.

That Martin kid might be a player, he said, if he can put on a little weight. He was catching everything that came his way when he worked out with the quarterbacks the other day.

Coach Von Driver said nothing but began, finally, to put on his clothes. He'd taken to dressing like a professional golfer of late after an extended run at imitating the khaki-clad former frat boys who made up the bulk of the university's influential boosters. His first year he'd tried to mesh the gelled hair standard in the northern industrial region with the official baseball cap of the southland, but in year two had opted, much to everyone's pleasure, for the modified tour professional look that coaches had long preferred. In this, his third year, he'd begun mixing in the occasional saucy chapeau: the winter fedora, the summer Panama, the occasional daring derby while on the golf course. Today, sitting on his desk, was a Tampa Straw with a colorful rainbow band as made famous by the golfer Chi Chi Rodriguez. Love knew this accessory was the coach's lone rebellion against the conformity required of the modern coach and it made him feel kindly and protective for a moment and regret, briefly, the many times he'd thought of him as simply a hairy cyborg.

Did I call you Coach Lowe earlier? he asked suddenly, sitting at his desk and eyeing the snappy Chi Chi number with a lascivious glare. He seemed, in fact, to be addressing the hat.

Love didn't want to lie, but then again he didn't really care that he'd been called the wrong name.

Maybe so, he said.

Well, it's Coach Love, I know that. And it looks like you're doing a good job with some of our young quarterbacks.

Thank you, sir.

Coach Driver stopped addressing the hat for a moment and looked Love in the eye, annoyed that he'd been interrupted. The five-second pause after he'd said his last sentence had led Love, mistakenly, to believe it was his turn to talk. He decided to count ten from now on before responding.

Meanwhile the head coach continued to stare at Love with his small eyes that constantly sprang forward then receded under his ever-twitching eyebrows. A bit like those snakes that pop out of fake cans of peanuts, thought Love. He could feel the vibration of the coach's knee shaking against the desk as well. The head man was all energy, that was for sure. One never saw him completely still.

We have this annual trip, said Coach Driver, calming his eyes and active brows. A trip for some of the coaches that we take every summer, where we go to several towns in the state and kind of give the boosters and supporters in the region a little pep talk. We try and hit up different towns each year, fan bases that usually travel to see us or just follow on TV and radio. It's a chance for the fans and alums to mingle with the coaches a bit and get to know them in a more casual setting. And hopefully we raise a little money for the program along the way. Most of the SEC schools do it, but we call ours the Pigskin Cavalcade.

Love had heard of it. The Cavalcade had once come to his hometown and most of the muckety mucks in town had talked of nothing else for days.

It sounds like fun, said Love.

Yes, of course, said Coach Driver. It's always nice to meet the home folks.

Love nodded, wondering how long it had taken him to work in

the word *folks* as a regular part of his lexicon once he'd taken the job in Dixie. For the home *folks*, those good *folks*, sure do like being called *folks*.

Coach Von Driver, or CVD as he was known in the football chat rooms, checked his watch, then hastily grabbed what looked like a printed schedule of his day's activities. With a jeweler's precision he checked off several items. Love assumed the schedule looked something like this:

1. Call in Coach Lowe and vigorously towel-dry self in his presence
2. Nude diagramming of plays for edification of Coach Lowe
3. Forget why I asked Coach Lowe into my office in the first place

After a few more notations he seemed to remember again that Love was in the room. He looked at his watch and then began speaking to it: in years past we've asked some of the graduate assistants to go with us on these trips. To help out with the driving, handle the golf clubs, just do errands, you know. I'd like you to go with us this year.

Love waited a moment to make sure Coach Driver was finished talking and also to give the timepiece first dibs at responding.

Thank you, said Love, I'd like to do that.

Good. That's the kind of attitude we like to see around here. I like a team player.

Love nodded eagerly and seriously as befit the team player that he was.

You'll be driving Coach Woody this week. You'll need to call him right away to make arrangements. I don't, under any circumstances, want him running loose around town. And you'll need to do all the driving. Is that clear?

Yes sir.

I don't expect you to babysit him every step of the way, but anything you can do to get him back to his hotel room at a reasonable hour will be helpful. I've heard that talking about two-platoon football will sometimes do the trick. And a grad assistant two years ago seemed to have good luck with drive-through Krystals. I grew up with White Castle, but down here I know it's Krystals.

He nearly laughed at this juncture, shaking his head at the eternal Mason-Dixon feud between the merits of White Castle and Krystals, and making no attempt to disguise where his sympathies lay.

Anyway, apparently Coach Woody loves those little square burgers. Of course a lot of the towns we'll visit won't have all-night little burgers, so you might have to improvise.

By this point, Coach Driver was facing the mirror on his side wall and carefully applying his hair gel.

So you think you can handle it?

The coach's reflection in the mirror made no reply, so Love said, yes sir, I can handle it.

All right. First stop is Goshen. There's a round of golf tomorrow. And then dinner at the country club. And then we'll hit Fairview for more golf and a banquet that night. Last stop will be the Parker Yacht Club. Here's Coach Woody's number. Call him right away. He's usually hard to catch.

Love took the small piece of paper with the neatly written digits from Coach Driver and said he'd contact Coach Woody as soon as he got home.

Make sure, said Coach Driver, that Coach Woody stays out of the lake. Last time we were at one of these godforsaken redneck *yacht clubs* he and one of his homeboys were doing cannonballs off the roofs of the pontoon boats.

Love smiled without knowing he was doing it and Coach Driver caught his eye in the mirror.

That stuff would fly twenty or thirty years ago, said the head coach. But this isn't the good old days anymore. As good as Coach Woody is and as popular as he is with the players, I can't have any freewheelers on the staff. You understand?

Yes sir.

Good. And Coach Lowe, if one team in twenty had a tight end who was both fast and could catch, nobody would run the two deep zone. But teams still run it, don't they? And with great success. What does that tell you about your tight end fly pattern solution?

Love didn't answer. He felt that too much information had been thrown at him at once.

Said Coach Driver, turning up the Bon Jovi again and wiping the excess gel from his hand on a nearby towel: I'm just razzing you, sport. Keep diagramming those plays. You might be the next Sid Gilliam.

Love offered a weak smile in return.

Coach Driver checked his watch and said: you can run along now.

Roar of the Crowd

As Love walked out of Coach Von Driver's dressing room, another young man came toward it. It was Sparkman, the other non-coaching graduate assistant this past year, and Love's sole competition for the now open position. Either he or Sparkman would find out, likely this week, which of them would be on the field, and which of them would stay full-time errand boy. Sparkman was wearing a 300 LBS BENCH PRESS T-shirt from Maryland, flip-flops, and a backwards baseball cap on his square tan head that showed only a glimpse of the blond crew cut beneath. His look, in short, was the classic surfer/linebacker love child as first popularized by Bryan *The Boz* Bosworth. In fact, Sparkman had been a linebacker for the Terrapins, a good one, and All-ACC his senior season. Whether he surfed or not, Love didn't know.

Lovey boy, my Lovey boy, said Sparkman.

What's up Sparkman?

Just going to see the boss man about this Cavalcade thing. You going too?

Yep.

Who you driving?

Coach Woody.

Oh man, that should be interesting.

That's what I hear.

Well, I'll see you down there. The big man asked me to drive him, so maybe we can drag race or something.

And with that, Sparkman continued his approach to CVD's dressing room. Love watched as he walked right in without knocking or calling first. Then heard him shout—literally shout—*what's shaking Chief?*

Love went over to gather his things, and as he did so, Sparkman let out a loud and raucous laugh. This confused Love. Never once had Coach Driver made him want to roar with mirth. Their exchanges usually had to do with a coffee that needing fetching or a brusque interrogatory about the location of a game film that Love had broken down. Love's end of these conversations amounted to nodding yes or no sir and the feeling that his eyes were wider than normal in the manner of a small, cornered creature of the night. And as soon as Coach Driver had left, Love would think of the point he'd rehearsed saying the night before in the event of such an encounter, some line to show he had what it took to be a coach.

They sure love that bootleg on the goal line, Coach.

And now it was Coach Driver's turn to belly laugh. Of course, he and Sparkman did have a prior connection, so that likely accounted for the jocularity now coming from across the room. Love had been appraised of that relationship on his first meeting with Sparkman back in August, which he recalled as going like this:

LOVE: Nice to meet you. How's it going?

SPARKMAN (scratching his ear): Fine.

LOVE: You're the other new grad assistant, right?

SPARKMAN (waving to the offensive coordinator over Love's shoulder): Yeah. (strokes his chin stubble and winks at the attractive secretary) That's right.

LOVE: Well, good to meet you.

SPARKMAN (playing some kind of calypso number, Harry Bela-
fonte maybe, on his stomach): My dad used to coach with Driver.
Those jokers cut their teeth together at Indiana. I've got a funny as
hell picture of them from the eighties if you want to see it. (yawns
and looks away)
    LOVE: Yeah, I'd like to see that.

As Love pondered how friendships made in Bloomington might
affect the open coaching position, Bon Jovi was suddenly cranked
up in the dressing room. When Coach Driver and Sparkman started
belting the impassioned lyrics in unison, Love decided now was as
good a time as any to get on down the road.

He entered the massive, empty stadium to find the JumboTron
on and the screen filled with a fifty-foot CVD. Love glanced toward
the screen without much wanting to just as the head coach was saying: *when you walk into Crafton Stadium, you walk into history.* He
then said something about *pride of tradition*, but Love had stopped
listening. He was trying to remember if this was the bank commercial or the one for the car dealership. Yes, it was the bank commercial
after all, the one where CVD gave an inspirational talk to players
assembled on this very field. Of course they weren't real players, that
was against NCAA rules, but either actors or beefy locals. Now the
camera was panning from one sweaty face to the next, each trying to
out-grimace the one before it with the weight of masculine intensity.
CVD's words were plainly motivating them. The actors/locals would
be opening a savings account soon.

Love put the bank commercial out of his mind as he neared mid-
field and took in the immensity and grandeur of the stadium. He
tried to imagine what it would have been like to play in such a venue.
The field seemed almost a separate entity from the stands, so well
situated was it for the viewing eye. It was the verticality effect, the

height of the stadium adding to the impression that what was below should be viewed with narrative distance, as one observes insects in a jar. Good play or bad, it happened in the naked wide open. In the stadiums he'd played in at Woodford College, a Division III school in Kentucky, the stands were so low, you hardly noticed them. Love had found it easy to forget he was being watched.

Standing on the fifty-yard line, he wondered how he would have fared in such a vast arena. His career at Woodford had been a good one. He'd been a three-year starter and the team had only lost two games in that time. But how would he have done here, where the stakes were so high and ninety thousand sets of eyes were on the quarterback? It would be horrible to throw a big interception with all those people watching. But to throw a touchdown pass? One to win the game? How loud it would be, how awesome.

Love smiled, catching himself lost in the roar of a phantom crowd. He wondered when guys outgrew that. Or if they ever did.

He'd made his way to campus, thinking that his first lengthy discussion with the head coach had been a success, all in all. Sure, he'd been forced to witness the floppy man dancing on a board trick, as well as a bare-assed coach diagramming plays. And true, the coach had forgotten his name during the majority of the conversation, made fun of the play he suggested, and failed to even mention the vacant position for the coaching graduate assistant. And the Bon Jovi, yes the Bon Jovi, that was the soundtrack the little man had danced to. There was no getting around that.

But still, he'd had an extended face-to-face with the coach, unusually intimate, yes, but a reasonable facsimile of normal human interaction nonetheless. He'd not known Coach Driver was capable of such a thing. And to top it off, he'd been asked personally to attend the Pigskin Cavalcade and to play what sounded like something of a pivotal role, namely keeping Coach Woody from getting his name in the paper and subsequently fired, a scenario that would hurt both the quality of the coaching staff and Coach Driver's popularity with the fans.

Coach Woody had been at the university for the better part of, what, forty years? First as a player, a hard-nosed end famous for his forearm shiver and spin move, then as defensive line coach nonpareil. He was a player favorite on the staff, an old-school coach who could still connect with his young charges. Love thought it stemmed from the fact that what you saw with Coach Woody was what you got and that he always shot straight with his guys.

He was now on the quad, en route to the Business School where the sports management graduate program was housed, to pick up his final paper in Advanced Psychology of Sport. On the way, he passed hideous undergraduate male after hideous undergraduate male, every bowl-cut one of them accompanied by a current or future Playmate. For a moment he weighed his own choice of college—small, private, studious—with the Hee-Haw Shangri-La of the state university. Had he made the right call? Spying now an albino troll giving a piggyback ride to Marilyn Monroe's granddaughter, he wasn't so sure.

He came to the Business School, and as was his way ran up the three flights of steps to the sports management wing. Upon arrival he passed two former women's basketball players who gave him the jockish half-nod of respect. Implied message: *what's up*. He returned the nod and headed down the hall toward Professor Hilliard's office.

His grades at this point were as follows:

Leadership Theories of Sport—A
Research Techniques in Sport—A
Advanced Biomechanics of Human Movement—A

LOVE'S WINNING PLAYS 25

A plastic file box was fastened to the door of Professor Hilliard's office and Love reached in and found his final research paper. He winced slightly as he read the title—*Applying the Principles of B. F. Skinner to High School Field Goal Kicking*—then turned immediately to the final page as all normal people do to check the grade. What he found attached to his own paper was the following typewritten note:

> *Raymond,*
>
> *Wish you'd spent more time on the psychological profiles of the three kickers. The sophomore sounded like a classic obsessive/compulsive and it made me wonder how this personality type was especially suited (or unsuited) for this highly specialized activity. The brief mention of his locker and his assortment of gee gaws (surreptitious Pokemon cards, sports bars stacked in rows of five, tiny hidden photo of American Idol singer, etc.) was fascinating and something you really could have scored points with.*
>
> *Also, more on the social ostracism of the soccer player turned kicker would have been nice. I believe soccer (European-style football) is still considered an effete sport in this region of the country. I know every time I mention it in my Introductory Sports Psychology class, the undergraduate men tend to roll their eyes and make remarks (often in a falsetto voice). I couldn't help but wonder if he'd been taped to the goal post or had his eyebrows shaved or been the victim of some sort of burning analgesic balm applied to his athletic supporter, all of which I've read about in my Psychology of Team Sports journals. Again, a small thing perhaps, but I was curious.*
>
> *Finally, I wondered if some of your reinforcing stimuli (bubble gum/Jolly Ranchers/et al.) were the proper choice for the offensive lineman, the third kicker in your experiment. Seeing as he rebelled at the idea of being a kicker, had in fact been forced into competing for the job by the coaches, I wondered if he might rebel as well*

against food as a reinforcer. Aren't the offensive linemen the largest
players on the team, and the least athletic? I wondered (somewhat
idly I'll admit) if he thought the choice of reward was an indirect
commentary, subconscious even on your part, about his size, dimen-
sions, and likely fondness for food items loaded with sugar. Might
vegetables have worked better considering his rebellious tendencies?

But aside from those quibbles I found this to be an arresting and
well-written paper. I was especially impressed with your creative
uses of the modifying elements (dropping your car keys while a sub-
ject was trying to kick, having the others make animal sounds, set-
ting your cell phone alarm to play Grateful Dead songs right as they
approached the ball, and so on). That their results improved steadily
as they grew acclimated to the distractions shows how much their
confidence and concentration had improved (though I was surprised
that the Dead are not popular with today's high schoolers. I've seen
them 26 times—HA!).

I was also impressed that the subjects scored so well when verbal
praise was the reinforcer. I think this bodes well for anyone consider-
ing a career in teaching or coaching. Excellent job, Raymond! I've
enjoyed having you in class.

Beneath the note a capital *A* was handwritten in green ink. Love
hadn't worked nearly as hard on the paper as he'd have liked to
because of his football duties, but hadn't half-assed it like a lot of
people did. He thought he'd shoot Hilliard an email sometime later
and thank him for the class. It was the young professor's first year
at the school and Love thought he often seemed a little lonely, calling after students as they left class to clarify some minute point, or
grasping at a flimsy excuse for small talk. And he obviously knew
jackshit about sports. But there was no doubting his sincerity and
that counted for something.

After popping into the graduate student lounge to look up directions to Coach Woody's house on the computer, Love left the building in a good mood, wishing only that he'd chosen a different band as one of his modifying elements. Hilliard in a tie-dye? Dancing arhythmically with all those other pale hairys to the Grateful Dead?

He'd try not to think about that.

Recipe for Love

On the way to the football complex to pick up his pay check for the month, he passed a group of university hostesses who were pointing things out to a goggle-eyed high schooler on campus for a recruiting visit. These hostesses, or university escorts as Love tended to think of them, were outfitted in extra-fitted business skirts and blouses whose buttons the wind seemed to play undue havoc with. As they walked with the young recruit, they kept up a steady assault of giggles and titters, arm touches and *accidental* hip brushes. And any second now, one of them would pull a letter of intent—abracadabra—from her push-up bra and the athletic department would have snagged another. The high schooler—slavering, sweating, and hyperventilating—looked ready to sign any form, army recruitment to Britney Spears back-up dancer, should it be pushed in front of him by the lovely hostesses.

How, thought Love, is that legal?

Arriving in the football offices, tidy and sterile as a doctor's waiting room, Love was greeted by two secretaries and a student worker named Julie whom he'd befriended in Advanced Biomechanics of

Human Movement, otherwise known as How We Run and Throw. A former college volleyball player, she had just completed the sports management program this past week and was now weighing a career as a high school biology teacher and coach against a profession where she might be able to earn a living wage.

She tapped out something on the computer, then looked up at Love. You get your grades yet?

Yep, said Love. Three C's and a D. Grad school is brutal.

She laughed and Love saw no reason to slow down. This was his first social contact with someone not involved in football in two days.

Hey, he said, are those hostesses allowed to give massages?

What?

Because they had some kid stretched out on the practice field with his shirt off.

Before Julie could respond, the office manager in charge of Love's paycheck said: you better be kidding.

I'm dead serious. They were lighting incense and had some wind-chimey music going. By the way, does the university cover the body butter or do the hostesses have to supply their own?

Come over here and get your check, said the office manager, before I massage the back of your head with this stapler.

Julie was now standing up and putting something away in a filing cabinet. She was a tall, athletic-looking young lady with a wicked grin—the grin was *fast*, if that made sense, flashing suddenly and unexpectedly and always in a way that seemed to catch Love a little off guard. He'd often thought he might like to ask her out, but she had a fiancé, a law school student at Georgetown, and was never around on the weekends. Nearly all of their interaction had come in class, at the grad lounge, or around the football offices where she worked as part of her assistantship.

So when does the book club meet next? asked Julie.

Tonight, said Love, trying to think of a way out of this conversation.

The grin was in full force now, one of the cockiest, winningest smiles he'd ever witnessed. He'd have liked to see her flash that baby after throwing down a spike in a volleyball match. A surefire irritant to the other team.

What's the book this week?

Love harrumphed a bit. Took the pay envelope from his pocket, looked at it strangely, then put it back again. *The Bon Bon Girls*, he said.

The what what girls?

Please don't make me say it again.

I thought you said something like *The Bon Bon Girls*, but I know that couldn't be it. Aren't you a football coach?

Sort of, said Love.

Man, that's worse than the one-eyed cat book. Okay, what's your question then? Is it as good as the one last week?

I'm not saying it out loud. No way.

Aw, come on. You can't hold out on me. I helped you answer the last one.

It was true. Last week's book club selection had been *Recipe for Love*, which chronicled the (mis)adventures of a recently divorced sous chef named Brylin who had decided to head to Prague, home of a world-famous culinary school, in search of the perfect soufflé. If she just so happens to meet the perfect man along the way, who is Brylin to complain? Mixing a true foodie's love of fine cooking, plenty of laugh-out-loud pratfalls in the kitchen/bedroom, and over thirty fantabulous recipes, *Recipe for Love* is just the book to warm the kitchen—and the funny bone—this summer.

As a member of the book club, Love had been assigned this question in advance of the meeting from the Book Club Supplement found at the end of the novel:

Were you surprised by Brylin's decision to intentionally lose the souf-flé championship so that Gustav could win?

Julie had written the following potential answers on a piece of paper during How We Run and Throw class and passed them over to Love:

1. Oh fuck off
2. Seriously, just go ahead and fuck right off
3. As soon as I finish watching Dora the Explorer, I'll answer that
4. I Gustaved into my handkerchief this morning and knew I should call the doctor

Love had laughed so hard and suddenly that he feared being called down in class for the first time since his freshman year in high school.

They had finally settled on the answer below, the answer that Love had given at that night's book club meeting: *No, I was not surprised that Brylin intentionally lost the soufflé championship so that Gustav could win.*

His response had been met with a brief awkward silence before Joel, the bread and fresh pasta maker in the book club, had rushed into the vacuum to say that he had been surprised—at first—because the soufflé championship had meant so much to Brylin. But after consideration, he thought it was the right way to conclude the book, choosing love over personal achievement. Love had nodded aggressive assent to this analysis and the group had swiftly moved on to the next question, which was:

Why, at the beginning of the book, did Brylin feel such ambivalence about her mother and her small-town upbringing?

• • •

So tell me, said Julie. What's the question this week? It must be a really good one.

Question #8.

And what does it say?

Love shook his head in the negative.

So you're going to answer for the book club but not even tell your grad school pal what it is?

No, I'm not answering it for them either.

Really?

Yes, really.

You seem torn. Either the question is that bad or the girl you like is that pretty.

Yes, he was torn. And yes, Brooke was that pretty. About fifty times better looking than anyone else who'd ever agreed to be seen with him in public. But were looks everything? No, she was smart, and funny too. But would he do the book club stuff if she were not, indeed, fifty times better looking than anyone else who'd ever agreed to be seen in public with him?

Of course not.

That pretty? asked Julie.

Love smiled but gave no reply.

So, I hear you're now an official member of the Pigskin Cavalcade.

Yeah, how'd you know that?

I filled out the forms for the per diems. You should have an extra check in your envelope to cover meals that aren't part of the official shindig. It's like fifty bucks a day.

Really? said Love, not believing this cash bonanza. Fifty dollars was usually his spending money for the month.

Not bad, huh? By the way, I think I'll be down there for a day, maybe two. I'm doing an internship for the alumni magazine and they want me to go down and take some pictures and write a little article. So you're going to have to hang out with me a little. Maybe fetch some drinks, that sort of thing.

Sure, said Love, least I could do.

Not sure if I'll be down for the second day or the third, or maybe both. You're on your own the first night though, sorry to say. You think you're ready?

I guess.

Have they announced who's getting that other coaching position yet?

No, not yet.

Julie smiled, a little wanly, Love thought.

Well, I'm pulling for you, she said.

Love said thanks and then was heading out the door, feeling, all in all, a bit better about his pending trip.

Question #8

His car was parked about two miles from the business building, the stadium, or anywhere else that anyone might want to go on campus, next to the railroad tracks and the fields of the agriculture department which had lain fallow for many a year. The day was now at its hottest, with few students milling about, and by the time he reached his car he'd need another shower. Perhaps it was the recent exchange with Julie, but Question #8 from the Book Club Supplement as well as tonight's final book club meeting were shaping up as something he'd rather not face.

The Bon Bon Girls detailed a group of single women in New York City who combined a love of gourmet food and sex. The book chronicled the assortment of men each woman dated/bedded and how their dating lives helped forge a tight bond of sisterhood. The title sprang from the central trope of the book, namely that each time one of the women had sexual congress with a new beau, she delivered a high-priced chocolate bon bon to all the other gals in the group. The treat chosen each time was a kind of clue to the other women about how the night had gone, and revealed some detail—emotional, anatomical, or other—about how the gentleman in question had performed in the boudoir. How these chocolate morsels arrived each time—wrapped in a pair of silk boxer shorts, carrier pigeon, baby stroller—was part of the delicious fun of the book.

It was Brooke, in her role as discussion leader, who had assigned Question #8 to Love. Not only could Love imagine no person in the world being willing to answer Question #8 in public, he couldn't even believe he'd had to read it in the privacy of his own home.

The fact that he'd been seeing her on and off for several months and still didn't know if he was meant to be a love interest or just the dreaded guy-friend didn't help either. About every fourth date, just when he was about to throw in the towel, he'd be invited in for a little time on the couch. On these nights, he felt very much like a romantic interest, very much like a Manhattanite who might one day be bon bon worthy. Their next time together, which might be a week, might be two, depending on Brooke's schedule and whims, he'd be back in the role of guy-friend, that lonely milquetoast station. Truthfully, he'd been so starved for social interaction since he'd moved to town, he'd have been fine just being friends. It was just confusing. At some point, Love hoped she'd fish or cut bait. Friend or Bon Bon, he could play either.

Regardless, he had to call her now. Maybe she'd let him bow out of book club tonight, considering the trip he had in the morning. He hit her number and hoped for the best.

After the exchange of greetings Love covered the phone and Gustaved slightly. Then he said: I don't think I'll be able to make it to book club tonight.

Why not?

Love paused. He thought of their Saturday at the campus aquatic center and that little yellow bikini, Brooke laughing and occasionally touching his arm in an intimate way as she read *The Bon Bon Girls*. The only thing that could have improved that moment was if she'd been wearing her little smarty glasses, the small, fashionable, black-framed ones that every sexy intellectual wore these days.

He'd once asked to try on the glasses just to be goofy, but she'd refused. From then on he'd been fairly certain the glasses were non-prescription and worn purely as an accessory. Did this matter? Of course it didn't.

I just found out I've got to go out of town tomorrow, said Love. And I need to pack and get ready for my trip.

Out of town? Why?

Love explained about the Pigskin Cavalcade and his role as chauffeur/aide-de-camp to Coach Woody.

That is so feudal, said Brooke with a laugh.

Yeah, I guess so. Anyway, I should be packed up by the time you get out of book club. Want to get a beer or a quick bite after you get out? I could meet you somewhere.

You told me it takes you like ten minutes to pack. Remember? That time we went to the lake and you said I was taking forever to get ready? Your exact quote: *I could pack for a weeklong trip to any-where in less than ten minutes.* That ring a bell?

Yes, said Love. I did say that. But I've never gone on this kind of trip before. I don't even know if it's casual or dress-up or what. I've got one sports coat, which I think doesn't even fit anymore. And four shirts that need ironing and no iron. And if I can find my dress shoes, they'll need to be polished.

It's called the Pigskin Cavalcade, right?

Yes.

I think rodeo attire would be fine.

Love laughed. He had to admit Brooke was funny when she wanted to be.

At any rate, he said, I won't be able to make it. Can we get together after? I'd really like to see you before I head out.

Brooke didn't respond for a long time and he thought she must have set the phone down. He could hear the TV clearly now and hadn't heard it at all before. Brooke, the burgeoning gourmand, had become a devotee of the Food Network. One night Love had watched a little of it with her and was alarmed by the number of times the word *foodie* was used. The word brought to Love's mind a sluglike orifice devouring gelatinous goo. Brooke had not yet started describing herself as such, but Love feared it was just around the corner. Poet? Fine. Intellectual? Whatever. Self-described book addict? Good for you. Foodie? No sir. Not on his watch. If push came to shove he supposed he'd even choose *fashionista* over *foodie*, hard as that was to imagine.

So how did you like the book? asked Brooke in a nonchalant voice that fooled no one on the line.

What?

Love was passing a couple of guys on their way to the basketball court and dared not say the title aloud. Plus his head was spinning from the foodie/fashionista choice. It didn't seem possible he'd found a word more inane, and possibly sadder, than *fashionista*. Was he being hasty?

The Bon Bon Girls. How did you like it?

It was okay, said Love. I don't really like reading about food that much.

You mean sex?

Sex is fine. I just prefer mine without all the food. I think it's a gender thing. Guys hardly ever write about food in their books.

Just drinkin, fightin, and fuckin?

Love laughed, a little nervously. He had some thoughts on why all the books they'd read in the book club had huge sections about food, long descriptions of meals and multiple in-text recipes, and so on, but thought maybe he needed a few more psychology classes before he offered those up. Likely a more sympathetic audience as well. And now that he considered it, he wasn't sure if guys were even allowed to use the word *gender* anymore, at least in academic circles. Obviously, it was time for a hasty retreat before the full-on rout.

Listen Brooke, he said, I like spending time with you. It's my first time in a book club. I'm one of three guys in there and the other two think I'm some idiot jock.

I thought you liked the book club, said Brooke. You said you enjoyed the camaraderie and intellectual stimulation.

Actually Brooke had used that phrase, had said after the discussion of *The Day Aunt Gertrude Burned Down the Piggly Wiggly*: don't you enjoy the camaraderie of the book club and the intellectual stimulation?

And Love had said: *yeah*.

I have enjoyed it, Love said, leaning back and staring at the sun as if hoping to be suddenly radiated or blinded or carried off by a passing bird of prey. He was next to the train tracks now and the guardrail had just descended with a great clattering of bells and lights.

It's your question, isn't it? You're embarrassed by it.

The train was coming by now with a great swooshing of sound, its horn blaring in Love's ear. He said: I can't hear you.

Your question! Brooke shouted. You're embarrassed by the question I assigned you!

Listen, said Love, also shouting. The train is going by. Can't you hear it?

He held the phone up for several seconds, then cautiously put it back to his ear.

I gave you that question because I thought it was the most interesting one!

Said Love: I . . . (holding phone up to train track) . . . can't (listening briefly) . . . hear you (holding phone aloft and shaking it with much gusto).

When he put the phone back to his ear, the line was dead.

Love Has a Visitor

Love walked into his apartment and immediately turned on the window unit: HIGH COOL. The little engine began to hum and Love took off his shirt to catch the icy breeze head-on. The apartment was stifling and smelled of the sweat of former tenants. During the heat of the day, like now, Love also thought he detected another scent, something akin to Eau de Urine, that emanated from the carpet, traditional toadstool in color.

Glancing now about the place, decorated to the last detail in *Modern Prison Living* style, Love considered again a trip to the Goodwill for things like a lamp, wall adornment, or kitchen table. What he saw in this combination den/kitchenette was the following: a couch bequeathed to him for being too outdated for his grandmother, a garage sale coffee table strewn with legal pads bearing the inscription *Love's Winning Plays*, the trunk he'd used to carry his meager possessions, and, atop this trunk, the last TV set with antenna attachment in the western hemisphere. His other room, the bedroom, was minimalist by comparison.

Cooled and ventilated, Love called the number he had for Coach Woody. As the phone rang, he wondered if there was a Mrs. Woody, but couldn't recall ever hearing mention of her. Single coaches, divorced or otherwise, were an anomaly, but then again, so was Coach Woody. The phone rang and rang and just as Love was about to hang up there came a strange noise, like a foraging bear on an animal show. There it was—a growl, a distinct growl. For a moment Love wondered if the animal had knocked over the phone and what he'd heard was the snuffling and slurps of the dog—he supposed it was a dog—testing the phone in gustatory anticipation.

Love said, hello? Coach Woody?

No sound came from the other party.

Uh, this is Raymond Love. Graduate Assistant Coach Love. I'm supposed to give you a ride tomorrow. I hope someone told you already. To the Pigskin Cavalcade I mean.

He stopped talking for a moment and waited. Most of the phrases he'd just uttered had sounded ridiculous, surely every proper noun. And the Pigskin Cavalcade, the sound of it, was starting to gross him out. He was no longer seeing footballs, but pork products and things muddily porcine. Was it Brooke's gibe about the rodeo? And my god, how many syllables were there in Graduate-Assistant-Coach-Love? That was a phrase that need not be uttered again.

Someone or something had decided to kick the receiver around a bit or else was using it to play air hockey, for Love heard nothing but swish-swish-clonk, swish-swish-clonk. In the background, a noise of some sort. Music? Yes, it was singing. Opera maybe. It was loud and not in English and the singer seemed to be lamenting something.

Okay, said Love in an apologetic shout, I'll try again later. I guess if I don't hear from you, I'll just swing by your house in the morning around eight.

He listened one last time, hearing only the occasional shallow breath from someone or something near the phone. Was Coach Woody dying? Should he call someone? Go by? Love's mind began to get a little creative. Was there anything about his position that didn't make him feel nervous and unsettled? Anything having to do with the full-time coaches, that is?

Love had been pacing around the apartment for an hour, trying, in vain, to find something on the television. Were there others without cable in this great nation of ours? He was considering moving the television into the other room to use as a bedside table when he heard a roughhewn knock, vaguely menacing in nature, at the door. Other than pizza delivery boys, this was a novel experience for Love, this knocking on door. Staring quizzically at the peephole as if this would surely alert the knocker that he was inquiring at the wrong residence, Love began a slow walk toward the door.

Open up, douche, said the voice from the other side.

Love thought: *douche?*

Put your pants on and open up, came the voice along with several simian slaps upon the door.

Who is it?

It's your teenage girlfriend. I'm pregnant, let me in.

Love was flummoxed. Perhaps some frat boy had the wrong apartment.

Come on, douche, my water just broke.

Sparkman. Of course. Love opened the door and there he was, Graduate Assistant Coach Sparkman, wearing, incomprehensibly, a blue and white seersucker suit, white bucks, and, in keeping with old-school tradition, a coaching whistle round his neck.

Come on in, said Love.

Sparkman looked around Love's abode in no more time than it deserved.

I like what you've done with the place, he said, adjusting the fattish knot in his tie.

Love said: I haven't quite got around to decorating.

Sparkman flipped a folder he was holding onto the coffee table and plopped down on the couch. You got a beer, Lovey boy? It's hotter than hell out there.

Oddly enough, the sight of his erstwhile rival dressed as a lost aristocrat from the planter class, and apparently some kind of planter who did a little coaching on the side, did little to improve Love's general sense of good will toward man. The fact that he was smacking his gum in the style of all devil-may-care twenty-first-century college coaches didn't help his case either. Nonetheless, a guest was a guest, so he went to the refrigerator and retrieved two beers, Pabst Blue Ribbons, which had been on sale at the market down the road. He handed the can to Sparkman and waited for a response. PBR was an inexpensive beer but it was not a bad one. In fact, Love liked PBR and would defend it publicly. He planned to brook no guff about the P, B, and R.

But Sparkman popped the can with no comment and drained down about half of it in a gulp. Then he chomped his gum a few casually aggressive times, moving it from cheek to cheek and popping it absent-mindedly, his mouth open during the entirety of the bubble gum's springtime adventure, no shortage of sloshy, saliva sounds either, before fixing Love with a wry smile.

You talked to the Wood Man yet?

Not yet, said Love.

Sparkman was sitting right in the middle of the three-person couch, his blocky head and shoulders now bobbing to the beat of a song—a *kicking* song no doubt—that only he, and perhaps other linebackers, could hear. Metal, man. As there was nowhere else to sit, Love found himself standing on the other side of the coffee table like a visitor in his own place, like someone being interviewed for a job.

Well, you better go ahead and track him down, said Sparkman while opening and closing the latest edition of *Love's Winning Plays*. Love stood waiting for a wisecrack about his tome, but none came. Sparkman hadn't read anything, had just grabbed something because he saw it, flipped it open then shut it again. A mild sedative seemed to be in order and Love wondered about the span of Sparkman's attention. He thought again of all the gum-smacking, *gum-showing*, coaches out there, feverishly chewing their cud. Was that what it took to make it to the top of the coaching ranks? Hyperactivity and aggressive gum work?

Love responded that he was confident of catching up with Coach Woody in the very near future.

Sparkman made no response but picked up and dropped again the folder he'd brought with him.

Coach Driver wanted me to bring this over to you, he said. It's the itinerary for the Cavalcade and tickets for you and Coach Woody to all the events, maps everywhere, tee times for the golf tournament, and all that shit.

Thanks.

Man, it's too bad there's only one grad coaching position coming open.

Sparkman yawned as he said this and drained the rest of the beer. Then, as Love had been waiting for him to do, he tooted a few times on the whistle.

What do you think? he asked, smiling now and trilling a marching number.

It's a good whistle. You coaching somewhere tonight?

Sparkman stood now and began some twisting of his upper body, and a little groaning, and still, give him credit, a fair chomping of the chewy stuff.

Nah. Me and a few of the coaches are going to some kind of bullshit lawn party down at that booster hotshot's place on the river. Sammy Dutch is the guy's name. I'm sure you've heard of him, a real jock sniffer. He'll be at a lot of this Cavalcade stuff. Well, I've got to bolt. I'm picking up Coach Driver in an hour.

Crushing the slightly dripping beer can and setting it on *Love's Winning Plays* as if it were a large coaster, Sparkman got up and made his way to the door. You got golf clubs?

Yeah, said Love.

That them? said Sparkman, pointing to the garage sale special collecting cobwebs in the corner.

That's them.

With an athlete of your caliber, I'm sure it won't matter. That said, if I don't smoke your ass tomorrow, I'll be very surprised.

We'll see, said Love.

Sparkman smiled and said: can you imagine the classic rock Driver's going to be cranking on the way down? Bon Fucking Jovi, man, for like four hours.

As he said this Sparkman made an aggressive air guitar motion, the earnestness of which Love couldn't discern. He couldn't decide which would irritate him more, Sparkman actually liking Bon Jovi or making fun of the coach whose gravy train he looked to ride for many a mile.

You have any idea what kind of music Coach Woody likes? asked Love.

Country and opera, said Sparkman smiling.

What?

You heard me.

No one on earth likes both of those.

Coach Woody does. He's an honest to god freak. Man can coach though, can't he? You ought to take your playbook over there and run some stuff by him.

Sparkman was smiling as he said this last bit and Love wondered for the first time if he was sharper than he'd first thought, maybe a lot sharper. Then tweeting on the whistle one last time, really fucking loud by the way, Sparkman bolted out the door.

He'd been dominated, pure and simple. From the moment Sparkman entered the apartment, he and his seersucker had set the pace and the terms. How could he expect to make an impression on anyone who counted if he let a guy like Sparkman get under his skin, another graduate assistant of all things? It was embarrassing. Head coaches had to deal with irritating people, irritating situations, around the clock: the media, boosters, prima donna players, their parents, administrators, every jackleg fan out there with a blog. You either had to be insensate or supernaturally confident to put up with all the potential irritants. Otherwise your head would explode.

Love popped another PBR, taking small solace that at least he'd not asked where the whistle came from.

Three beers in, Love, not a big drinker, decided to call Brooke. He'd been dialing Coach Woody for the last few hours and received nothing but the busy signal. Woody was indubitably dead. Now, at ten p.m., Love was beginning to second-guess, slightly it must be said, his decision to skip the book club's final meeting and its discussion of *The Bon Bon Girls*. The phone began to ring and Love thought: maybe food and sex isn't that bad, the two of them together, maybe that's really what girls like to read about, sex and food, chocolate in particular, all swirled into one exotic fondue, and with a lot of explicit details about both, the lushness of the bon bon, the various adjectives for the male apparatus. He seemed to recall that many of these adjectives sounded vaguely foodlike too.

But would Brooke ever let him do something warm and fonduish? Would she ever discuss his apparatus in food terminology with other hungry gal pals?

Love sure hoped so.

Of course Brooke didn't answer. There'd been zero chance of that all along. Now, to leave the lonely message or no? His number would show up anyway. What if she were out with that guy who'd claimed to have wept a few weeks back at the close of *My Southern Girlhood: A Memoir of Momma, Elvis, and a One-Eyed Cat Named Sue?*

Maybe it was just the PBR talking, but Love could almost understand that fellow's sentiment as he recalled the last scene and the girl playing *Love Me Tender* in her bedroom after the cat funeral, the funeral of One-Eyed Sue, and then her mother bringing in a plate of Mississippi Mud Cookies, her specialty, still soft and warm from the oven.

As Brooke's voice recording came to a close, Love found that he was slightly hungry as well.

Hey, it's me, he began. Hope the book club went okay. I'll be out of town till the end of the week. Would love to see you tonight if you're free. Well, you've got my number (forced awkward laugh here). See you.

Brutal. Romped by a cell phone. The Bon Bon Girls would have a field day with that one, playing it over and over at Cheryl's loft apartment, eating sushi and drinking some cocktail Love had never heard of, bantering quickly and all at once about what a very lame marshmallow (their word for unworthy mates) was Love. Yes, there'd be nary a bon bon for Love in the SoHo district anytime soon.

He tossed his phone in the air and let fly a vicious kung fu kick upon its descent, missing badly and knocking himself into the coffee table in the process. Afterwards, he mused for a little while on Brooke and her yellow bikini, Brooke in her hiking shorts, all the many clothed, albeit barely, ways in which he'd witnessed her, and felt a pang that he'd never see her in the purely natural state. Yes, that ship had sailed. All because of Book Club Supplement Question # 8.

• • •

He'd packed and half-heartedly called Coach Woody ten or so times and was just about to turn in for the night. His alarm was set for six a.m., the standard since he'd been with the coaching staff. Woody was dead all right, or run off to some mountain man's cabin way off in the sticks not to be found until he wanted to be. That panting though. Would a dying man sound like a big dog, a hungry and inquisitive one? Perhaps. At any rate, Love's ticket to the Pigskin Cavalcade looked unlikely to be punched or at least punched on time. Could he be blamed for Woody's death? He didn't have to tell about the call, but of course they might check phone records.

His teeth were brushed and flossed, his bag neatly packed at the foot of the bed, the minor mess he'd made put away, along with Sparkman's crushed beer can—a high school move if you asked Love—and now the covers were being turned back.

Well damn it to hell, said Love, getting out of bed and throwing on his shorts and T-shirt. Grabbing his bags and the directions to Coach Woody's house, he headed out the door. The clock said 12:35 in the a.m.

Coach Woody

The directions he'd gotten from the computer brought him to a small subdivision of sixties-style houses out on the west side of town. Two quick turns on dark and silent roads led him to the driveway of a brick rancher which looked in the blinding glare coming from its exterior lights, its windows, its wide-open front door, like a small casino set down in a suburban desert. Even with the windows up in his car, Love could hear music blaring from the house, if opera could fairly be said to blare. The singer was quavering in Italian to the world at large and Love had the sudden impression that at any moment this house would rise up and begin floating through space, a brilliantly illuminated ranch spaceship, manned by a panting dog in a space helmet, the American Laika who so loved his telephone and his opera.

Cautiously, Love got out of the car, leaving the keys in the ignition, for a quick getaway perhaps. Somehow all of the light and all of the volume, especially the foreign and melancholy nature of the volume, made the house seem the emptiest on the street. Love looked around. How were the neighbors not roused? Why were no cops swarming the place? The yards were large and fairly well spaced, but the dog or deranged killer who'd answered the phone was testing the speaker capacity of a really nice stereo system and apparently all of the neighbors were too deaf or too drunk to hear.

Pavarotti? Was that who was singing? Of course Pavarotti was the only opera singer he could name. Surely there were others. He walked across a lawn that was well above his ankles and approached the open front door. Pavarotti was crying now, soaring and trembling in ways that made Love especially jumpy. This was the kind of music often played in a horror flick right as the body was discovered. Love pulled out his cell phone and dialed a 9 and a 1, leaving the final digit to be punched the moment he was falling to the ground with a lacerated liver, victim of a scythe to the midsection. And still so many bon bons yet to be delivered in his name.

Upon entering the domicile, Love's first thought was: what's that smell? His second was that if he kept on his current track of home decorating this was where he would eventually land. Minimalism on a large scale. A den, a couch, a blasting stereo. Not one thing adorning the plain white walls other than a nature calendar from the year before. On the television grainy black-and-white football players running in a staccato slow motion pattern. Were guys that slow back then or was this a trick of the eight-millimeter film? Man, they looked slow. Of course, they were all white, so maybe that explained it. A Doberman sat on the couch, his head leaning over the opposite end and lapping at something Love couldn't see. His guess would be a bloody body. The music was so loud the dog hadn't heard him walk in. Love worried that startling the beast as he lapped the blood of his beloved, massacred owner might warrant a maiming of the first order. Perhaps the dog would recognize his voice from the phone. One could hope.

At this moment the singing paused for a brief moment, replaced by the delicate tapping of a thin-skinned percussion instrument, not unlike the dying beat of a human heart. Love cleared his throat, once, twice, three times. The dog turned his head then and Love heard what sounded like sobbing, man or canine impossible to tell. The pooch gave Love a mournful glance, then went back to his gentle lapping over the far edge of the couch.

Love walked toward the object of the dog's tenderness. When he arrived he found a large older man lying flat on his back on the floor, head to couch, bare feet sticking out the open patio door, curtains whipping gently against his toes in the breeze. It was Coach Woody, dressed in a terrycloth bathrobe and wearing huge seventies-style sunglasses, something De Niro would have worn back in the day. Two moths flitted about his head, nimbly avoiding the affectionate dog's saliva shower. Love crept forward until he was near Coach Woody's knees, which were exposed, as were some other things that Love thought best not to consider. He crouched down until he was nearly face to face. The singing had commenced again and seemed to be building toward something loud and powerful. Love had to bend down even further to ascertain the particulars, but Coach Woody was breathing all right, heaving more like it.

Love said quietly, Coach Woody, are you okay?

Slowly, painfully, somewhat dramatically Love realized a few minutes later, Coach Woody lifted a finger to his mouth in the classic shushing mode.

Can I get you anything, Coach Woody? Do I need to call an ambulance?

The music had risen to a crescendo now, though Love would have bet good money anytime in the last sixty seconds that the music could get no louder or more angst-ridden. The simple fact was some Italian heart was breaking now, really breaking, not just being casually abused as before.

Coach Woody lifted his glasses in a measured, pained way. His eyes were closed, but Love could see the tears welling behind the closed lids.

Act II, he said. Otello saying goodbye to joy. Not now.

Then he made a quick, irritated motion with his hand in the general direction of the kitchen and said, whisky's that way.

Love walked to the kitchen with the dog following, wondering if Coach Woody had meant to say *Othello* with an *h*. The kitchen was almost identical to his grandmother's, down to the wallpaper, a rather dainty pattern in tan and orange of assorted kitchen items. Against this quaint backdrop, the mauled phone was splayed across the floor, looking well lubricated and much the worse for wear. In the corner, two bowls sat empty and Love filled one with water and the other with dog food from a bag propped up against the pantry door. The dog came over and sniffed with immoderate disdain at the food, then took a few perfunctory sips of water. He seemed used to better fare.

The one item displayed on any of the kitchen counters was a bottle of George Dickel whisky. Love found a glass and mixed himself a short one. When he got back to the den with his highball, Coach Woody was still prone on the floor, dabbing at the tears running below his Super Fly shades. His hand was out, as if in need of something. Love tried to avoid looking at the baby sea lion dangling between his legs, but didn't have complete success. Seriously, what was that? He'd seen smaller animals stuffed and mounted in a museum. Even more seriously, what was the record for seeing naked coaches within a twenty-four-hour time period? This was the offseason, for crying out loud.

My glass is on the floor by the stereo, said Coach Woody in a scratchy, overwrought voice. Make me a drink, Coach, and don't be timid with your pour. But first, turn off the music. I can't take the final two acts. It gets sadder than hell from here on out.

Love turned off the stereo and returned to the kitchen, with the voluptuary dog at his hip, wondering how this was the same man who handled three-hundred-pound defensive linemen, the most menacing men on the field, like so many babes in swaddling clothing. He was thrilled, and embarrassed to be so, that Coach Woody had not only recognized him but had addressed him as *Coach*. Most of the staff passed him in the football complex like an adjunct professor they vaguely seemed to recall from the semester before.

He made the drink with ice and whisky, skipping water altogether. He'd paused to look at what he assumed were family photos on the refrigerator, smiling men and women older than he was, and a gaggle of little kids on Santa's lap or banging a pail on the beach. Coach Woody as grandfather? It seemed odd to consider.

When Love looked back toward the den, he saw that Coach Woody had removed his sunglasses and turned off the overhead light. He was standing up close to the television, following the silent black-and-white action with his finger on the screen.

WHAMMO-BAMMO! he shouted suddenly, then commenced a quick, menacing buck dance where he stood. All-American, my ass!

The old coach then did a nifty power move around the couch, as if he were shooting a gap in the line, before resuming his spot in front of the television.

Coach, he said, how about grabbing a couple of burgers out of the fridge for Oskie. That dog won't eat dog food anymore, I've spoiled him rotten. Then bring my drink and come watch this hit on Landry Burns. There's no audio, but by god, my ears are ringing after that one.

He was shaking his head, and in the spectral glow from the set, his shaggy formless mane of gray hair made him look as if he could be a truck driver, an unreconstructed hippie, or a circuit-riding Methodist preacher of the wild-eyed nineteenth century. That is, it was the long hair not of someone trying to make a point, aesthetic, political, or otherwise, but of someone who didn't clutter his mind with minutiae like the cutting and combing of hair. But it was the wild-eyed preacher image that Love thought most captured the moment.

Love opened the refrigerator and found a plate with ten fat

grilled burgers on it. Oskie was nosing his head into the fridge and sniffing with particular fervor at two of the treats and these were the ones Love snagged. He emptied the bowl of dog food back into the bag and placed burgers in their stead. Oskie set to and was finished by the time Love gathered the highballs and made his way back to the den.

Woody was standing a foot from the television, remote poised and anxious looking in his hand. On the screen a football player was laid out on the field, his legs splayed and helmet skewed. His hands gripped the single-bar facemask, which had been twisted to such an extent that he seemed to be looking out the ear hole. Several teammates were trotting toward him, their earnest faces disbelieving that *this* man was down.

Tell me your name again, said Coach Woody. I remember you from the film room when you were breaking down the Mississippi State game, but I've lost your name.

Love gave his name and Coach Woody nodded without giving any indication the information had just sunk in.

That Otello you heard, that was the great tenor Mario Del Monaco. Some folks say his phrasing lacks nuance, but I think that's a crock. You heard him. Was the man feeling it or not?

Love had to agree he was feeling it.

Damn right. Absolutely right. I'll bring that CD and a bunch of others tomorrow. You'll be humming *La Bohéme* by the end of the week. You're welcome to stay here if you've got your stuff with you. I'm just watching old game film and having a nip or two. Seven o'clock is a damn early wake-up call outside of football season, but they got us golfing and hobnobbing and god knows what else. Making patch quilts for all I know. They tell me that's what you've got to do these days. But just so you know, this is all bullshit, this Pigskin Stampede or whatever they call it. Complete and utter booster bullshit. Don't mistake coaching football—

teaching young people, I'm talking about—for all the horseshit
you're in for this week.

Love nodded his head vigorously to indicate that he too was
against horseshit.

But this here, said Coach Woody, pointing at the television
screen. This game, blocking and tackling, running and catching.
Well, you know. You played ball. Anyway this damn Landry Burns
from Baylor was supposed to be the greatest end in the game. First
team All-American. Cover of *Look* magazine with his uniform all
muddy and making a mean face. Slower than smoke off shit. Well,
come watch what we did to him back in the 62 Cotton Bowl. After
we got finished with him, he didn't know his ass from the Dallas
airport.

Never once did Coach Woody ask Love why he was there, why
he'd shown up in the middle of the night. Perhaps his driver showed
up at this time every year. Love found it strange and went back and
forth about whether to head back to his own place or not. The clock
on the DVD player showed they were closing in on one o'clock. He'd
be up in five hours no matter where he slept. Now Coach Woody
was rewinding the game film, the slow and small-looking players
moving jerkily in backwards motion.

He turned to face Love, his face older looking in the light from
the television.

Getting the game films on DVD is nice these days, he said. Easier I guess, compiling information, especially for specific situations
like goal line or third and long. But man, every time the light goes
out in the film room, I get a little nostalgic for that clickety-click
of the old eight-millimeter reel-to-reel, that kind of gentle scratchy
sound. It's too quiet these days when you go in to break down film.

He gave a rueful smile as if aware of how silly this likely sounded
to a young man.

You want to see how we warmed up in those days? They filmed the whole pregame. I guess cause it was a bowl game. It's pretty interesting if you like that sort of thing: high step strut, carryokie, drum major, all those running drills we used to do to warm up. Like looking into a time vault.

I'd like to see it, said Love.

Good, good. Make yourself another drink if you want to, then set there on the couch with Oskie. He likes to watch me slobberknock Landry Burns too.

Cat Napper

Love felt like the man in the iron mask. No, that wasn't it. He felt like his head was made utterly and completely from lead. It sat upon his shoulders like some heavy material that would yield to no jackhammer, no matter how relentless the operator of that fine machine was. He did marvel that the burly man at the helm was able to find the spots in his concrete noggin that seemed most likely to yield to his assaults. You had to tip your hat. This fucker simply wasn't going to give up.

They'd been on the road for an hour now and his only accompaniment during that time was the tree-felling snores of the slumbering Coach Woody beside him. They were in Coach Woody's Cadillac, a luxury ride to be sure, heavy on the leather and so cushy in all the right spots. Yes, the donut pillow could be safely stowed away. All was plush, soft, and warm.

It was so comfortable that Love could barely keep his eyes open. He'd been awakened that morning from dreams of sleek and friendly dolphins. At first the dolphins had been sea maidens and Love had been making some rather good and wet time. Frolicking about, slipping and sliding hither and yon. Then he was riding a dolphin and feeling not the least self-conscious about his own nude form. The dolphin was taking him for quick rides under the water, but Love could hold his breath for only so long before he had to coax the slippery mammal upward for breath. On occasion Love would recall the nubile sea maidens he'd befriended earlier and would search about for them, but always to no avail. Still, once he got used to the nude dolphin riding, he found he rather enjoyed himself.

It was when Coach Woody's Doberman had finally wet his face completely and most of his hair, and was making moves toward his neck and chest, that Love came unwillingly into the conscious state. As friendly and affectionate as the dog was, Love still felt disappointed that this, a canine face licking, had been his nude dolphin ride, and likely the source of his time with the frolicsome maidens as well.

He'd come groaning from the guest bed, roused Coach Woody from the floor where he'd slept sans pillow or blanket, turned off the television, thrown Oskie a burger, and started the coffee. They were on the road twenty minutes later and looking, if they were lucky, to be skidding into the parking lot of the Goshen Country Club just in time for lunch.

He'd gotten a maximum of two hours sleep. Once the film study had got going in full, the whisky seemed to go down a little smoother. They'd watched the whole of the 62 Cotton Bowl, pregame and halftime included, and replays of Coach Woody giving the old Whammo-Bammo! to that tin soldier of an All-American, Landry Burns, ten or fifteen times, forward and backward. They decided that backward was actually more enjoyable, seeing Burns prone, then flying to an upright position. Coach Woody would pause the action here, Landry—the big bad All-American—unsuspecting in the moment before hell's fury was unleashed.

After that Coach Woody had brought out several game tapes featuring teams that ran the Single Wing formation with the triple-threat tailback. Play by play, with frequent rewinding and slow motion, Coach Woody had described the intricate blocking schemes they were using. He'd also given a fairly thorough tutorial on the substitution patterns of two-platoon football. Love had enjoyed all the backfield motion and the tailback's razzamatazz with the ball, but around the fifteenth quick kick he felt ready to call it a day.

I thought you were a football coach, said Coach Woody.

It was late. Love was licked. Fraternities had been kicked off campus for less than this. With a gathering of strength and what liquidity still survived in his system, he managed to say: I'm not a coach yet. I'm a non-coaching graduate assistant.

Guest room's that way. Spider McCoy's about to make his catch to put the Demon Deacons down for good. But if you're tired, you're tired.

Love limped to the bedroom, looking back only once. When he did, he found the Doberman eyeing him with a mixture of pity and disappointment. It was plain in the dog's eyes that he had much to learn about Single Wing football. Love's final thought before landing face first on the bed was that he couldn't believe he'd dodged out on the term *coach*.

Next to him now, Coach Woody made noises like a bubbling still, plorping and wheezing and slurping. In the harsh sunlight that streamed in from the window, his tan and wrinkled face looked ready for planting. Corn here. And a nice row of tomatoes in that furrow. Love noticed as well that the hairs that grew from his large, twisted nose, broken how many times, were positively Rastafarian and moved to a gentle island beat. Occasionally, a bear cub would poke his head out of the underbrush that grew within the coach's left ear. Poor lost little chap.

It occurred to Love that growing old might be a right pain in the ass.

• • •

He'd just placed his hand on the eject button, feeling that maybe three hours of Willie Nelson's Greatest Hits was enough for the time being, when Coach Woody woke as if poked with a hot iron. As Love casually moved his fingers from the vicinity of the stereo, Woody let fly an elephantine groan and a series of machine-gun farts. There ensued several pleased yawns and a hyperbolic shaking out of ye olde cobwebs. Casually unscrewing the cap from the army-style canteen he'd packed for the trip, he drank heartily and with relish.

Nothing like a catnap, said Coach Woody, wiping the excess water that ran down his chin. You learned how to catnap yet?

Not yet, said Love.

If you're going to stay in coaching, it's imperative, absolutely imperative, that you learn how to steal ten, fifteen minutes here and there. It's the only way you can keep up with the pace.

Love looked at the clock. Unless Coach Woody snored, farted unabashedly, and jerked every five or so minutes while awake, he'd been sawing logs for the past three hours, or almost the entirety of the Red Headed Stranger's catalog, however you wanted to measure it.

Love nodded insincerely.

Yep, if you can steal ten, fifteen minutes, you wake up feeling like a new man.

How do you feel after a longer sleep?

Oh, I can't nap for more than thirty minutes or so or I'm grumpy the rest of the day.

So you're feeling pretty good now?

Fit as a fiddle.

They drove for a few minutes in silence. Love had to admit Willie Nelson was better than he'd expected overall, but as the greatest hits started over again, he thought a little change of pace might not be a bad thing.

Say, you seemed to be implying something a few minutes ago.

What's that? said Love.

I get the feeling you think I slept longer than I did.

Love smiled though it hurt his face to do so.

Am I correct?

Love continued to smile.

Coach Woody reached over and ejected Willie Nelson with true showmanship and flair.

I'd like to know just how long you think I slept?

Three hours, said Love. Maybe a bit longer. There at first I couldn't tell if you were sleeping or doing some kind of meditation. It was a humming noise I'd never heard before.

Huh? What? You don't know what the hell you're talking about.

Coach Woody looked at the clock and pointed. It showed 10:50.

At ten thirty, he said, I looked at the clock and figured I had time for a quick catter before lunch. I noted the time because I figured to eat lunch before noon and knew that would put me right on schedule.

Those noises you made as we left your neighborhood sounded suspiciously like snoring to me.

Coach Love, I respect your opinion, and I respect your integrity, but you are simply mistaken on this front.

They drove on in uncomfortable silence. Normally Love wouldn't have challenged the veteran catnapper on such a trivial point, but he found that his head, rather than feeling better as the day wore on, was feeling much, much worse.

What are you wincing about over there?

What?

You're wincing, said Coach Woody. Wonder if it might be a kidney stone.

No, I just had too much to drink.

You're not lactose intolerant are you?

No.

Do you have one of those gluten deals? Cause that kind of shit winds me up. Maybe we should stop and get you a gluten-free cracker.

I'm not allergic to gluten.

All right. Thank god. Gluten allergy, my ass. All right then, was the pain down low and kind of in your back?

Love thought about it. He rarely got sick and never paid much attention to pain or minor ailments.

I guess so, he said.

Well then, I'm telling you, my money's on a kidney stone. You'll need to keep an eye on that one. I won't tell you about the one I had. But if you ever wondered what it'd be like to give birth to a sharp rock through your pecker, you'll know soon enough if a kidney stone's what you've got.

Love didn't like the sound of this at all and for a few minutes he concentrated on breathing slowly and calmly without calling attention to himself. He thought any number of over-the-counter remedies would likely fix him up right, but no matter how he tried, Coach Woody's image of jagged geode nativity could not be shaken. He decided he needed more caffeine, more water, something greasy from the potato family to eat, and a jar or two of antacids.

I really don't think it's a kidney stone.

Coach Woody shook a concerned and parental head. I sure hope not, he said.

As they drove and Love's hypochondria—or was it hypochondria?—began to get the better of him, the thought crossed his mind that perhaps all this kidney stone business was a little psychological payback for the catnap controversy of a few minutes past.

I'm positive it's not a kidney stone.

Coach Woody, riffling through his portable CD carrier, nodded and said, good, good. A little bite to eat will likely buck you right up. You ready to stop for lunch?

Aren't we supposed to have lunch at the Goshen Country Club?

Aw, those things always run late. I'm hungry, aren't you?

The clock showed that it was nearly eleven. If they didn't stop, they'd be on time for the appointed lunch. He visualized the aggressive-looking itinerary that Sparkman had delivered from Coach Driver the day before. The thought played around in his mind that any slip-up regarding the delivery of the Woody package would doom what little chance he had for the graduate coaching position.

We'd better keep rolling, said Love. I can hang on for another hour or so.

Coach Woody laughed in a dismissive way.

My friend, you can't go through life scared shitless. If you're worried about Coach Driver, I'll handle that. He'll know it's my fault if we're late, not yours.

I don't know.

Hell, man, you're already on the staff. He won't fire you this late.

Love cleared his throat.

I'm still kind of hoping to get that coaching position.

I thought you had that already.

No, there's only one slot. It'll come down to me or Sparkman.

That fellow who's always laughing and joking with Coach Driver? Wears his hat backwards and always wants to slap hands with everybody?

That's him. His dad was on the staff with Coach Driver at Indiana. I'd say it's already been decided, but if not, I wouldn't want to ruin my chances.

Coach Woody nodded and put a new CD in the player.

This here's Roger Miller, he said. Listen, you do what you want, but I think anybody who's any good at coaching will get a job eventually. You can't worry yourself to death about job security, that'll drive you crazy. I mean, if you're doing your best and doing a good job and it's not good enough for whoever you're working for, then to hell with em. If they show me the door here, I'll find something else. Worse comes to worst, I'll just mosey down to Walmart and be one of those greeters who bug the shit out of people when they walk in the door.

You'd miss coaching, said Love.

No I wouldn't. Listen, I been fired four times. Three of those were staff changes. The head coach gets the ax and all the assistants go packing too. Unless you're just lucky as hell, you got to start out working at these Kansas States, and Iowa States, all those schools with *state* in their names. More than likely, you're going to get the ax sooner or later.

Love nodded. He thought that was likely the case.

One of those firings was a solo job though, said Coach Woody. One of those pink slips I earned all by myself.

How's that?

Had me this defensive coordinator I was working under out at Wyoming. My first job out of college. He was a big good-looking guy, big talker. Had just gotten divorced and taken up with this girl fresh out of college. Best-looking gal in the state. Just beautiful. Anyhow, he wasn't worth shit as a coach but knew how to butter up the head man. Anyhow, I'm coaching the linebackers for the Wyoming Cowboys, lowest piss ant on the staff. Well this fellow—his name was Brandt Bookhouse—he'd been giving me the high hat ever since I hit town. I don't know why. Probably cause I was as big and good-looking as he was.

Love laughed.

You don't believe me?

I believe you.

Get on that Internet sometime and find you some old pictures of me. Shit, hell, I'm still good-looking, what are you talking about?

Love smiled but said no more.

So whenever I'd seen him on campus or out at this one little beer joint in town called Daddy Fat's, he'd just walk past me without saying a word. Or if we were all out as a staff, he might say hello if the head coach was around. Head coach at Wyoming was Slick Wampler. Pretty good coach. Didn't know shit about the forward pass or any offense but the Wing T, but his boys would hit you. Anyhow, I wouldn't have minded the high hat if that was all, but on the practice field, he'd just ride me up and down. And I don't mind getting ridden. I been saddled up and rode by the best of them. You try getting your ass scorched by Ray Chuck Johnston when it's a hundred and twenty degrees down in Lubbock, Texas and see how you like it.

Love couldn't tell if he was being addressed, or if the question was rhetorical. Coach Woody was either suddenly pissed off that he—Love—had never had his ass scorched off by Ray Chuck Johnston or was mad at the memory of his own scorching ass or mad that a piss ant like Brandt Bookhouse thought he knew how to administer one.

Said Love: I don't believe I'd like it.

Like what, son? said Coach Woody in a distracted, angry manner.

Getting my ass scorched down in Lubbock.

What the hell are you talking about? Ray Chuck Johnston's been dead forty years. Died out there screaming at some redshirt defensive lineman. You know what his last words were?

No sir.

You big fat tub of blubbery, buttery shit. I'll teach you to titty-push your way to the quarterback. Then he dropped dead as a stone. Right there on the practice field. Half the players were still laughing when he hit the ground, already dead. Stroke. Oh, he was salty all right, but I loved him. So did the players. If he wasn't hollering at you, it was damn funny.

They rode for about a minute in silence, Coach Woody moving from his earlier anger to a kind of melancholic Zen state, blissfully recalling the lively days in Lubbock.

What we were talking about? I clean forgot.

Getting fired at Wyoming.

Oh yeah. Brandt Bookhouse. That's an arrogant-sounding name, isn't it? Anyhow, what he was doing was calling me Hondo.

Like the John Wayne movie?

Yeah, I know, it sounds like a compliment. And the right guy calling you that it would be, somebody who liked you. Well, I'd bought me a Stetson and a pair of rattlesnake-skin boots when I first got out there. Corny, I know. But it was my first time out west, and I was hankering for a cowboy hat and pair of boots soon as my feet hit Laramie. Well, Brandt Bookhouse gets to whenever he sees me, he'd say, in this real hokey drawl, *here comes old Hondo. Everybody best take cover.*

Love was smiling at Coach Woody's western drawl, and how he rolled his shoulders and head as he repeated the line.

It's funny, I admit it. I can almost laugh at it all these years later. So I was coaching linebackers and he was defensive coordinator and on the practice field every time one of my guys would miss a tackle, he'd say, *goddammit Hondo, can't you get your boys to tackle?* A good head coach will usually chew his assistants out in the locker room, in private. Even a hell raiser like Ray Chuck Johnston would really only embarrass an assistant when he was trying to make everybody mad, when the whole team was just kind of fatting around and he finally just had to send a message. And I don't think a coordinator should ever do it in front of the players. You agree?

Yes sir.

Old Brandt Bookhouse liked to play head coach too much for my liking. So one day after practice, late in the season, a right shitty season at that, I said something in the locker room to a lot of the

other assistants about what I was going to do the next time Brandt
called me Hondo or even looked at me funny. Brandt wasn't in the
locker room at the time and I was mad and more or less just talking to myself to blow off steam, you know. But as soon as I said it,
I knew I meant it. And I knew that you couldn't just say things like
that, something that provocative, behind somebody's back. Not if
you were any kind of man at all. Now some coaches don't mind
going behind other coaches' backs, but I never did truck with that.
What about you?

No, I don't truck with that.

So later that night, a big group had gone to Daddy Fat's for a
burger and beer, and there was Brandt Bookhouse standing by the
jukebox with a couple of coaches picking out songs. I walked up
behind him and waited. I was very peaceful and serene in my decision. So he turns around and I give him a little nod, like *come over
here a second*. So he follows me over to the corner with this little smile
on his face. Not a cocky one. Curious, I guess. We get to the corner,
just the two of us. No one else in the bar even knows we're talking.
And I said: Coach Bookhouse, I just wanted you to know that I've
been telling people that if you call me Hondo one more time, or ride
me in practice, I'm gonna whip your ass and steal your girlfriend.

Love laughed suddenly and loudly.

Coach Woody had the beginnings of a small smile working as
well.

What did he say? asked Love.

He looked at me for a second like he hadn't quite heard me or
still couldn't believe what I said, so I said: I just thought I ought to
let you know. And he kind of stands there for awhile longer with a
dazed look on his face, then he says, okay, thanks for telling me.
And walked back to the big group at the table.

When did you get fired?

Right after the season. Coach Wampler called me in and said

he understood Brandt and I didn't get along and that he didn't want any discord on the staff. I understood, no hard feelings. And twenty-four hours later I'm on the road heading back home. Figured I'd just take up at the shoe factory like my daddy. Later that summer, Ray Chuck Johnston called and asked me to come on down to Texas Tech.

Coach Woody took a long sip from his canteen and looked out the window at the passing cows, the power lines dotted with birds.

Love had been turning one aspect over in his mind though.

Did you even know Brandt Bookhouse's girlfriend?

No. I'd said hello to her a couple of times but that was it. For the record, I don't normally use that kind of language when talking about a woman. I was just trying to make a point with Mr. High Hat. For emphasis you know.

So you were just kind of bluffing on that part.

Not at all. It was a two-part deal, a two-part promissory note. I could have had it notarized.

But if you didn't know her and she was in a steady relationship with Brandt Bookhouse, how could you be sure you could steal her away?

I don't know. Haven't you ever just set your mind to something? If he'd called my hand I would have taken him out to the parking lot and jerked a knot in his ass right then and there. I might have got on the phone to his girlfriend right afterwards and asked her out, or I might have waited a day or two. I hadn't thought through all the particulars. Hell, she was way too good for Brandt Bookhouse. She was a classy gal. He'd out-kicked his coverage with her, for sure.

Love didn't say anything but could feel Coach Woody looking at him.

Listen hotshot. You might not believe me. But right then, right at that moment at Daddy Fat's in Laramie, Wyoming, Brandt Bookhouse believed me, I'll tell you that much.

They rode on in a silence listening to the idiosyncratic rhythms and lyrics of Roger Miller. After awhile Coach Woody said: I reckon I might miss coaching after all. You're right on that. But if you don't think that was a two-part deal out in Wyoming, you don't know your ass from a hole in the ground.

Love fought back a smile but said nothing. When they passed a beat-up sign on the side of the highway for Debbie's Diner, Coach Woody said, that place'll do, and looked at Love as if he'd just called him Hondo.

Love thought it best, all things considered, to go ahead and pull over.

Sparkman on a Roll

Love knew they'd already missed lunch, as well as the par three contest, but thought they were still in good shape for the shotgun start to the round. First prize for the par three was a new set of golf clubs and Love was a little dismayed not to have had a crack at them. But so be it. He'd safely delivered the goods, although a little late, to the Goshen Country Club and that was the important thing. He was heading toward the trunk for their clubs and golf spikes when Coach Woody grabbed him suddenly by the elbow.

Listen, he said, if you get in a bind talking to one of these old-timers, just ask them how their garden's doing. That'll do the trick.

All right.

And if you can, I'd recommend staying away from all the fatcat boosters. The regular folks who show up are usually all right. Very nice and sometimes a little nervous. They're excited to meet the coaches and you might have to do a little extra to make them feel comfortable.

A grad assistant?

Yes. You've got the word *coach* in front of your name and that means all the world in these little towns. Especially coach at *the* university. The fatcats, though, they won't bother talking to you. Some of them think I'm not even worth talking to and only the head coach will do. Do you know how to spot em?

Love admitted he did not.

The old ones are usually beefy and red-faced and kind of have a satisfied look about em. Their hands are usually fattish and tan. First thing you do is check their hands. Hadn't pushed a mower in forty years. And whichever town we go to, they'll have folks shuffling and bowing around them like they're hot shit.

Seriously?

Yes. Anyhow, the old boosters will want to talk about *their* football days, and none of them were worth a shit. Or the time they hired/fired a coach. The young ones, the ones in their thirties and forties, will talk about how big and fast the players are. They'll get this kind of glazed, moony look in their eyes and use words like *ripped* and *cut* a lot. Some of them will ask questions about body fat percentage and things like that. They're usually kind of licking their lips when they're talking about the players and jingling the change in their pockets.

No way, said Love smiling. You're exaggerating.

You wait.

It can't be that bad.

Maybe not, said Woody, getting out of the car and heading toward the trunk. Hope reigns supreme.

Love was nursing a gaseous domestic draft, cold though, under a banner in the tent that said: GOSHEN SUPER BOOSTERS WELCOME PIGSKIN CAVALCADE! Next to him was Coach Jackson, the running backs coach and only non-white-bread face under the tent. Of all the coaches, Love knew him the best.

Too many white people make me nervous, said Coach Jackson.

Love laughed.

They're gonna break out the Kenny Chesney any minute now, I can feel it.

Love grinned and shook his head.

They're gonna start line dancing.

Love took note of the crowd. He had to admit it, an impromptu Cotton-Eyed Joe wasn't out of the question.

> Now Golfers, dosey-doe
> Pull out your putters
> And swing em as you go

Are you here for all three days? asked Coach Jackson.

Yeah. What about you?

I'm one and done. Heading to the beach tomorrow with my wife. So sucks to be you, my friend.

Love was smiling about this, smiling that Coach Jackson would get a well deserved vacation after the long year, when Sparkman strolled up wearing—did Love's eyes deceive him?—plus-fours. Knickers, that is. Knee breeches. But there were no Scottish Highlands here. No bagpipers. No crusty toothless caddies slurping down foamy ales at the nineteenth hole. Love looked on, spellbound. And yes, that was a matching derby cap upon his knotty linebacker head. Knee stockings too. All in the university's colors.

He grinned at Coach Jackson and stuck out a fist for the en vogue *bump*.

Coach Driver dared me, said Sparkman. My dad told him he'd sent me this get-up and Coach D was dying to see it. Pretty sweet, huh? Old school to the max.

Jackson gave him the briefest of bumps, fearing, it seemed, that the very whiteness of the outfit would rub off on him in some osmotic and permanent way. Gone then: moves on dance floor, street cred, athletic ability, innate fear of khaki.

Shit, man, Jackson said smiling. Coach Driver should have paid you too.

Man, every babe in this place is digging me. This outfit shows *confidence*. Like a kilt. You wouldn't believe how many of the chicks have commented on it.

If you say so.

You guys going to let me hit that keg or not? said Sparkman, twirling an upside-down cup on his index finger. He pumped the keg a few vigorous times, adding a slightly orgasmic face in the process, oldest frat boy move in the book, ye olde pumping-away-at-it stroke. After the cup was filled he seemed to notice Love for the first time.

What's up, Lovey boy, he said, offering his fist for a little bumpdom.

Love looked at the fist. As long as he could remember, he'd made an honest effort to avoid all man-touches other than the traditional and suddenly anachronistic shaking of hands. On the athletic field or court or when prompted by older or much younger people, Love could be moved to slap five, almost exclusively of the down-low variety. For pure lack of cool, Love thought nothing could top the high five, especially as perfected by the golfers of the United States Ryder Cup Team. But with this fist bump business he wasn't so sure.

Sorry, said Love. I don't man-touch.

What? said Sparkman, laughing.

Love extended his hand in the traditional greeting that had served their Anglo-Saxon forefathers so well and repeated that there would be no man-touching today.

Coach Jackson laughed and Sparkman did too. Then Sparkman double-pumped his fist and said, come on Love, give it up. Give me a little bump.

Love assumed that his weapon-free hand was evidence of his essentially friendly status. Would knights from foreign countries fist bump or high five while mounted on steeds heading in opposite directions? Love thought not.

Can't do it, he said, smiling a bit as he withdrew the offered hand.

Okay, douche. But it's uncool to leave a brother hanging. Isn't that right, Coach Jackson?

Coach Jackson looked at Sparkman, jarred by the man in the plus-fours laying down such heavy lingo. Love thought perhaps he felt less a sibling to Sparkman than Sparkman hoped.

That's between you fellows, said Coach Jackson. We don't teach you guys any of our good shakes anyway.

Man-touch, shit, said Sparkman, reaching again for the beer tap. Well anyway, to hell with it. I believe it's traditional after hitting a hole in one to spring for the beers. So get your cups up, gentleman and douche, this round's on me.

That was a good shot, man, said Jackson. One bounce, then right in the bucket. You going to break in those new clubs today?

I don't know. They're just like the Pings I've already got. I might just sell them.

Trying not to choke on his beer, Love thought of his own golf clubs, twenty years old and outdated when he bought them. He'd never even heard of the person who endorsed his clubs, but the garage sale special fit his high school budget. He'd long assumed the signature belonged to some professional golfer from the sixties or seventies, but now he wasn't so sure. A famous caddy perhaps? A Putt-Putt champ? A golf announcer? The inventor of the Ryder Cup high five?

The Pigskin Cavalcade

Sparkman had just replayed the par three winning shot, not just closest to the pin but an ace, crediting his golf panoply and the crowd's approving murmur of it as a driving force behind his *sweet stroke*. He nodded his head fondly at the memory and took a satisfying swig of his brewski.

Hey, he said to Love. I met this girl last night at Sammy Dutch's lawn party who said she knew you. Said you guys were in the same book club.

Coach Jackson shot Love a sardonic smile at the mention of *book club*, but said nothing.

Brooke, said Sparkman, that was her name. Book club? What the hell, Love?

Love ignored this last bit with a dignified scratching of his face.

Man, she was nearly hot enough to make me join a book club. You guys just book club pals or what? No way you're hitting that.

Before Love could answer, Coach Jackson said: what's her last name?

I don't remember, said Sparkman.

Sampson, said Love.

That's the AD's daughter, you know, said Coach Jackson.

Love thought about it. Somehow he'd never gotten around to asking about her parents, or at least not in much depth. Maybe he'd asked and she'd dodged the question. He usually felt too distracted by her good looks and constant talk about art and literature to form a cogent sentence, much less a probing interrogative. About all he knew about Brooke's parents was that they lived in town. The athletic director's daughter? Couldn't be. She hated sports.

You sure? said Love.

Brown hair, olive skin, very attractive?

Yes, said Love and Sparkman at the same time.

That's her, boys.

Love and Sparkman took sips from their beers, silently taking in this new bit of information.

She came to this thing last year, said Jackson. I bet she's here this time too.

As Love processed this development, mulling the different ways Question #8 from the Book Club Supplement to *The Bon Bon Girls* had complicated his life, Coach Woody strolled past, hollering, come on, hot ass, we're up.

Love grabbed his clubs and caught up with Woody. Immediately, the craggy coach began talking out of the side of his mouth lest he be overheard. Love assumed the two men behind them were their playing partners for the day and that Woody was trying to talk surreptitiously.

Now listen, he said, you get the young dipshit and I'll take the codger. You got that? No negotiations. That young guy's hands are sweating all to hell and he's already breaking down games from last year with me. I'm sorry, but I got you on seniority on this one, so that's just the way it's going to be.

Two golf carts were waiting for them at the first tee and Coach Woody, rather obviously, Love thought, lingered before committing his bag to one or the other. Wherever the young guy went, he was going opposite. Doing as he'd been told, Love delayed as well.

The young guy, a short, stocky type in billowing khaki shorts and a high-billed golf cap, threw his bags on the cart nearer the tee box and said: Coach Woody, looks like it's you and me.

Woody looked angrily once at Love as if this were somehow his fault, then grudgingly placed his bags where he least wanted them. Love's partner, the old-timer, was tall and gray looking with skinny legs poking out of his Bermuda shorts. He wore a golf shirt and a wool vest ensemble in the school colors. Love thought it a trifle warm for a vest, hovering as it was around ninety, but had little knowledge of the circulatory system of a pensioner. The fact that he apparently hadn't any hair on his body no doubt increased whatever nip was in the air. The man smiled once at Love, placed his bag on the other cart, and headed toward the tee box.

Despite the tension and his embarrassing golf clubs and the fact that he only had three balls, one tee, and a soiled and ripped glove too pitiful to display in public, Love couldn't help but be excited. Before him lay the nicest fairway he'd ever seen in person, lined on both sides with mature trees and fairway traps white and glistening in the sun. It was the first course he'd ever played with fairway sand.

Love's playing partner appeared to be loosening up, holding his driver straight-armed in front of him and rotating his trunk six inches to either side. He was grunting slightly under the duress.

Henry Rice, the man responded after Love had introduced himself.

And other than the words *yes, no, good shot*, and *thank you*, this was all he spoke for the first eight holes of the round.

Love was only two over after eight and thrilled he'd yet to lose a ball. He was playing so surprisingly well that he'd nearly been able to strike from his mind the image of Sparkman dressed as a fancy stable boy. It was amazing what a good round of golf could do for the spirits, and he found himself whistling away in the cart as they headed the hundred yards down the course to where Mr. Rice's drive had finally come to its hippity-hop rest.

As the spindly linksman took the first of his seventeen practice swings, Love thought that he seemed happy enough despite his vow of silence on the course. Then again, perhaps he wasn't talking because he'd gotten stuck with a no-name graduate assistant. Didn't people pay money to come to these things to rub shoulders with the head honchos who made it happen on the field? Was Love considered part of that, a celebrity by proximity? If so, what were his responsibilities to the boosters? What, exactly, was he supposed to say or do?

Mr. Rice swung and hit his best shot of the day, a fairway wood that made it just past the drives of his three golfing partners. As he watched the ball bounce, a quick smile passed over his face.

When he was back in the cart again, Love said: good shot.

Thank you.

Ahead of them, Travis Trotter, Coach Woody's playing partner, was preparing to hit out of turn. Love's ball was a good ten yards behind the young superbooster's, but such was his hurry to get back in the cart and diagram plays, offer personal tips, and recount his own football exploits on the junior varsity gridiron to Coach Woody, that golf etiquette must by necessity take a back seat.

A fly or something landed on Travis Trotter's ball and he swished his club around several times. This was the longest Love and Mr. Rice had been in the cart without moving and Love was beginning to feel the pressure of silence, of his role or non-role as university dignitary. He would have thought it preposterous, ludicrous, to pose as a university delegate only an hour before, but now he wasn't so sure. Perhaps he was a certified member of the Pigskin Cavalcade after all, and with that came the entitlements—and responsibilities—of membership, namely keeping the boosters happy.

How's your garden? said Love.

Not worth a flip.

Too much rain?

That's it.

Love couldn't tell if Mr. Rice was done or not. His face had a kind of faraway look to it as if winded, or sated, by the previous exchange. Then to Love's amazement he spoke again:

You know what I like?

What's that?

A pepper sandwich.

What's on it?

Peppers.

Love wondered if he could keep up his end of the exchange. He'd grown so accustomed to not speaking the last hour that it was as if he'd lost the ability to converse. It was then that the muse paid him a visit:

That on white bread?

Yep. With mayonnaise. Plus a little black pepper.

Black pepper on a pepper sandwich, huh?

Well, that's according to personal taste. But that's the traditional way.

Up ahead, Travis Trotter was pumping his fist and shouting, *TNT*, as he did after every shot that he liked. Love guessed that perhaps his middle name started with *N*, but the derivation of the nickname wasn't a subject he planned to pursue.

As TNT began his short-legged strut back to the cart, Coach Woody turned to look at Love. On the side of the cart, he was moving his hands back and forth in the universal sign for switching up. His plan, obviously, was to swap partners at the turn. Love put the cart in motion and pretended not to see.

MacArthur Gets the News

At the turn, folks milled about under the hospitality tent, eating pigs in blankets and brownies, sipping on lemonade and beer from the keg. Love had taken passes the several times the beer cart girl came by with her wares, but now, after nearly two hours in the hot sun, he thought he could have another cold one without too much effect. The one thing Love was not going to do, absolutely not going to do at any point during the trip, was get drunk. Coach Woody and all the rest could do as they pleased, but Love, in a role of responsibility specifically granted by Coach Driver, would play it straight down the middle. A beer here, a beer there to be social, but that was it. Any chance, however slight, he had for the coaching position depended on his ability to keep the Wood Man out of trouble.

A logjam had developed at the tenth hole as a result of the hospitality tent and the wait was longer than Love expected. After gulping down a barbecue sandwich and several cookies, discreetly procured one subtle time after another, he was ready to get back on the course. He'd actually birdied the ninth hole, invigorated perhaps by his part in the pepper sandwich roundtable. And Mr. Rice himself had managed a par as well and was now to be seen sipping on a draft and making an arching movement with his hand as he described his miracle shot on nine to another codger of similar rank and style. For a moment the Cavalcade seemed as one.

Coach Lowe, snapped a harsh voice from somewhere outside the tent. This voice, a shrill bark really, like a ferocious medium-sized dog whose stub of a tail has been stepped on, made the use of an on-field whistle completely unnecessary. Turning and starting at a near jog, nearly knocking over the food tray and a few innocent bystanders in the process, tripping over a sprinkler, skinning his shin and spilling his beer, Love heeded the call of his head coach. He felt suddenly feverish, and pungently so.

Yes Coach, said Love when he was five or so feet away, voice cracking in a pubescent way.

Coach Driver did not immediately look at him. Standing on the tenth tee, he continued to take his driver back with methodical—menacing—patience, then hold his phantom swing at its height for several seconds. He repeated this a number of times without ever glancing up until Love began to imagine he'd heard his name called. The whole first month of the season that voice had haunted his sleep. A short punch of voice shouting *COACH LOWE!* and he'd wake from his sleep as to an air raid siren.

Which was strange since no one ever called his name at practice, much less Coach Driver.

Blood was trickling down his leg from its recent scrape with the sprinkler, and Love was on the verge of slinking away in search of a bandage when Coach Driver, from the frozen position of his abbreviated swing, spoke:

I gave you an itinerary, didn't I? For the Pigskin Cavalcade?
Yes sir.

Was it abbreviated? Or was today's lunch listed? I'm wondering if I gave you an incomplete itinerary?

No sir. It was the full itinerary. Today's lunch was clearly listed.

The head coach then swung his club with full force, catching a bee who had been resting peaceably on a blade of grass with a faint *ppfht* of contact. Love couldn't see where the bee landed, but the swing had been solid, leaving Coach Driver with what was likely a five-iron to the green if he decided to play the insect.

I'll expect you, and especially Coach Woody, to be on time for the rest of the events this week, said Coach Driver, looking at Love with his bugged eyes and eyebrows twitching to and fro.

Love found that he was nodding in a wobbly-headed fashion at the coach. Might he be truly deranged?

If there's one thing I don't like doing, it's answering a lot of questions about where my subordinates are. I had twenty people asking where Coach Woody was today.

As Coach Driver said this, he casually swished the club in front of Love, a foot or so from his knees. Deciding this was some sort of test of nerve, Love held his ground. This proved harder to do as the head coach's swing—waggle to be precise—gradually rose to just below belt level.

Yes sir, said Love. I understand. I'll have Coach Woody on time from here on out. You've got my word.

From nowhere a smile crossed Coach Driver's face.

I'm guessing it's Coach Woody's fault and not your own that you guys were late.

Love considered his response, considered the undecided coaching position waiting to be filled.

I can't blame Coach Woody, he said. We were both hungry and decided to stop for lunch.

His head coach kept the waggle going, back and forth, just below Love's belt buckle. He seemed to be having a hard time getting comfortable with the club.

Coach Love, I assume you know we have an open position for a coaching graduate assistant.

Yes sir.

We'll be deciding who gets that position, the coaching staff and I, here in the next few days. The big advantage to this position of course is that it is often a springboard to a regular, paid position on a major college coaching staff, which is where most graduate assistants would like to be. You were aware of this?

Yes sir.

If it were me, if I were a graduate assistant, I'd be doing everything I could to look responsible, to look like someone who could, one, handle a leadership position, and two, be a solid and upstanding team member. That's just me, of course. Then again, I always knew I wanted to coach at this level. Not everybody does.

That's what I want too. I want to be a college coach.

Nodding his head and walking toward his golf bag, Coach Driver said: I'm glad to hear it. Let's just say, no harm no foul on this one then.

Love stood there, trying to look as much as possible like an upstanding team member.

I think I'll be teeing off soon, said Coach Driver, heading toward the practice putting green and talking over his shoulder. How about running over and getting me a barbecue sandwich?

Okay, said Love.

Do they have side dishes?

Yes sir.

Give me a couple of sides too. Anything but cole slaw. And tea to drink, unsweet with lemon.

Yes sir.

Oh, said Coach Driver, turning to face Love as if something important had just come to mind. If they've got any pie, get that. Unless it's something with cooked berries. Like blackberry or blueberry. Cooked fruit is okay. But absolutely no berries. If there's no pie, just grab a brownie or cookie, it doesn't matter which. But try and get something without nuts.

Got it.

Oh, one more thing. Not too much ice in my tea. Like five or six cubes. Half the time you get more ice than drink. I hate that.

Yes sir, said Love, trotting off, I got it.

You got to trade with me, said Coach Woody. This jackleg dipshit TNT or whatever he calls himself is trying to tell me what line stunt we should have run against Kentucky down on the goal line last year.

They were standing under the hospitality tent, waiting for their group's turn on the tee.

Well, I guess it takes all kinds, said Love with a smile.

I'm not sure it takes all kinds, but we sure as hell got em. You gonna change or what?

What stunt did he suggest on the goal line? Are you talking about that draw play when they scored in the fourth quarter?

Now damn it.

I'll switch, said Love. But I'm playing out of my mind. I hate to mess up my mojo.

Aw, you'll be fine. He won't be quizzing you and thinking he's auditioning for a job on the coaching staff.

You've got to tell him though. Didn't he pay extra to get paired with you?

I'm going to say I feel bad about this old-timer getting stuck with you for eighteen holes and promise to sit at his table tonight at dinner.

Are you?

Oh hell no. I plan on hitting the nearest steakhouse in town as soon as we get off this golf course, then getting the hell out of Dodge first thing in the morning.

You can't do that, said Love.

Before Woody could respond, a great roar came from the tenth tee as Coach Driver's playing partners commenced hooting and hollering over his latest drive. Perhaps a few celebratory pistols were fired in air. In response, the head coach offered a modest shake of the head and an aw-shucks grin. For a moment Love thought he lip-read the words: *even a blind squirrel finds an acorn every now and then.*

There, it was complete. The Bon Jovi fan from Syracuse, New York was well on his way to becoming a good ole boy, with all the privileges and prestige that that entailed. Tonight, at the secret pig roast on a booster's private hunting preserve, they would drench him with Jack and Coke, Rebel-yell the school fight song, and blood his face from a deer fatted on daily grain and killed from an SUV with a high-powered rifle. Afterwards the coach would be treated to more bare-bottom paddle spanking than any man could desire.

No deal then on the switch, said Love. You've got to go to dinner tonight or it's my ass.

What? What? What?

No dinner, no switch. Deal's off. I like the old-timer anyway. Once we got to talking about gardening, the whole conversation opened up. He was telling me about his war days in Korea. Did you know he served under MacArthur? Hell of a poker player too, apparently. He was fixing to tell me about the day Truman recalled the General. Apparently Mr. Rice was in MacArthur's quarters the day he got the news.

What? MacArthur? Hey, I gave you that garden tip. You've got to switch.

No way.

MacArthur? Was he an aide to MacArthur? Was he ever up on the Yalu River?

He mentioned the Yalu. But that was the last hole. He was supposed to finish up when we got started again.

What was his rank?

Love shook his head. No more information regarding the ever-interesting, ever-surprising Mr. Rice would escape his lips.

Aw, you're bullshitting.

Love smiled but made no confession. He was, of course, completely bullshitting. No man of this generation could resist MacArthur.

Listen, said Love, Coach Driver just gave me a firm talk about us being late to this thing. He doesn't want it to happen again. And if it does, I'm in trouble, not you. So we have to go to everything and get there on time. And that includes tonight's dinner.

Oh bullshit to that.

As the old coach said this, he scratched at his sunburned forehead in an agitated manner. He'd not worn a hat. And he'd applied no sunscreen. These old cats were going to get their Vitamin D, come hell or high water.

Coach Driver chewed that ass, did he?

Not sure it was a chewing, said Love. But I felt he got his point across.

You're still aiming for that coaching position, huh?

Yes.

I hate to break it to you, but I don't much favor your chances. That other fellow's been working it pretty hard with the head man.

As he said this, he motioned toward the keg where Sparkman was yukking it up with Coach Vaughn, the offensive coordinator. And if his eyes didn't deceive him, Coach Vaughn was filling his, Sparkman's, cup. The four trips Love had made to fill, precisely, and exactly, Coach Driver's snack order burned ever hotter in his mind.

Yeah, said Love. I'm not holding out a lot of hope about that coaching position. But until it's been announced officially, I want to take care of business.

Coach Woody slapped a big hand with ruined knuckles on Love's shoulder and gave him a few painful thumps.

No job's worth a whole hell of a lot of asskissing. But all right. I'll go tonight. I'll just have to find some other way to ditch my sweaty little coaching friend at dinner. Hot damn, you'd think he was Chuck Noll or something.

With that Coach Woody headed toward the throng of people under the tent, looking for TNT to break the sad news. He stopped after a few steps and turned back to Love:

He was really there when MacArthur got the news?

Love laughed, shaking his head in the negative.

Goshen Super Booster

What do you bench, by the way?

Love said he didn't know.

I cranked 315 the other day, said TNT, grabbing a club and heading toward his ball in the fairway. Was watching that kick-ass Brett Favre commercial at the gym, the Wrangler one where the guys are playing pick-up football. Got jazzed and just cranked it out like it was nothing. Man, that commercial gets me fired up as hell for football season.

If Love remembered correctly, the commercial being referenced was a slow motion, sweaty, touchy affair featuring smiling middle-aged actors in some simulation of football. The background music was the classic rock song *Ain't Seen Nothing Yet*. Watching the commercial late one night after drinking several Pabst tall boys, Love had been struck by the amount of blocking in the simulated game. He wondered who would want to block in touch football. Why not just send everyone out for a pass? Did they take a vote with guys clamoring to play offensive guard? Was it because of all the extra touching the lineman got to do? And did they do an actual snap where Favre put his hands under some Wrangler-butted center? Why were they all smiling so much during the game, especially when they closed in to fondle the famous quarterback? And finally, was the song, *Ain't Seen Nothing Yet*, a not so subtle hint about what lay in store for these worked up middle-agers after the preliminaries were over? Would it be straight to the Turkish baths or what? Or would they prolong the foreplay a bit with a few brewskis at the sports bar while watching the latest offerings of the Golf Channel?

TNT had just launched his third shot onto the green, which left him with what looked to be a five-foot putt for par. On the other hand, Love's own game had gone due south with the switch in partners. Love thought Nicklaus himself would be hard-pressed to keep his composure with a loaded stick of dynamite in the same cart.

TNT! came the shout from the fairway and then his slow strut back to the cart.

Getting into the cart, he held up an open palm for the Ryder Cup high five. As a university representative and half-ass Cavalcade celebrity, Love felt obligated to oblige. But it cost him some to do so, both on an emotional and spiritual level.

As they made their way to the green, TNT said: Do you wear Wranglers?

No, said Love.

TNT nodded in an unsurprised fashion. You ought to give them a try. They're a good fit. Lots of room in the seat and thighs. Kind of like those old Levi button flies.

Was he really having a conversation about men's jeans? He was, he definitely was. Slowly, Love discerned the ploy. He and the dynamite man had been tied after nine, but now Love's game had been detonated by a true master of psychology.

Said Love, casually: so, did you play football?

Oh yeah, said TNT, flooring the golf cart and passing Mr. Rice in midswing with no decrease in speed. I played fullback and linebacker.

Just as Love figured. Fullback. Read: back-up lineman of indeterminate designation. And linebacker. I.e. kick-off coverage team, senior year only. He'd met the old high school fullback/linebacker combo dozens of times.

I bet you liked to hit, said Love.

TNT gave a leering smile. You got that right, buddy. What about you? You ever play any ball?

Yeah, I played at Woodford College.

Never heard of it.

It's a Division III school in Kentucky.

Oh. Division III. I thought about playing at that level, but decided why bother? Especially when I could spend the next five, six years chasing tail at the university.

Love managed to gather himself after this exchange and hole his long putt for a double bogey. Meanwhile, Coach Woody and Mr. Rice were playing in an offhand fashion, putting quickly so as to get back to their conversation about the paucity of quail in the region and their fondness back in the day for the fried version of that wild fowl. As the rotund former fullback of Never Was High lined up his par putt, he muttered to himself: man up, TNT, man up.

As the *man up* phrase was one that Love found especially embarrassing for those who shared his gender, he wasn't particularly displeased when his playing partner gagged his putt. Nor when he yanked the comebacker as well.

TNT stalked back to the cart muttering about the bullshit greens.

Did you get a six? he asked.

Yes, said Love.

TNT nodded and made two quick marks in the score card. Flooring the cart, he said: can't believe I bogeyed that fucker. Easiest hole on the course.

Bogey?

Love counted shots: drive into trees, punch out, good third shot to green. Missed par putt. Missed comebacker. Tap-in. Yes, it added up to six. Or as Love sometimes liked to call it, *double* bogey. Though Love wasn't fond of anyone who kept better count of his opponent's strokes than his own, there was his role as university envoy. What could he say? Did he even care?

Yes, he sort of did.

They arrived at the eighteenth hole to find one group on the tee and another waiting. Now there was no way around it, no shot to hit or divot to replace, Love would have to hear more of TNT's offerings on the sports world and karaoke night domination. My god, he might even discuss his tail-chasing days on campus. Love's mind began to race. He might want to talk politics. Or deer hunting. If he mentioned *Tuesdays with Morrie* or some other motivational book by a sportswriter or coach, Love wouldn't be held responsible for his actions, university envoy or no university envoy.

TNT commenced chuckling now in a feigned way and Love knew the moment of truth was at hand.

That missed putt reminds me of this story from my annual golf trip to Myrtle Beach that me and my college friends take every year.

Love nodded.

It was the eighteenth hole and I was up one skin. Small bets. Hundred a side. You know the skins game? Like they have on TV?

Love made a motion with his head that could have been interpreted two ways. The first interpretation would be *yes, I've heard of the skins game*. The second interpretation would be a little closer to *it's fine with me if you don't finish this story.*

TNT went with the first interpretation.

Had me about a ten-footer to take home the bacon. And I'd been playing terrible all day. Just ham-and-egging it all over the course. Then pulling one out of my ass every three holes or so. All the guys were razzing me, you know how frat brothers are:

Hey TNT, bet you blow up on this one. Bet ole TNT is about to explode all over this putt.

Love quietly began to weep.

Then he realized that the junior booster wasn't really talking to him, that his attention wasn't even required. TNT either didn't care if people listened or was so used to talking to air, to blank horrified faces, that he no longer noticed. Love relaxed a bit. How bad could it be?

So I look up from the putt and say, let's add ten lap dances to the bet and a handle of Jack. Well of course they jumped on it. They knew I was just talking trash, and like I said, I hadn't made diddly-squat when it counted all day. So what do you think happened?

Your friends charged you en masse, swinging their three-irons above their heads like flails?

TNT was still waiting for an answer. The one above hadn't quite made its way out of Love's mouth.

You made the putt, said Love.

Here, and it was so predictable Love couldn't believe he hadn't seen it coming, the little keg-o-dynamite offered up another high five, and said: *you got that right, soul brother.*

The look now on TNT's face was pure bliss, his absorption in the fabricated tale complete. The putt would land with a satisfying plonk, the defeated phantom friends would whoop in feigned indignation, the handle of Jack bought, laps danced upon. At closing time, TNT's favorite practitioner of the burlesque would request a nightcap. And who was TNT to deny a lady?

In short, not to complete the Ryder Cup moment would be the equivalent of telling a child there was no Santa Claus. What good could come of it? And what need to destroy such wondrous suspension of disbelief? Besides, they were legion, these TNTs, populating the frat houses and sports bars, the golf courses and boardrooms, *manning up*, every one of them, over their birdie putts, their Texas Hold Em, their trips to Vegas no matter what the little lady says. And so it was that Love met the offered palm with a gentle palm of his own, answering the modern and ubiquitous and oddly poignant call for yet another and another and another: *man-touch*, that so bespoke the death of the American male.

I won't tell you what all happened in the strip bar, said TNT, other than the ten lap dances turned into about fifty and someone who shall go unnamed ended up on stage dancing his ass off to *Back in Black*.

It sounds like fun, said Love, feeling more tired than he had in a long time. The long night had finally caught up with him, and so had his round of golf with the boosters. He wondered how coaches did this year after year. How did they not go crazy?

Said TNT: When are yall going to get somebody up there who knows how to coach quarterbacks anyway?

Errand of Mercy

At the hotel, Love lay on his bed, trying to sleep and watching with one eye a show about great college football games of the last decade. He wanted a nap, needed a nap, before dinner at the country club, but his catnapping skills were still in their infancy. He'd have had a better shot at sleep if he just turned off the television, but after going so long without cable, he wanted to get all the TV he could.

Luxuriating in the nether region between the dim and innocuous voice of the football announcer and the Land of Nod, he thought he heard his name called. Like the voice on this television, whoever was calling seemed to do so from a great distance, and Love couldn't tell if he now resided more in the real world or the dream one.

Coach Love. Can you hear me?

Coach Love. I need you for a minute.

It's an emergency.

This last sentence was delivered much louder than the others, as if the person had been trying to whisper before and had discerned the futility of that tactic. Love shook himself awake sluggishly. He had been asleep. In your face, catnappers!

The voice was Coach Woody's and seemed to come through

multiple doors. Loud as the cry now was, it was still muffled, barely intelligible. Love roused himself fully and hurried through the door that adjoined his and Coach Woody's rooms.

Entering, he called out loudly and firmly, heralding not only his arrival but his willingness and capability to handle whatever crisis might be at hand. He'd never felt more alive or ready. There was something to that catnap business after all. What he said was what any well-trained and capable southern lad would say when beckoned from afar by an elder:

Sir?!

Coach Love?

Yes sir.

The voice that had been calling him came from behind the closed bathroom door, sounding slightly spent with the effort of his summons.

Coach Love, have you had the pleasure of trying this hotel's brand of toilet paper?

No sir.

Well, I believe they must make it here on the premises.

Love wasn't sure how to interpret this so he went to default response: yes sir?

I'm thinking they must go around collecting wood chips and bits of sandpaper from local construction sites. And probably a fair smidge of pine bark from the nearest patch of woods and whatever shards of glass they can round up in the parking lot. Then they just whip it all together down in the basement with some Elmer's Glue and hot sauce.

Love kept his own counsel, continuing to stare at the bathroom door in front of him as if he were conversing with it. At no point must his mind imagine what sat within. He heard the sound of a belt buckle hitting porcelain, then a seat squeaking about, then some impatient ruffling through something. The monologue continued throughout:

Two days of this and a man'd be saddle sore for a month . . . I'd pay twenty dollars extra to get decent toilet paper . . . And who needs this shampoo and conditioner and shit. Hand lotion? Well goddam . . . Coach Love, never skimp on ketchup, dress socks, toilet paper, or a sports coat. You'll get your money's worth ten times over if you pay for quality . . . I once stripped paint off an old desk . . .

After a spell, there came the sound of shoe scuffling and grunting. Some sort of primitive ballet was afoot beyond the threshold. Delicate and treacherous balance—the grasping of the nearest solid thing—casual blasphemies regarding a Job-like fate—and then—voila—a twenty-dollar bill peeking beneath the bathroom door.

Get yourself a four-pack too, came the breathless cry from within.

This cry coincided with the heavy crash of weight descending, the grimacing power lifter dropping his bar after the three-second buzzer has rung in the clean and jerk.

What brand?

Charmin. Be sure it's ultra soft and not just ultra strong. And don't even think about that Angel Soft load of malarkey. If that's soft enough for an angel, then it's an angel with a cast iron asshole. And don't even get me started on that Quilted Northern horseshit either.

Got you, said Love.

And pick me up two or three Slim Jims if they got em.

Okay.

You like Slim Jims?

Not really.

What do you like, Funyuns?

What? He'd been under the impression that this was something of an emergency situation. Now they were fully engaged in a discussion of snack foods.

No, said Love.

Well, get some pretzels or something sweet if you like. My treat.

Hey, that sounds good. Get me a fried pie if they have em. Any old kind. Those individual sized things you see in these small markets sometimes.

Love heard a significant pause, as if Coach Woody were waiting for a response or thinking of some other treat that might tickle his fancy, perhaps a morsel suggested by Love himself. But the time seemed ripe, so Love got while the getting was good.

When he returned, he let himself into his own room and stood there for a moment beside his bed, deep in concentration. On the television, a head coach was showing no mercy to an innocent piece of gum. Seriously, whence sprang this phenomenon? Open-mouthed coach-chomp seemed the stylistic order of the day, with the mandible working like twenty, the tongue flickering here and yon, the wad of gum bobbing like a raft on a wild river ride. Did they not know the camera was on them?

From the other room came the faint and tuneless humming of an unknown opera. All the way home, Love had been contemplating the denouement of his adventure, namely the delivery of the 2-ply package. He passed through the den with a determined step and announced his arrival at the bathroom door in a deliberate, no-nonsense manner.

I've got your toilet paper, he said, eyeing the doorknob with a furrowed brow.

Good, good. You get the Slim Jims?

Yes.

What about the fruit pies?

They didn't have any. I assume you meant the homemade kind and not those packaged things like Hostess makes.

No, hell no, I didn't want those packaged things. That's not fruit in there. It's some kind of rubbery substitute.

I got you a cinnamon roll.

Here there was a pause, as if working over the notion of cin-namon roll as replacement for homemade fruit pie. Apples and oranges to be sure. Love had thought it was all Slim Jim, the Slim Jim forefront in the mind, with the fruit pie as something of a side dish. Now, the wind had changed. The old boy had his heart set on some fried lard and sugared fruit all right.

That'll do I guess.

I'm just going to toss it in, said Love.

The cinnamon roll?

No, the toilet paper.

Oh yeah, got you, of course. But hey, don't throw it in, you'll break something. Just open the door and hand it to me real quick.

It was clear the time for lines in sand had arrived. He felt firm about this. The Rubicon had been crossed, consequences be damned.

I'll just toss the package in.

No. Hell no.

But the door was open, opened quickly, and Love tossed the goods in a sidearm Frisbee motion without care for accuracy. The door was just shut as the Charmin hit the bathroom mirror and began ricocheting to parts unknown.

In Love's mind: a reflection of Coach Woody in a compromised position, nude to the core, hands raised, hoping—too late—to catch the package on the fly. Then the sound of glass crashing and gen-eral mayhem on prescription bottles and toiletries and other myster-ies of the geriatric loo.

Well I'll be damned, there goes my Old Spice.

Love didn't respond. He thought the collateral damage well worth it.

That one's on you, buddy boy.

Listen, said Love. I'm not saying I haven't enjoyed this conversa-tion, both of them, in fact. But I'll talk to you when you get out.

Coach Woody chuckled at this and was soon humming again the opera of the day. All seemed right with the world. Whatever toiletries had been lost was as nothing to the satisfaction of the Charmin Ultra.

Love lay on the bed watching ESPN Classic, a replay of a game played two years ago. He was contemplating the use of the word *classic* when Coach Woody walked in, fresh as a powdered newborn, and sat on the opposite bed.

When did coaches start chomping gum all the time? said Love.

Woody pointed to the television. You mean Pete Carroll?

Yeah. It's like he wants us to see his gum. All the coaches do it now. Why?

Hell if I know, but that guy down at Nebraska who looks like a plumber's gonna break his jaw if he's not careful.

They stared in dumb silence at the screen. The camera had been on Carroll for quite awhile now as he stalked the sidelines in a hopped-up fashion, alternating cocksure smiles with displays of his gaping facial orifice.

Woody shook his head: it's the damnedest thing I've ever seen. I'm sorry you brought it up.

Love nodded. The whole spectacle left him feeling sad and grossed out.

Actually, said Woody, I think it started with Bowden. Trying to look casual, you know, nonchalant. I like Bobby, and he's a hell of a coach. Nobody'd heard of Florida State before he came along, but anybody who thinks he's loose just doesn't understand human nature. And then he had some success and I guess coaches just started copying him. Trying to look cool under pressure, you know. Hell, look at Spurrier with his visor. Now half the young coaches wear em. Let me tell you something, if some guy coached in a smoking jacket and bikini briefs and had success, you can bet your ass there'd be a run on both items before long in the coaching ranks. Gum chewing one day, bikini briefs the next. Who the hell knows?

You ought to work in the occasional visor, said Love. I think it would suit you.

Listen, I understand a visor on a hot, sunny day. Keeps the sun out of your eyes and your head doesn't get hot. It's functional. But a visor at night? That's a fashion statement.

Love laughed.

A man wearing a visor at night thinks it looks good. Otherwise he wouldn't be wearing it. It serves no functional purpose. Bear Bryant wore the houndstooth hat, and a lot of the old coaches wore hats back in the day. You know, hats like a man wore when he was dressed up in a coat and tie. Dressing like that told your players you expected them to take care of business and do things the right way and play like men. Why any coach thinks looking like a half-ass golfer at night inspires young men is beyond me. Dressing like that says: let's go play some golf. Let's go look like silly asses out there. Would having your coach dress like a golfer make you want to go out and pop somebody?

No, said Love, I don't think so.

Of course it wouldn't. A coach who wears a visor and has a good team is winning despite the visor. Whereas a coach in a dress hat was worth three to seven points. There at the end, Bear's houndstooth was worth ten points, minimum.

Love smiled.

That goddam visor though? That's a message being sent I can't decipher.

The Banquet

Love sat at one of the fifteen or so round tables spread out around the banquet hall. The room was wood paneled and a little dark, but did offer a picture window which Love spent his time gazing out of when he wasn't eyeing the door in anticipation of Brooke's late arrival. But thus far, neither she nor her supposed father, the athletic director, had shown. Love remained skeptical that Coach Jackson had his facts straight. It just seemed too unlikely.

At the front of the room was a raised dais that served as both the speaker's platform and guest of honor table, much in the fashion of the few wedding receptions Love had attended. Earlier the food had been blessed by a middle-aged representative of the Fellowship of Christian Athletes. Throughout the prayer the woman sitting next to him had harrumphed and fidgeted. She'd even laughed when a long pause that seemed to anticipate the *amen* finale led into another round of blessings for the local high school students about to graduate, recently elected delegates to Congress, and the waitstaff who brought forth the *tender blessings* about to be consumed.

At this point she'd nudged Love with her elbow, pointed with her fork, and said: I'm sorry but iceberg lettuce, bacon bits, and ranch dressing do not a tender blessing make.

Love wasn't sure how to reply so he didn't. Then, during the first course, the iceberg wedge of note, she'd maintained her silence and merely looked about the table with a kind of riveted distaste. She was an attractive lady in her forties with long curly hair that seemed to swing all about the room, She wore impressive jewelry on her pale left wrist and hand, a hand that was constantly snaking out over the table to snag a roll or butter square, and never mind if she had to reach over Love to snare it. Her whole demeanor fascinated him, contrary as it was to the buzzing earnestness which filled the room. Still, he made no attempt at conversation. She seemed an artful saboteur, accidental or otherwise, of anyone who might have pretensions to a coaching career.

What made this especially interesting was that the woman was Coach Driver's wife.

Across the table sat Clay Dibble of the *Bugle Register*, the most prominent sportswriter in the state. He was a small, moustachioed, reddish man whose few stubborn locks of hair had been superglued into glistening place sometime in the previous decade. He now undertook to strike up a conversation with Mrs. Driver.

As he did so, Love wondered if she remembered the article Dibble had written back in the fall about Coach Driver's decision to try a fake punt late in the game against LSU, a game they'd gone on to lose. Love had thought it a mean-spirited piece and one that falsely accused Coach Driver of panicking under pressure. But maybe that was par for the course when you were that high up the coaching ladder. Maybe Mrs. Driver didn't even bother with the sports section.

It was Clay Dibble's style, more than anything, which interested Love, namely his strict allegiance to the declaratory sentence, his six-word sentence maximum, and his eschewing of the multisyllabic as a kind of Frenchy artifice. Love and Julie had passed many a humorous moment in the graduate lounge reading Dibble's articles aloud in a kind of stunned, possibly wounded, deer hunter voice.

*Saturday was a cold day. A perfect day for football. Maybe the punter
didn't notice. He sat at his locker. His head hung low . . .*

On the other hand, weirdly, perversely, every once in awhile,
Clay couldn't help but work in the fact that he was something of a
man about town, a bon vivant of the art and culture scene, name-
dropping a surrealist painter here, a favorite jazz performer there.

*Jazz lovers could relate. Bird Parker fans in particular. The pass was
clean and true. The catch sure. A riff begun and ended . . .*

Likely it was this quirk of personality that accounted for his current question to Mrs. Driver:

Have you seen the Georgia O'Keeffe exhibit at the Jeffree
Museum?

No, I haven't, said Mrs. Driver, reaching over Love for the pepper shaker and knocking his shoulder in the process.

It's quite good, said Clay Dibble.

An older woman sitting next to him nodded her agreement.

We drove up last week to see it. It's superb.

Clay Dibble looked at the woman, who alternately smiled at him
and the head coach's wife across from her. If there was to be a conversation, she wanted in.

Pass the rolls, please, Mrs. Driver said to Love.

He did as requested, and as he handed over the basket of bread,
she looked at him for the first time and grinned rather conspira-
torially. Taking a bite of the roll, she smiled quickly at the waiting
sportswriter, the waiting old lady. She then placed a hand in front
of her mouth and said sideways to Love: Georgia O'Keeffe, my ass.

Love had the feeling the comment had not just been heard, but
filed away, when the sportswriter's moustache bristled and red-
dened in response.

Mrs. Driver leaned a bit toward Love and said in a slightly—very
slightly—lowered voice: what do you think of Clay Dibble's work?

Love glanced across the table. He didn't want to be rude and obviously talk about someone else at the table, but the elderly O'Keeffe fan was yakking away to the sportswriter, despite his obvious chagrin, and Love thought it safe to respond.

Well, he likes short sentences.

Yes. And you know what else he likes? He likes writing about people screwing up. College kids who drop a pass. Players who get arrested. Some old coach who's gone bankrupt. What he doesn't like writing about is a good game or a great player. He's a glorified gossip columnist is what he is. And he wants to talk to me about Georgia O'Keeffe? Ha!

Love had noticed this predisposition on the sportswriter's part himself. But he'd long assumed there were two kinds of sportswriter, those who actually liked sports and those who didn't, and hadn't given it much thought.

Have *you* seen the Georgia O'Keeffe exhibit at the Jeffree Museum? said Mrs. Driver slyly.

No maam. I've never even heard of that museum.

Very good. I'm glad to hear it. Did you say maam?

Love recognized his mistake. She was much too young and vibrant and intimidating to be called maam.

I think I did. It's a habit, I'm afraid.

She pinched his cheek in a mock matronly way and said, I'll forgive you this one time, sonny boy. But only this one little time.

Giving his cheek one final tweak, she released him with a smooshy kissing sound.

Across the way, Clay Dibble took note of this exchange, his colorless eyes beading across the table even while maintaining a half-hearted discussion with the friendly old lady about Georgia O'Keeffe. It was clear the old lady considered Clay Dibble a pretty fair celebrity catch. Love thought all in all he could have done a better job of faking his end of the conversation.

• • •

Up on the dais, the head of the Goshen Super Boosters was looking over his notes, a sign that his introduction and Coach Driver's
remarks were fast on the heels of the main course and dessert. Joining them at the head table were Coach Woody, a few local political types, and a big, smiling man in a fancy suit and eyeglasses
that looked a little too dark—yellowish and opaque—for the current lighting. He sat on the opposite end from Woody and was now
motioning for someone in the crowd.

As Love began to cut into his chicken finger entrée, he noticed
that the man in the dark yellow glasses had been successful in his
summons. For there at the end of the dais stood the smiling and—
again—seersucker-suited Graduate Assistant Sparkman.

This confused Love. The seersucker two days in a row. Actually the last ten minutes had confused him: the nervy coach's wife,
the reddish sportswriter, the mysterious beckoning man in the yellow shades.

So you're not an art poseur, said Mrs. Driver. That's good. And
you look much too earnest to be a sportswriter. Please tell me you're
not some sort of coach, but just a handsome, taciturn, polite young
man I've had the good fortune to sit next to, one who has accidentally stumbled into this godforsaken event and has not come of his
own volition to talk about FOOTBALL in the spring of the year.
Isn't it baseball season?

Yes, said Love.

And golf?

Yes.

Tennis too, I suppose.

I think so.

Tell me you've come here by accident.

I'm afraid not, said Love smiling. I'm kind of a part of the Pig-skin Cavalcade.

Please never utter that phrase again. It reminds me of some sort of greased pig contest at the county fair. Or pork skins. Or an X-rated *Porgy and Bess*. Which president was it again who liked pork skins?

The first President Bush, I think.

I would have thought it was Clinton. Man of the people, you know. Calling in the pigs at Arkansas. *Soo—Eee!* But I believe you are correct.

Up on the front table, Sparkman was setting a drink down in front of Daddy Yellow Glasses, whose cowboy boots were now sticking casually—why the H not—out from under the table. In payment for service rendered, Sparkman received a sly wink and finger-pistols engaging in catch-you-later fire.

Mrs. Driver pulled out a mirror and applied a fresh coat of lipstick.

I like this conversation so much better than the one with that poor unfortunate sportswriter. Now tell me, are you the young man who picked up our son from high school last month when the little brat lost the keys to his car?

That was me.

Did our son thank you? I believe you had to drive him home, get spare keys, then drive him back to school.

Yes, Love lied. He thanked me.

I don't believe you. But I appreciate being lied to.

Mrs. Driver was looking toward the front table and smiling in an amused manner.

I believe Coach Woody is trying to get our attention. It looks rather dire. Shall you attend to him or shall I? The master of cere-monies is craning his neck and jiggling things in his pants under the table. I can't see that for certain, but I'm sure that's what he's up to. It's a sure sign of a booster in pre-speech mode. We need to act fast.

Up front, Woody was waving two fingers on the side of the table in the classic surreptitious beckoning gesture.

Love pretended not to see.

Coach Woody began making a swift jerking motion as if hustling a player off the field before the ball is snapped.

Smiling, Love waved a little toodle-loo to the old coach.

Coach Woody now appeared to be trying to lead a small aircraft to the terminal, such was the rollicking and multi-directional waving of his hands.

Well? said Mrs. Driver. You or me?

I'll go, Love said, pushing out of his chair.

Make it two.

Excuse me?

I'll have whatever Coach Woody is having.

With Mrs. Driver whisking him forward with a *run along* hand, Love made his abashed way to Coach Woody.

I see you're sitting next to Mrs. Driver.

Yes, said Love, is she crazy?

I don't know. I don't think so. She's a hoot though, I'll tell you that.

She's already insulted Clay Dibble.

Good, good. He can't be insulted enough for my liking. But listen, this fellow up here is ruffling his notes all to hell and clearing his throat every four seconds, and I need you to run down to the bar and get me a little drink.

What bar?

The bar. Where are you from? Goddam, every little redneck country club has a bar. What the hell you think these guys come out here to do, play golf? It's probably the only place in the county with liquor by the drink. Now run along. The bullshit's about to start flying up here and I need a little fortification. No one told me this was going to be a dry affair.

I don't know.

What? Oh don't give me any bullshit.

You want me to go to the bar, order a drink, then come deliver it to you with all these people out there looking up here? And Coach Driver too?

Boy, are you an only child? Did your father play the acoustic guitar while wearing sandals? Did your mother have a kiln in the house? Now can you get me a drink or not? Cause one of us is heading to the bar. I don't care which.

You don't mind if everyone here knows you're drinking?

Well hell no. But if you're worried about it, get me a gin and tonic in a water glass, no lime. Walk up here real smooth and leave the drink and take my water. Don't you know anything?

Love could tell the old boy was in bad need of a replenisher and decided to throw caution to the wind. He liked his chances of pulling off the maneuver better than the irritable Hondo on a mad dash for firewater.

Mrs. Driver said to get her whatever you were having, said Love. Do you think she meant a cocktail?

Well, she didn't mean iced tea. Now get the lead out and get going. And I strongly advise one for yourself. You're in for a solid sixty minutes of the worst kind of horseshit.

Gridiron Gurus

Only in the process of delivering the contraband cocktail did Love realize he'd seen this bit of subterfuge before, namely Sparkman's delivery of a few minutes before to the mystery cowboy. Then Love's brain began to work as twenty, sequencing the permutations as follows:

Booze errand + Front table + Sparkman in seersucker + Sparkman is asskisser + Sparkman at lawn party the day before + Brooke at party talking to Sparkman + Casual mention of important booster host of party = Mystery Cowboy is Superbooster Sammy Dutch, lead chevalier of the Pigskin Cavalcade, hirer and firer of all things athletic.

Which raised the following questions:

What angle was Sparkman not exploiting?

What butts were safe from his inquiring nose?

As Mrs. Driver drank her fortifier, she smiled slyly into her glass and blatantly ignored her husband at the podium.

Witnessing this, Love wondered how she might begin to act once the liberation juice had her in its thrall, and wondered further, what was his precise liability as banquet room bootlegger, should she begin to hurl brickbats at innocent fans and sensitive sportswriters willy-nilly.

From the front table, Coach Driver said: *be the first man up, and the last man down.*

His better half patted Love's arm and mouthed: *this is so delicious!*

Only rather than mouthing the words, as is the custom, she said them aloud and with a fair amount of lip-smacking gusto before casually sticking the drink in Love's face and insisting he take a sip.

Coach Driver said: *one board is just a board. But eleven boards can build a wall.*

The people at their table were torn between watching Mrs. Driver or the coach at the dais. Love could tell, however, by the weight of many eyes, that spectacle looked sure to win out over coach-speak should it come down to a vote, so when Mrs. Driver shook the cocktail an inch or two from his nose and insisted he take a sip, he complied. No need to give the voyeurs more than their money's worth. Once he did, all eyes were back on Coach Driver, who was now walking the crowd through his *Isosceles Triangle of Success.*

Coach Driver said: *the winner knows the price of work is high and the price of quit is cheap.*

Only the sportswriter, who'd likely heard enough coach-talk in one lifetime of rubber chicken banquets, was paying no heed to CVD. The novelty of a coach's wife sharing cocktails with a graduate assistant had him enthralled and he looked on with unabashed interest. Then much to Love's chagrin, he pulled a small pad and pen from his corduroy jacket and jotted down a quick note.

On the dais, Coach Driver said: *whatever we do, we do together. Whatever we don't do, we do alone.*

By this time Mrs. Driver was slurping noisily on her ice, getting the last bit of medicinal value from her G and her T. Love had stopped paying attention to the speech not long after Coach Driver said: *the efforting team affects. The nonchalant team is affected.*

Love was pretty sure *efforting* wasn't a word. Also, was *enthused* a word? Coach Driver had said it about twenty times in his speech.

Then everyone was clapping and Coach Driver was leading the suddenly standing crowd—the standing O!—in a rousing a cappella version of the school fight song. Talk about enthused! Goshen Super Boosters were!

Next to him, Mrs. Driver said: well, the show's over. I don't know about you, but I'm ready for a nightcap. Point the way to the bar. The next round's on me.

Love had tried to flag down Coach Woody as soon as he'd left his table, but the old coach had been mobbed by enthused well-wishers as soon as he tried to leave the dais. He was standing now with one foot still in the banquet room and one inching ever so slowly—but persistently—toward the bar. Meanwhile, TNT, the squat golfer from their earlier foursome, was pushing his way toward the front, efforting with every fiber of his being for quality face-to-face time with the university institution. He had the look of someone ready to *man up* with a chalkboard. X's and O's were on his mind.

Thinking it best to consult with the Cavalcade veteran before venturing into the bar area, loaded as it might be with land mines and Sparkmans and eccentric coaches' wives, Love lingered in the hallway, smiling and nodding at the good-hearted fans who filed past, recognizing him by his unfamiliarity as one likely affiliated with the university gridiron squad. Love returned nods and smiles in what he hoped was an earnest fashion. He had no idea how to act and felt like something of a charlatan for receiving the goodwill intended for true staff members.

Then an unusual sensation occurred in Love's pocket.

Was it?

It was.

The cheery vibration of his cell phone hopping about like a Mexican jumping bean. His first masochistic thought was that it was Brooke, come to her senses at last and ready for a nude read-aloud session from *Feast, Travel, Meditate*. This happy notion—complete with visuals, glasses, etc.—came and went in the span of four seconds.

As he was deciding whether or not to take the call, Clay Dibble, moustache twitching, capillaries aflame in lovely autumnal hues, moved in his direction.

Thought Love: vamoose, young Love, vamoose!

He stood now on the tenth tee talking to his mother. They'd run through the weather, what he'd had for dinner, his father's obsession with the new riding mower, and the complete itinerary for the Pigskin Cavalcade, before she finally got to the point at hand:

Have you heard anything about the coaching position?

No maam.

Any idea when you'll hear?

This week probably. But don't get your hopes up, Mom. The other guy's almost sure to get it.

Oh, you don't know that. I can't imagine he's more qualified than you.

At any rate, I should know one way or another in a couple of days.

Well, that position on your father's staff is still open.

On the side porch where Love had exited, a furtive-looking figure stood gazing out into the night. Clay Dibble was on the case, no doubt about it. Were there no books he needed to write about forty Saturdays in forty stadiums or something? Surely a hungry audience awaited.

Your father said you'd be a great offensive coordinator. He thinks the kids would really respond to you.

Love smiled to himself. His mother was torn between pulling for his ambition and her own, namely having him back in the old hometown, riding to work with his father, eating supper a few times a week at the house, a wife and grandkids one day, the little ones acting as ball boys when they got older just as Love had done for his father's team as a youngster.

It's nice to have that option, he said. But even if I don't get the coaching position, I can still do what I did this year. I'm still on the staff.

Do me a favor and don't mention this to your dad. He wants you to do what you want to do. He knows you've always wanted to be a college coach.

On the porch, Clay Dibble made one last sweep of the area, then headed back inside to investigate god only knew what. Perhaps thirty years of interviewing bored coaches and half-naked college boys made anything out of the norm potentially interesting.

I love you Mom, said Love. I'll let you know as soon as I hear anything.

He'd made a cautious entry back into the country club and was moving stealthily down the hall in search of Coach Woody or Coach Jackson, the two surefire friendly faces he could count on. Inside the bar, Rascal Flatts could be heard. Actually Love had no idea what band was playing. It just sounded kind of rascally and flatt.

He was making his way toward the barkeep for one—and one only—beer when he was beckoned at full volume from a foot away.

What's up man? Hey listen man, I need to ask you a question.

It was TNT, accompanied by an elfin man with a pen in his

pocket and a serious look. Only one glance told Love there was nothing casual about this fan's allegiance.

Love tried to move his body sideways so he could give token response to this request while also hailing the bartender, a fetching country lass with dimples and an alert manner. He much preferred her alertness to the intensity with which the duo regarded him. It was plain they were about serious business and Love, like it or not, would soon be privy to their machinations.

Unfortunately, Sparkman was now doing some kind of parlor trick involving three glasses of water, a pack of matches, and a coaster for the bartender's pleasure, one sure to involve several steps and a fair amount of audience participation, and it would be some time before her attention would be diverted. With Zen-like calm, Love threw in the towel and turned to face TNT and the angry elfin man full on. He could wait five more minutes for a beer.

Love checked the clock. Had he really been here for thirty minutes, empty-handed and dry of throat, listening to TNT and this small man who called himself the Gridiron Wizard? The Gridiron Wizard ran an Internet chat room devoted exclusively to the athletics of the university. This chat room was called Gridiron Gurus.

Below is what Love learned about the team he thought he was associated with:

TNT: Us boosters usually know things about as fast as anybody. If it happens at practice that afternoon, it's usually in Gridiron Gurus before I crack my first after-work Jack and Coke. The Wizard is super-connected.

GRIDIRON WIZARD: Thanks for the props TNT. If I could get a few minutes with Coach Woody for the message board it would mean a lot to the guys.

TNT: This fellow here is on the staff. He might be able to help. Hey, sorry, what's your name again?

Love gave his name.

GRIDIRON WIZARD: You're not a coach.

TNT: He's a grad assistant.

GRIDIRON WIZARD: I've never seen him on the field. Only grad assistants I know are Pickering and Oerchslin. And of course Sparkman, who didn't coach this past year. I've got the whole staff memorized. Managers and trainers too. Even the ball boys.

Love explained that he was like Sparkman, one of two non-coaching graduate assistants.

GRIDIRON WIZARD: You weren't in the media guide.

Love told him he'd been hired late, after the guide had already gone to press.

At this the Gridiron Wizard asked him for his name again, then took out paper and pen and made an irritated notation. It was clear he was going to force himself to memorize the name of a non-coaching graduate assistant to insure totality of knowledge, a knowledge until this moment he had deemed complete. It was clear as well that he found such a task unseemly and extraneous.

GRIDIRON WIZARD: You know Sparkman's dad coached with CVD?

TNT: Of course I know that. You think I'm some kind of hack?

GRIDIRON WIZARD: Last year on one of the Cavalcade stops Sparkman's dad and Coach Driver swapped yarns. I was lucky enough to be at the next table and could hear just about every word. It was kickass. They told this one about . . .

Every time Love started to make a break for the bar, he'd be asked a question:

TNT: Have you ever seen Royal with his shirt off?

Love said he wasn't sure.

TNT: I've never seen a guy that ripped.

GRIDIRON WIZARD: I know. Absolutely cut. At the spring game, I was standing on the fence talking to Kurt Dobson, the SID, when Royal had to change jerseys. We just looked at each other like, *that ain't right.*

TNT: Man, what do you think his body fat percentage is?

GRIDIRON WIZARD: I asked Kurt that very thing. He said it was right at seven percent last year. He said when they tested this year, it would likely be closer to six percent.

TNT: Mine was somewhere between six and seven percent when I was in high school and training my ass off. I wrestled too. Then I went to college and got introduced to the keg stand and everything went to hell in a handbasket.

Everyone laughed here except for Love. The Gridiron Wizard mentioned that even though he lived at home during college—had the whole basement to himself, it was sweet—he too had drained a few drafts in his day.

Love said that all this talk of beer put him in the mind of one.

TNT: So you don't get on the field at all? Do you not want to coach? You want to be a recruiting coordinator or something? Man, if I was anywhere near the field, I don't think they could keep me off.

Love said that actually he would like to coach. He mentioned his informal work with some of the quarterbacks the past couple of weeks.

GRIDIRON WIZARD: Well, god knows we need a quarterback and a quarterback coach too. I don't know why they don't hire Rocky Delonte over at Wingo State. I know it's NAIA, but that guy's a mastermind. I checked them out during our off week last year and they put up pinball numbers on offense. There's no defense for what he's running.

TNT: I remember your post on the board about CRD. I'd love to see old Rocky at the helms.

GRIDIRON WIZARD: Hey, did you play ball anywhere?

Love said he'd played at Woodford College.

GRIDIRON WIZARD: Oh. Division III. How did you get this job then? I thought only D-I guys could get on staff.

Love shrugged and said he didn't know. The thought dawned on him that maybe he'd had enough of this expertise without the benefit of any form of alcoholic diversion.

TNT: All right. You've been working with the QBs. Maybe you can settle a bet for us then. Who do you think is going to be the field general next year, Freeman or Delaney?

GRIDIRON WIZARD: Off the record of course.

Love thought about it. Considered as well the way they'd spent the entirety of the conversation peering over his shoulder should a more important staff member come along. Considered the general tone of the chat and their battle between being completely unimpressed with everything about him, and their obvious preference to have some Cavalcade representation in their football discussion, no matter how lowly or beneath their standards he might be.

Love said that you didn't hear it from him, but that Anthony Scott had lit it up this spring.

GRIDIRON WIZARD: Anthony Scott? Really? He didn't even play in the spring game, and I haven't heard anything about him from my sources.

Love said he'd spoken too freely already.

TNT: I heard there were like six scouts from other teams at the spring game to check us out. I thought the offense was even more vanilla than usual. Did they hold him out because of the opposing scouts?

Love held his hands up in surrender, unable to confirm or deny anything else.

GRIDIRON WIZARD: I saw the Florida scout with my own eyes.

TNT: I thought it would have to be somebody down on the depth chart. Freeman and Delaney suck ass.

GRIDIRON WIZARD: Scott ran a 4.3 in high school. He threw a pass from the fifty-yard line through the goal post. On his knees.

TNT: Maybe he figured out the offense finally.

GRIDIRON WIZARD: I know for a fact he didn't fail any drug tests this last go-round. I've got that straight from a member of the training staff. That's verified. That's absolutely verified.

TNT: Could you tell us if he's likely to start the first game? Just in your opinion.

GRIDIRON WIZARD: It will go no further.

Love smiled enigmatically, shaking his head as if *sorry, sorry, said too much already*. Then he made his unapologetic way to the bar and a well-earned frosty mug.

Spontaneous Yodeling

Love was sitting at the bar, waiting for Coach Woody to be free of booster well-wishers. What he was hoping to do, tonight or sometime, was to sit around with some of the experienced coaches and talk football, strategy mostly. What would a defensive coach think about attacking the two deep zone with go patterns to the tight end? That sort of thing. There was so much he didn't know, especially about how the defensive side of the football would react to certain sets, react according to down and distance. What did they anticipate? What was the one thing they wanted to protect? What would be left vulnerable in the bargain?

He felt marginally guilty about the misinformation he'd fed the Gridiron Gurus about Anthony Scott, the supposed dark horse candidate to be the starting quarterback come fall. The truth of the matter was that he'd seen the moody and recalcitrant player with his bags packed, standing in the lobby waiting for a ride home, only the day before. He'd not attended a class since February and had, despite the Gridiron Wizard's rock-solid information, failed a drug test of late. Sometime later this week, or early the next, the athletic department would tell a disinterested world that the Anthony Scott era at the university was at an official close.

Love thought wistfully what he might have done with Scott's size, speed, and arm.

He was about halfway through his beer, moving imaginary players here and there in his mind, matching wits with the great defensive coordinators of the land, when he felt a tap on the shoulder. He turned to find Mrs. Driver standing there, looking impatient.

I'd prefer not to wait on my husband and was wondering if you could run me over to the hotel.

Love had not anticipated this. He stared blankly at the woman, his mind still flashing signals from an imaginary sideline. There was no gameplanning for this sort of thing.

I came straight from the airport and haven't rented a car yet, said Mrs. Driver. Von and I don't travel together on any football outing. I refuse to be completely at the whim of his schedule and that godforsaken cell phone.

Love continued to stare at Mrs. Driver. She was taller than he'd remembered and thin in a way that spoke of high energy and low patience. He wondered how two highly inpatient people could coexist in the same house, but maybe it was better that way. He assumed the adult Ritalin factory in the basement would be running round the clock.

Mrs. Driver snapped her fingers in front of Love's face.

Have you been rendered deaf and dumb by this godawful affair? Well, I can't blame you. I remember my first jaunt through the football booboisie. I started to yodel about halfway through. I had never yodeled before and haven't since. But there I was, over a breaded chicken thigh, yodeling like there was no tomorrow. A Slim Whitman tune, as I recall. Are you familiar with Slim Whitman?

I don't think so.

I believe it was *Indian Love Call* that I began spontaneously yodeling that night. The funny thing is, before that night I'd never heard of Slim Whitman, and I'd surely never heard *Indian Love Call*. It was nothing more than spontaneous combustible yodeling brought on by circumstance.

I'm supposed to drive Coach Woody tonight, said Love, quickly and with a kind of lunging desperation to his voice. I'll need to talk to him.

She pointed over to the corner table where Woody was holding court for a group of people. He had beer bottles lined up in formation, and was moving them here and there on the table, clanking blocker upon defender, to show how he taught his linemen to shoot the gap.

There's your man. I'll be out in the parking lot.

Love hustled over to the table and asked to speak to Coach Woody in private. The onlookers, disturbed by the interruption, seemed ready to crack their beer bottles in two and brandish them in a menacing fashion at Love. Woody hushed the murmurings only by asking for another beer and promising to be right back. This appeased the villagers and they put their weapons away.

What is it, my boy? I'm about to send all kinds of hell at the BYU quarterback in the 81 Sun Bowl.

Saying this he leaned over the table and did a quick swim move with an empty bottle of Bud that was playing defensive line. It was apparent to Love and all the onlookers that the Coors Light was a sitting duck in the pocket.

Love motioned Coach Woody to follow him out the side door that lead to the patio overlooking the eighteenth hole.

You've met a girl, said Woody smiling. Is it that bartender? Good work, boy, good work. By all means take the car. No questions asked. I'll hitch a ride with somebody back to the hotel, no need to worry about me.

No, there's no girl, said Love. Coach Driver's wife just asked me to give her a lift to the hotel.

Hhhm. Well. Okay. She wants you to drive her home then? Okay. Okay. I got you. I read you. She's probably tired of the dog-and-pony show and just doesn't feel like waiting for the head man to be through shaking hands and kissing babies. Yeah. Yeah. That's it. Of course. Just run her on over there, and I'll be here when you get back. That's it. No problem. Nothing to it.

So you think I should do it?

It's the head coach's wife. Of course you should do it. In fact, you should do it no matter what lady asked. You are a gentleman, aren't you? I've badly misjudged you if you say otherwise.

Love looked at him with what hostility he could muster. He was pretty tired.

You'll be here when I get back, right? I'm just going to jet over there and turn right around.

Said Woody: where would I go?

They were in the elevator of the four-story hotel when Mrs. Driver asked if Love liked her husband.

Love thought about it and could come up with no answer he found satisfactory.

He's a good coach. I'm glad to have my position.

That's what I thought, said Mrs. Driver. I don't care for him myself sometimes.

Love didn't like the drift of the conversation. The car ride over had been a rundown of all the stops she and the coach had made during his rise from graduate assistant to head man: Bloomington, Moscow, Fresno, Starkville, Norman, etc. A year here, two there. A house constantly half-packed, a life lived in boxes and always the new neighborhood, the new school for the kids.

When they'd arrived, she'd asked him to follow her up to the room to move the suitcase she'd wrenched her back hefting onto the bed. He wasn't too sure about this, but found no good way to say no without suggesting he was afraid of some sort of monkey business.

The deserted lobby had been a welcome development, as was the empty floor when they exited the elevator. Now Mrs. Driver stood in front of her room, key card in hand.

In case you're wondering, she said, my husband's room is on another floor.

Love had not been wondering. It was a development that surprised him. When he heard the clear ring of the other elevator about to stop on their floor, Mrs. Driver was putting the key card in upside down. Then she tried it wrong side out. Love wished she'd hurry it up. The elevator doors began their slow slide open and Mrs. Driver was still trying to figure out the hieroglyphics of the arrow, which now pointed up.

Love held out his hand and the card was passed over. He inserted the arrow down as required and the lock clicked. Taking the handle and opening the door, Love waited for Mrs. Driver to get in the room. His back was to whoever exited the elevator and the footsteps that seemed to have halted mid-step. The door closed behind them and Mrs. Love set her purse on the desk and immediately kicked off her heels, one of which clumped noisily against the air conditioner. In the hallway, there was no sound, though Love should have been able to hear receding steps or the clicking of a door being unlocked. He had the impression—paranoid, he knew—that someone was standing just past the door, maybe flush against the wall, out of the peephole's range.

He stood in the foyer of the room, nervous and alert. Mrs. Driver, meanwhile, was shaking the empty ice bucket. Love observed that neither queen-size bed was burdened by a suitcase, dumbbells, or any other heavy item, unless that *Vanity Fair* weighed more than it looked like.

It looks like the bellman moved the suitcase after all, said Mrs.

Driver. Would you mind filling up the ice bucket? I brought a nice bottle of chardonnay I'd like to chill.

Love hesitated, torn between wanting to get out of that room as quickly as possible and concern about whoever might be lingering in the hall. He couldn't tell if he was more worried about his job or Mrs. Driver's reputation. She sat down in a chair with her stockinged feet propped up on the far bed. He knew he wasn't supposed to notice such things, but Mrs. Driver seemed to have quite nice legs. He'd not spent much time around attractive fifty-year-old women—smart, confident, and slightly scary ones—but in different circumstances he thought he might enjoy it.

You're welcome to join me for a glass, said Mrs. Driver.

Thank you. But I'm in Coach Woody's car and he'll need a ride back.

Shaking out her hair with a slender hand, Mrs. Driver said: if I know Coach Woody, he won't have any problem finding a friend to give him a ride. Have a glass of wine. I'm sure you haven't had a moment's relaxation all day.

Love thought about this. It was true. It was also true that nothing about staying in the room, with or without a glass of wine, would be relaxing. Cougarific maybe. But not relaxing.

I'd better run along. I'll get that ice though.

Mrs. Driver stood up and grabbed the ice bucket from atop the small refrigerator. Handing it over to Love, she smiled and said:

So you hope to be a college coach some day? A head coach?

I believe so, said Love.

And you'd also like to be married one of these days, I assume?

Yes, I think so.

Make sure your wife has a life of her own then. I always did, and it's kept me from going absolutely out of my mind.

Love felt decidedly nervous. Mrs. Driver and he were standing two feet apart, with only an empty ice bucket between them.

She looked at him forthrightly, bemusedly. She seemed to find him funny and a little sympathetic. The handful of girls in his limited experience had not prepared him for such a scenario. He found her quite attractive.

I'll get my own ice, she said, reaching now for the bucket. You better run along. There's no telling where Coach Woody might be skinny-dipping at this very moment.

Love walked down the hall feeling weak legged, relieved, and slightly let down. He pushed the button for the elevator and stood there waiting, more confused than anything, but also titillated in a way that left him disappointed with himself. He was standing thus when he sensed something just down the hall, in the small alcove marked VENDING. Whether it was simple intuition or a minute sound—the gurgling rumble of the icemaker—he wasn't sure. The elevator door opened and then shut without Love getting on. He stood there, turned toward the alcove, waiting with a kind of electrified patience.

As if counting ten after the close of the elevator door, a reddish face and moustache peered cautiously, ever cautiously, around the corner of the alcove. But even in this caution, there was a brief look of pleasure and pride, the look of one who thinks he has escaped an unusually close call. And then this face was met by the gaze of Love.

The face popped back behind the wall.

Just for fun Love punched the button for the elevator again. When the door rang open, Love waited patiently to see if the hide-and-seeker could resist looking. He could. His patience or terror was limitless. The door closed again without Love aboard. Half a minute passed. The air was charged with anticipation and Love couldn't help smiling to himself. He was going nowhere.

Suddenly out popped Clay Dibble from the alcove. He strode

past Love as if he carried a soda or an ice bucket or some tasty treat from the vending machine and wasn't, indeed, empty-handed. He appeared to think that a head held high and a brisk step was a suitable bluff.

How's it going? said Love.

Clay Dibble had just passed him, and paused dramatically as if addressed by the wastebasket in front of the elevator. What? Oh. Yes. Hello. How are you?

And then he resumed his march down the hall and presumably toward his room.

You're Clay Dibble. The sportswriter.

Yes, that's me, he said, stopping painfully in the hallway.

I sat across from you at dinner tonight at the country club.

The sportswriter knitted his brow in thought, in sincere recollection, but couldn't seem to place Love.

I was sitting next to Mrs. Driver.

The sportswriter shook his head. Apparently Love had done nothing to command his attention at dinner. As he tried to place Love, his hands fidgeted here and there. He looked to be regretting the absence of an ice bucket.

An ice bucket much like the one Mrs. Driver now left her room carrying.

She walked toward them nonchalantly but at a fair clip.

Am I missing a discussion of Georgia O'Keeffe? I see you have your pen behind your ear, Mr. Dibble, and your notebook handy in the old shirt pocket. Perhaps you're preparing for an interview.

The bard of the SEC was at a loss for words. If he'd found the time later on to pen the moment, it might go something like this:

He stood shitting in his pants. His syntax was all that remained. The short sentence. The easy words. Neither art nor jazz would help. The coach's wife glared. His heart beat loudly. He would have to change pants. And shower of course. He wondered about the punter. On the

perfect fall day. Perhaps he had felt this way. When he'd seen the large
defender. The one who would tackle him. Quite hard to the ground.
The sportswriter had never been tackled. It would probably hurt. A jazz
riff played in his head. But he couldn't tell whom. Maybe Miles Davis.
Maybe Kenny G.

Or are you just back from the pork belly banquet? said Mrs.
Driver. I thought I heard someone scuttling about the hall earlier.
In fact, I'm almost certain I heard scuttling right outside my door.

Yes. No. I'd just.

Here he pointed in an ambiguous manner toward the alcove and
began patting his pants in the classic *no change unfortunately* mode.
Love pushed for the elevator. Much as he'd like to continue to watch,
the prudent move was to fetch Woody.

Little ghost crabs scuttle, said Mrs. Driver. You see them at the
beach, usually at night, making their sneaky, frightened scramble
for food. You must be hungry. And you have no change. Wait here,
my friend. I insist. I have change in my room to spare.

That's fine, there's no need, said the sportswriter, taking a few
tentative steps toward the elevator. I must have gotten off on the
wrong floor.

Utilizing the traffic cop's signal to halt, Mrs. Driver said: Wait
here. I insist. I hate to see a man deprived of his midnight snack.
And your floor might not be chock-full of goodies as mine undoubt-
edly is.

The elevator bell rang at that instant and Love entered without a
word. During the whole of the conversation Mrs. Driver had treated
him as invisible, as necessary to the scene as the exit sign or the
small couch on the opposite wall. The elevator doors began to close
and his eyes went to the downcast sportswriter glued to his spot in
the hall. He seemed to be ruing something specific. Love wondered
if it had anything to do with minding your own business.

• • •

Woody was gone. That this surprised Love was in itself a surprise. Of course he was gone. He was gone the moment Love walked out the door on his mission of mercy and slight horniness. Technically that last part, the horniness, came later, but now Love had a hard time taking it out of the initial equation. Perhaps it had been there all along. But any way you sliced it, Woody was gone into the night.

The bar had cleared out in the brief time he'd been gone, and no other members of the coaching staff were in attendance. Only one table in the corner remained and Love didn't immediately recognize any of the holdouts. He was about to ask the bartender for the directions to any local watering holes—there couldn't be many—when he was hailed by a loud, brusque voice from the corner:

You there, young coach, come on over here and introduce yourself to Uncle Sammy.

Love turned to find the big man in yellow shades waving him over, with several smiling locals looking on.

With a reluctant step Love headed his way.

You son, he said, pointing with a cigar, are a graduate coach. I'm just guessing because I've not made your acquaintance. But you look like a coach, and you're too freshly scrubbed and eager looking to have been around long. Tell me your name and what your coaching specialty is. I always like to meet the up-and-comers.

As he spoke, he looked at Love, but seemed ever aware of his audience, six or seven men, men of standing by the ease with which they sat in the country club bar. Local men of standing, yes, but they were now watching a statewide man of standing, a university man of standing.

Love gave his name and coaching background as requested.

A quarterback coach, you say? said Sammy Dutch, nodding

emphatically around the table to give the impression of being impressed.

Yes sir.

Well then, by god, you've got a good chance of being a head coach one day. Yes sir, I can see it now. You'll leave here pretty soon, knock around the business for ten years or so, and if you do a good job and get with good programs and catch some breaks, who knows, I might hire you here at the university. This staff here will be long gone by then. It's just the nature of the game. Folks need change. But here in about a decade, I might be hiring a man who looks a lot like you.

Love didn't smile and he didn't reply. The men around the table were laughing and trading knowing looks, and when he'd finished talking Sammy Dutch had given the group a broad and obvious wink.

Relax, young man, said Sammy Dutch, crinkling his eyes like a fairly drunk Santa. Coach Driver's doing a good job. He's not going anywhere soon. I'm just talking hypothetically, you see. Let me buy you a drink. Least I could do. Loosen you up some. What's your poison?

I appreciate it, said Love. But I believe I'd better get on back to the hotel.

I understand, I understand. How about on your way out, you tell that little gal at the bar that I'd like another JB and soda if she's not too busy. Thank ye Chief.

Love nodded and said it was nice to meet him.

It wasn't, of course. But he didn't have anything else to say.

He made stops at four bars in town that the bartender said might still be open, glorified pool halls and small-scale juke joints, but the wily coach wouldn't prove that predictable. Running up and down the main road in town several times, he tried to organize the many events of the day, his first sampling of the life of a football coach outside of the playing field. But he was too tired for such, and on his third leg past the closed up strip malls, the Walmarts and Applebees, the pawnshops and junk stores, the churches scattered here and there along the way, he said to heck with it, Woody would show up before they were due to head out in the morning or he wouldn't.

The Fade Route

With his bags packed and ready beside his chair, Love sat surfing the Internet in the hotel lobby. It was seven a.m. and he'd slept well. They were due in Fairview in four hours, and though the drive was less than two hundred miles, Cavalcade members were already packing cars and going over directions to the Fairview Resort, a mountain golf and tennis community spread around a man-made lake.

Woody was still unaccounted for and Love had come up with no plan for how to proceed in his absence. His thought was to remain in the lobby for as long as it took for Woody to show. If that were the next hour or the next day, Love saw no way around this course of action. He had the man's car and no one cared if Love showed or didn't in Fairview. What the people wanted was Coach Woody.

On a whim, he thought he'd check out Gridiron Gurus, on the off chance that the Gridiron Wizard had updated information regarding the Cavalcade. It turned out that he had indeed, under a topic header reading:

Ladies and Gentlemen,
Introducing Next Year's Starting QB.

Gridiron Wizard (Ninja Master of Gridiron Gurus): Greetings Gurus. I'll be posting reports all week from the Pigskin Cavalcade. And my first one is a whopper. After a discussion with a prominent young booster and a key member of the staff at the Goshen Country Club, I have it on good authority that the starting qb for next year is almost certainly going to be Anthony Scott. This is off the record info, so I can't divulge more, but these sources have proven veritable in the past. More information as I get it.

Ballstud: Wow Wizard. That's a real bombshill. I'm guessing Scott has finally gotten himself straightened out. Does anybody know if he's in the Bible study group that meets over at Bella's Cafe on Tuesday evenings?

Ballstud: My bad. I meant bombshell! Got so carried away by the news I forget to spellcheck. By the way, that Bible study is players only. Not sure if I made that clear. I showed up one Tuesday to participate, only to find out it was players only. The guys were kind enough however to let me sit at the next table and listen along. Just an FYI.

TNT: Great insight as always, Wiz. Also, I can confirm the above information. The staff member told me the same thing: re Scott. We're going to kickass next year!

KidGenius: Man, if Scott plays half as hard as he drank last fall, we are going to kickass. I was down at Flippy's one night after the Southern Miss game and me and Scott knocked back fifteen pitchers. By the end of the night, I was riding him piggyback down the Strip. It was pretty awesome until he puked!

Ballstud: Does anyone know where CVD currently worships?

KidGenius: Who gives a shit!?! As long as he wins ball games!

Ballstud: I give a *%#&, that's whom.

KidGenius: I can tell you where Anthony Scott likes to drink if that will help—ANYWHERE AND EVERYWHERE!!!

Ballstud: Sigh. It's after midnite so all the kiddies are on here playin. Some of us GROWNUPS would like to have a serious conversation every now and then on the board. Oh well. I'll check back in the morning when the ADULTS are back in charge. God bless you all, even the kiddies!

KidGenius: Yeah, you check back in the morning. I just cracked another beer and I plan on being here awhile, large and in charge! Anthony Scott! Holy Shit!

Classof72: Hey Wizard, I was wondering if they still do that par three competition on the first day of the Cavalcade. And if so, who won? P.S: Not all of us oldtimers are in bed, KidGenius!

KidGenius: Rock On! Class of 72. Ballstud took his ball and went home. He's so easy!

Gridiron Wizard (Ninja Master of Gridiron Gurus): Graduate Assistant Coach Sparkman won the par three with an ACE! He pocketed a brand new set of clubs for his trouble.

Classof72: Thanks Wizard. His dad coached with CVD as I recall. Sounds like he's got a bright future. Hope we can keep him on staff.

Gridiron Wizard (Ninja Master of Gridiron Gurus): You are correct. CVD and Lance Sparkman broke in together on the Indiana staff. From what I can tell, the apple doesn't fall far from the tree with his son. Sharp guy. Very sharp.

KidGenius: Does anyone know where graduate assistant Sparkman worships? I want to stalk him.

Ballstud: Very funny KidImmaturus.

KidGenius: I knew you wouldn't leave! Sucker!

Ballstud: Wife is snoring to wake the dead. No way possibel to sleep. Now if you think you can carry on an adult conversation without resorted to foul language, maybe we can have a desent discussion.

KidGenius: Oh fuck that.

Ballstud: I'm gone.

Love had enjoyed what he'd read until he'd come to the part about Sparkman's bright future. And he was truly sorry to see Ballstud go this second time. Once he was gone, KidGenius had no real adversary and his entries lost their spark and verve.

After several pages of entries, mostly talk of Anthony Scott's bench press and squat capabilities, his personal best in the forty-yard dash, the time in high school when he threw a ball through the goal post from the fifty-yard line on his knees, and a bit more about his drinking and body fat percentage, Love picked up the topic again on page 6, which opened with this entry posted at 5:30 a.m.:

Ballstud: Hey guys, don't know if you seen or not, but today's paper says Anthony Scott has left school. Don't know where he's transferring, but sounds like three strikes and you're out. Wonder who put the Wizard on a bun steer.

Ballstud: Before all you grammer Nazis jump my case, it should have read: bum steer. Not bun. Haven't had my coffee yet.

FootballFreak: I can't imagine anyone saying Scott had the remotest chance of starting. I was in Military Science class with him freshman year and he was dumb as a sack of rocks. And that class was easy as shit!

Classof72: Ha! Glad to hear Military Science is still a popular choice on campus. I took it three semesters. Easy A. And I think I was hungover ever single class. Crazy for Wizard to get something this wrong. Anthony Scott as starting quarterback? That's ridiculous.

FootballFreak: I'm hungover right now!

Ballstud: Agreed Classof72, very out of caracter for Gridiron Wizard to miss this one.

FootballFreak: I think you meant character.

Gridiron Wizard (Ninja Master of Gridiron Gurus): Just read the paper myself. I'm on my way to Fairview in just a few minutes. Have no idea where my source got his information. This shocks me. Sorry to all for putting out the misinformation. Will get to the bottom of this and report back. My bad, guys! Thought this was a solid lead.

Ballstud: Thank you for correcting my typo, FootballFreak. And good luck next week in the national spelling be.

• • •

Love's chat room reverie was interrupted by the bullhorn voice he'd heard in so many dark dreams:

Coach Lowe! Coach Lowe!

Love jumped up as if electrocuted and jerked his head about looking for Coach Driver. Moving without direction, he galloped from the chair and circled around the row of couches separating the lobby from the front desk.

Coach Lowe! Coach Lowe!

Yes sir! Yes sir!

They bumped into each other as Coach Driver, turning left, rounded the corner on two wheels. Even upon collision the fiery coach failed to brake or reduce speed. Love had given the coach a good knock, but by lowering his shoulder and applying a slight forearm shiver to Love's midsection, Coach Driver soon had the right of way all to himself.

Coach Lowe, where is Coach Woody?

Obviously Love didn't know.

He also didn't know how Coach Driver could have guessed he was in the lobby. Maybe he'd just started hollering as soon as he left his room, kept it up during the elevator ride down, and picked up steam once on the bottom floor. As far as Love could tell it would have continued out into the parking lot, perhaps even when the car was driving down the road, his head out the window, hollering: Coach Lowe! Coach Lowe!

I'm sure he'll be here any minute, said Love.

From where? Is he in his room? I've called ten times. No answer.

I bet he went out for breakfast. Probably to Cracker Barrel.

We have a free breakfast here. The hotel provides it. I had it this morning. Aren't you supposed to be driving Coach Woody? How

did he get to Cracker Barrel? Aren't I talking to his driver? Why is
he at Cracker Barrel? Why aren't you with him?

At this point, Sparkman came down the hall, pushing a cart loaded
down with baggage. He gave Love a smile and a wink but passed on
without comment. Coach Driver spotted him as he passed and said:

Thanks Sparky. I appreciate the help with the bags.

I've had three different calls, said Coach Driver, yesterday and
today from people wanting to play in Coach Woody's foursome.
Important people. Check-in at the course is eleven sharp. Sparky's
loading my bags in the car right now. Where are Coach Woody's
bags? Where are your bags? Where is Coach Woody? Where is Coach
Woody's car? Where do you think he is?

Love felt himself blinking with each new query. He wondered if
the head man was trying to make a point, about urgency perhaps,
or if a chip in his brain had come loose. He wasn't sure if an answer
was expected from his end, so he stood there for a few seconds, as if
in a strong wind tunnel, to see if more questions would pour forth.

Well, said Coach Driver. We can stand here all day with our
heads up our asses or we can get some answers.

I'll round Coach Woody up right now.

You'll what?

I'll get Coach Woody.

So you know where Coach Woody is?

Somebody looking for me? said a hoarse voice behind them.

Coach Driver and Love turned simultaneously to see the big
coach come walking in, looking like something the cat drug in,
assuming that that something was another cat, one who'd recently
swallowed the canary.

Coach Love, I should be ready in five, said Woody. I'll just meet
you down here in the lobby.

Love smiled at this Christmas miracle. Without this pleasant turn of events he might have been there for hours, facing a bulldog prosecutor intent on a full accounting of who/what/when/where/why.

That same bulldog was now being patted lightly on the back by the old coach, much in the manner of a favorite uncle to his Nervous Nelly nephew. That Woody was wearing the same clothes as the night before was impossible to miss, as was the fact that his hair had been styled at the Mad Scientist Salon.

Coach Driver, did you remember that Fairview is my old hometown? I'm betting they have a parade in my honor.

As Coach Driver blinked his bug eyes and tried to adjust from the earlier hard-nosed persona, he sheepishly relayed the news of the various people who wanted to spend time with Coach Woody in Fairview.

Woody, agreeable, smiling, laughing, putting the high-strung coach at ease, said: sure, sure, whoever you like. Just let me know what you need me to do.

Witnessing this exchange, Love wondered about Coach Driver's feelings for Woody. Was he just too much of an institution to treat like another assistant? Was he just that good a coach and too much of a player favorite? Maybe respect for age and years of service? Or was it simply that Woody made him relax, that looking over at the big, confident coach in the locker room before a big game put CVD at ease? Woody had coached with and against everybody, he'd seen it all. Yet each Saturday he looked like someone who couldn't wait to get out on the field. Today we get to *play*. Perhaps there were times Coach Driver needed to be reminded of that.

Whatever it was, Coach Driver now managed a smile, gave Woody a mock punch on the shoulder, and headed toward the parking lot.

Once he was out the door, Woody turned to Love with a wry apologetic grin.

Looks like you had a close call, he said. Sorry about that.

Love smiled despite himself.

I assume you don't want to hear any excuses.

No, said Love. I don't think so.

I never do either. Well let me get a quick shower and we'll get on the road.

It was as if a sewage treatment plant had married a paper mill and produced a noteworthy offspring. No, that wasn't quite right. It was like a goulash made from rotten eggs, guano, and sun-ripened monkey cages. No, worse. Much much worse.

Sorry about that one, partner, said Coach Woody, rolling down the window. For that one, I must apologize.

How much curdled buttermilk had the old coach consumed the night before? How many Gouda cheese frittatas? Love spent the next few minutes pondering what the worn and ill-treated system next to his was trying to digest. Chive tofu? Pond algae? Eye of newt?

In a miasma such as this, Love found it hard to appreciate either the opera they now listened to or Coach Woody's commentary upon it. The singer was Giuseppe di Stefano and Woody was praising his phrasing and something about his tone or timbre, Love couldn't recall. The funk in the car was affecting his hearing and his attention span. It seemed neither time nor place for discussions of high art.

What do you think is the worst play and the best play down on the goal line? he asked.

Huh? What? You want to talk football during *La Traviata*?

I think so.

Woody reached for the stereo and lowered the volume.

All right, he said. All right. You played quarterback in college, correct?

Correct.

Did you all ever run the fade route down at the end zone?

Yes, we did.

Pretty regular?

Yes, I'd say so.

You liked to throw it too, didn't you?

Yeah, I liked to throw it.

That high, fading touch pass is real pretty, isn't it?

Love smiled. Yes.

Your receivers loved it too, didn't they? Especially those big tall rangy ones.

Yes sir.

Did you complete a lot of em? Score a lot of touchdowns with it?

Love considered the question. The more he thought about it, the more his answer surprised him.

No, he said, not really.

You know why?

No I don't.

I'll tell you why. Cause it's the shittiest damn play in football, that's why.

Love laughed.

Sit down one day next fall when we've got an off week and watch college football all day long. You'll see twenty fade patterns on the goal line. And maybe one will be a touchdown. And every time they throw that big ole piece of shit, the announcer's voice will get excited and the crowd will get loud. You know why?

Why?

Because when it works—that one time in twenty—it looks real easy. Just pitch and catch. That's what the announcers will say: *just a little pitch and catch.*

Love laughed. Woody's imitation of a peppy announcer was pretty good.

You know why else they like it?

Love admitted he did not.

Because the announcers and the crowd and the coaches that call that shitty pass don't know a damn thing about putting the ball in the end zone. The fade is the all-time, the all-time, give-up call. You just throw that butterball up there, it's incomplete of course, the field goal team comes out, and no one ever calls it what it is: a chickenshit call. You might as well kick the field goal on third down. Look at how much space you have to work with. The pass has got to be just right. Right height, right angle. And you got about four feet in the corner of the end zone to work with. All the cornerback has to do is play the angle, then get an arm in there and start swatting away. Doesn't matter how tall he is. I've seen little midgets out there breaking those fuckers up. Jockeys and dwarfs and Munchkins from *The Wizard of Oz*. If you ever see a coach call the fade, you know he's saying, I have no idea what to do here. Let's just hope we get lucky. And the fans won't whine about it and the reporters won't second-guess him because it *looks* so easy that one time in twenty it works.

Love remained silent. Coach Woody seemed a bit worked up.

You ever play any defensive back? In high school or anything?

Yes sir, said Love. I played both ways until senior year.

Did the fade scare you?

No.

Why not?

What you said. Plus you always knew it was coming if you were guarding a tall guy.

Any route you hated to guard? Down on the goal line I mean.

Love considered. The slant, he said.

Yes, by god, the slant. One cut and the corner's boxed out. Little guy, big guy, it doesn't matter who's guarding the receiver. You've got em angled out. Receiver's throwing it to the ref before the DB's got his jock on straight. Did you like to throw that one too?

Oh hell yes.

Then why did you ever let your coach call a fade? You should have checked off every time.

Love laughed.

Now, when you're a head coach, are you ever going to call the fade, or are you going to make a real call, and not give the first goddam how the fans and media might react?

No, I won't call the fade.

Good, good. I might make a coach of you yet. Now turn that opera up and I'll teach you a little about music.

Resort Living

They were staying at the Fairview Resort, one of those pricey, casual establishments that dot the southland, and provide golf, tennis, swimming, hiking, etc. for the reasonably well-to-do in the region. Most of the guests for this stop on the Cavalcade were staying at the hotel proper, a large faux hunting lodge surrounded by pine trees that sat upon a hill overlooking the lake. The coaches, university employees, and a few of the choicer boosters were being housed in cabins, twenty yards or so apart, that stretched around a large cove on the south side of the lake. The cabins were walking distance from the lodge where all of the Cavalcade activities would be held, and each came with a deck and boat-less dock.

The golf course had been no harder than the one the day before, but Love had hacked up eighteen innocent fairways that had never done him any harm. He sat now in the high-ceilinged den, half listening to one of the ESPN channels and gazing out the sliding glass door to the deck outside. They had a few hours to kill before the dinner program and he thought he'd like to sit outside with a beer for a spell sometime that afternoon. It looked peaceful out on the water and Love found the entire setting tranquil and relaxing. A few fishing boats, their quiet trolling motors putt-putting, moved in dragonfly fashion along the shoreline, but otherwise the lake was free of human activity.

He was stretched out on the couch, feet propped up on the coffee table in front of him, when Woody came in from his fifth catnap of the day, looking as if he'd finally caught up on the sleep he'd missed the previous two nights. After guzzling a glass of V-8 in the kitchen that adjoined the den, he let out a loud sigh of satisfaction and joined Love in front of the television. It was NBA playoff time and the sportscasters were discussing strengths and weaknesses of each team. Love was still looking out at the lake when Woody said: what does that mean?

What?

Score the ball.

It means score.

Then why do those sportscasters keep saying *score the ball*? I've heard *shoot the ball*. And *score*. And *score baskets*. But not *score the ball*. Why not just say: he can score. Or he's a scorer. It's not necessary.

I don't know, said Love. I think they just try to invent phrases sometimes, hoping they'll catch on and people will start saying them. It's mostly for young guys, I think, these sports shows. My dad won't watch em.

Old guys like us already know what razors we like, what beer we drink, and what car we want to drive. I watch a game on a Sunday and I don't know what the hell half the commercials are talking about.

They sat in front of the television as a series of fast-paced advertisements with X-Game-type characters came and went. Then there was one for the older set. It was the erectile dysfunction ad where the courtly older gentleman and his surprisingly hot and much younger wife/date/paid-escort are dancing the night away. During their dance, the couple share a number of knowing looks, and the woman is fairly licking her lips at the sexy senior. Both seem well aware of the pharmaceuticals pumping through the dance master's veins, and confident that what blood is left in that dried-up system of his will soon be hurrying to the designated spot.

Love found watching the libidinous couple pretty uncomfortable even when by himself. It seemed well past the time when they should be heading to the room. Frankly the old coot looked a little too pleased with his store-bought stiffy as well.

Throughout the commercial Woody had maintained a studied silence, whether from discomfort or empathy Love didn't know.

That's a happy-looking fellow, said Woody as the ad came to a close.

Yes sir, said Love.

How do you think his family feels when they see their daddy acting in something like that?

Love shook his head. He didn't know.

Actors are a different sort, aren't they?

Love agreed that they were.

By now, Coach Woody was looking intently out the sliding glass door.

That there's a tufted titmouse, he said in a whisper. Hey, he's got him a nut or a seed. Grab us a couple of beers and let's sit out here on the deck and watch that joker go to town. He'll sit there and jackhammer like hell till he cracks that sucker open.

They'd been on the deck for only a few minutes when a huge boat came flying down the coastline opposite. Two riders were being pulled behind the boat on an oversized inner tube. One of them was a stout surfer-type with a blond crewcut. He looked as if he'd recently won a new set of golf clubs and had coined the word *douche*. The other was a tan young woman in a yellow bikini, who likely belonged to a book club, and might or might not be the daughter of the athletic director.

Love and Coach Woody watched the boat circle the cove in silence. As it got closer, they could hear the music blaring from the stereo and the laughs of the couple on the inner tube. Now they could see that the driver of the boat was Sammy Dutch, sitting with one foot propped confidently on the dash in front of him. The music was Kenny Chesney—the official voice of the SEC—which Love found both appropriate and unfortunate.

As the boat and inner tube came past the deck where they sat, Sparkman held up the *hang loose* sign and hollered: Coach Woody!

Brooke looked once toward them, then turned her head in a casual, heedless way, smiling as before at the antics of Sparkman. The little white soles of her feet as they passed by were impossibly pretty and Love wondered if he might now cry.

By god that looks like fun, said Woody. Riding along on that big tube.

Love nodded sadly in response.

Almost wish I'd gone with em.

Why didn't you?

Well, as much as I like riding on a boat on a pretty day, I don't care to spend any more time with Sammy Dutch than I have to. Now if I was a younger man and I'd known that gal in the two-piecer was coming along, I might have changed my mind.

Coach Woody thought about this for a minute, looking at Love the whole time. Love hoped his face didn't look as sad as he imagined it did. What he wouldn't give now for the goofy, horndog expression of the aged Lothario of the erectile dysfunction commercial. So happy it was. So hopeful.

No, said Woody, I stand corrected. Even when I was younger there was nothing that could entice me to spend any time I didn't have to with Sammy Dutch. I'd have passed then too.

Love nodded, feeling perhaps a little better.

That Sparkman fella sure gets around, doesn't he? Every time I turn my head he's talking to somebody important.

Love agreed that he was the social type.

Well, you know, there's two ways to play it. In football or anything else. You can try and asskiss your way to the top or you can just do it your own way and figure if you're good enough at what you do, you'll get there eventually. I'll say this, the first way, the way of the asskisser, is unquestionably faster and easier.

Here Woody paused, as if letting the first option sink in.

But the second is a hell of a lot more satisfying.

Love smiled. The old boy was trying to cheer him up.

Said Coach Woody: I met my first Sammy Dutch when I was out at Wyoming. He was an oil man like this one we got here. Only difference is he earned his money, or stole it fair and square, depending on which group in the state you believed. It was Sammy's granddaddy who was the wildcatter and made the first bundle. Sammy's been on the family tit from the first go. He was up at the university a few years after me. They gave him a scholarship cause of his daddy, but he couldn't play a lick. I think he got himself a varsity letter his senior year, one of those sympathy jobs for coming out to practice for four years, but I don't believe he ever got in the game. But you wouldn't know that by the way he flashes that conference ring around, would you? Yeah, now he's a big tough hombre, ain't he? Making and breaking coaches and university presidents too.

Love wanted to know if he was as powerful as all that.

Well, yes and no. He gives more money to the university than anyone. So everyone wants to keep him good and happy. And he did just about single-handedly hire our current coach. And he could fire him too. But here's the thing that Sammy and all the Sammys around the nation don't realize. There's always a new Sammy waiting. What he's doing has always been done. And it will always be done, at least as long as the money in college sports is as crazy as it is. Sammy dies, or Sammy gets caught doing something he shouldn't, then the new Sammy will emerge before the year's out. Nature abhors a vacuum, you know.

Is that why you never became a head coach? You didn't want to have to deal with the Sammys of the world.

The old coach smiled.

The Sammys. And the press. And the fans who take it way too seriously. Don't get me wrong. There's a lot of good fans out there, loyal as can be and supportive. They're in the majority actually. But that nutjob minority, the ones who claim to live and die it, and bleed the team colors, and throw things after games and cuss at their wives and so on, well, they're just too batshit crazy for anything. No, I like being a position coach. Watching the guys improve and mature and start to learn who they are. Listen, for all the horseshit that goes on, there's still nothing better than game day in my book. Don't you agree?

Love said that he did.

While they'd been talking, Sammy Dutch and his fun crew had steamed back into the cove, circled it once with boat horn blaring the university fight song, then dropped anchor in the spot which seemed most easily viewed by anyone on shore. People were now leaping into the water with flotation devices and drifting lazily and casually in the middle of the lake, beer koozies in hand, laughs and shouts aplenty. The soundtrack was Lady Gaga, but even this couldn't sway Love from the thought that it looked pretty fun.

Hey, who's that young lady over there waving at us?

Love turned in the opposite direction and there, on the next dock down, was Julie, his grad school friend arrived at last.

Love shouted hello and smiled and waved in return. He was now standing up and facing his friend, but even in this posture he could feel Woody's eyes on him. Several seconds had passed. Coach

Woody cleared his throat and knocked his beer a few ornery times on the deck's rail. When Love turned in his direction, he found the coach wearing an incredulous scowl. Love gave the old coach his same goofy smile. Out in the middle of the lake, the boat party was still splashing and frolicking and singing-along to *Cheeseburger in Paradise*. Even this couldn't diminish Love's feelings of sudden serenity. He had an ally now, one his own age and of similar sensibility. Tonight he wouldn't feel nearly so outnumbered. Without really knowing he was doing it, he waved at his sports management cohort again.

Well for the love of god.

Uh? What is it?

If they put your brains in a tiny little gourd, they'd rattle like hell.

Coach Woody said this as if he'd just witnessed a defensive lineman attempt to titty-push his way to the quarterback, fall to the ground to avoid contact, injure his tubby ankle in the process, then sit on the field and wave for the trainer with more energy than he'd shown all game.

This is right embarrassing, said the old coach.

Oh. You think I should invite her over?

You were dropped on your head as a tot. That much I know. But from what height? My guess is way the fuck up there.

Love held up a confident hand to indicate the message had been received and that further postscripts would prove superfluous.

You want to come over? he hollered. We got some beer.

Giving a quick wave of assent and indicating she was on her way, Julie ducked into her cabin with that cocky, cheeky smile on full display.

Said Woody: you finally got that gal in the yellow two-piece to look this way.

A Man Called Snort

Love asserted—for the third time—that he did not, in fact, have a kidney stone, despite Coach Woody's dire predictions on that front.

Since she'd arrived, Julie had been encouraging Woody's dabbling in the medical arts and other philosophizing on the subject of Love's phlegmatic nature. Words like *torpor* and *lethargy* were bandied about. Though Coach Woody hadn't directly alluded to it, Love was sure the whole topic had been instigated by his belated invitation for Julie to join them on the deck. That they were now on that same deck, drinking beer and conversing with the woman in question, seemed not to have lessened Woody's despondency regarding Love's hardiness, intelligence, and adaptability in the Darwinian sense. His doubts about the future of the Love family line were apparent.

So you haven't noticed a general lack of energy lately? said Coach Woody. General fatigue is often a symptom of a kidney stone.

Before Julie could respond, Love argued that his energy level was actually quite good, kidney stone or no.

Maybe it's gumption, I mean, said Woody. Young lady, you

know this young fellow better than I do. How would you rate his gumption?

Julie took a sip from her can of beer. She was wearing running shorts and looked even taller than usual with her long legs stretched out before her.

Gumption? Like having confidence, seizing the day, making his own destiny? That sort of thing?

Yes. Exactly. Does he have what it takes?

Would you consider joining a book club to impress a girl gumption? Or just good old-fashioned desperation?

Depends on the girl. Wait. What? Book club? What kind of books did you read?

Love said he couldn't remember the titles and asked if anyone needed another beer. He was just heading to the kitchen.

There was *Feast, Travel, Meditate*, said Julie. And the one with Elvis and the one-eyed cat. And what was the one with Gustav, the lovesick crepe maker?

Woody had a confused look on his face after this conversation. That one about Elvis, he said, was it any good?

No, said Love. Absolutely not.

Well what about the gal then? The one you joined up to impress? Every man I know has done something crazy trying to impress a woman. I'll usually give a fellow a pass on a deal like that.

Love considered explaining that he hadn't joined just to impress Brooke, that he'd always liked reading and thought he'd enjoy a little socialization away from football, but it didn't seem worth the effort. His attention was directed out on the lake, where the Sammy Dutch outing had turned into something of a Cirque du Soleil on water, with Sparkman flying off the bow in a series of acrobatic somersaults and Brooke striking the occasional yoga pose when Lady Gaga seemed to call for it.

Love had still not answered the question about the woman in question, the prompter of Book Club Love, when out on the lake Sparkman yelled: hey Brooke, check this out.

Wait, said Julie, squinting out toward the boat. Did that guy just say Brooke? Wasn't that your book club girl's name?

Love nodded.

Isn't she the athletic director's daughter?

I think so, said Love. I just found that out recently.

Julie smiled and looked over at Coach Woody.

I think we've got to give him a little credit here, she said, jerking a thumb in Love's direction. Squiring the AD's daughter, even accidentally, has to count for something in the gumption department. Love, I'm starting to think you should have answered your book club question after all.

Before the inquisition regarding Book Club Supplement Question #8 could begin in earnest, a voice came shouting into the den and through the open sliding glass door. All three of them turned instinctively toward the back of the cabin.

The voice was low and growling and country as it came onto the deck:

I swore there was two things I was gonna do before I die. The first was join the circus. And the second was to whip Bill Woody's ass. Well, the circus just left town but Bill Woody's sitting right there in front of me. Now get up, big fella, and make a young boy's dream come true.

Snort, said Coach Woody, Miss Duncan's not here to break us up this time. You best think twice.

The mysterious visitor had his dukes up and was moving in Woody's direction with a steely gaze, a veneer broken only once to cut an approving glance in Julie's direction. He was unusually thick, his hairy, freckled arms roped with the muscles one gets doing farm work or operating heavy machinery. His hair was long and stuck out all sides of his well-worn baseball cap. He wore a short-sleeved shirt that said FAIRVIEW VOLUNTEER FIRE DEPARTMENT and gray work pants. Though he was half a foot shorter, his thickness and overall feral appearance convinced Love he'd be a formidable foe for anyone, even Hondo, who sat grinning before his approach.

Then the stalking pugilist smacked fist upon palm and jabbed once to within an inch of Coach Woody's nose. Soon after the old coach's hair was being tousled and swirled in an affectionate way.

Best friend a man could have right here, he said. By god, I'd take a bullet for ole Bill Woody.

Love was being grilled by the curious on the deck about the plot and philosophies of *Feast, Travel, Meditate,* and was trying to put into words the basic notion that while exotic asparagus and travel by rail were sources of inspiration for the spiritual seeker, true feminine fulfillment must come from within. Also that it was important to be plucky.

The synopsis of *Feast, Travel, Meditate* had befuddled Snort, Coach Woody's friend from the old days. He scratched his face in a distracted manner.

She ate asparagus every night of the week?

Just the week the asparagus was fresh down at the Piazza, Love explained. She'd prepare it a different way each night. Then the next week, she might experiment with capers or fresh leeks. Just whatever was in season week by week.

So the whole book, or a lot of it, was just about eating?

Well, she traveled quite a bit, so there was a lot of description of different European cities. And she meditated, of course. There was a Belgian yoga teacher named Henri who was pretty important. He taught her the whole philosophy of eating what was in season. The idea was to live in the moment and to use what was at hand in the natural world. Henri's philosophy was that all we needed was either inside of us or very near at hand. If you meditated, and shopped locally grown, that seemed to take care of a lot of problems.

Wasn't there any romance in it? asked Snort, that old romantic at heart.

Oh, she and Henri wind up together. They end up buying a bed and breakfast together out in the country. It had a happy ending.

Well that's all right then, said Snort, shaking his head fondly. I like a happy ending.

At this point Julie and Woody could be seen looking out toward the lake and smiling. The object of their attention was swimming toward shore, swimming in fact right for the dock that sat below their cabin. Out on the boat, much of the pizzazz seemed to have gone out of the floating party despite the peppy Dixie Chicks song now being played. It wasn't a bad song, though it did make Love feel more than a little girly and free. In fact, he'd used that phrase several months back when Brooke asked how he liked it.

BROOKE: How do you like this song?

LOVE: It makes me feel girly and free.

BROOKE: You're not nearly as funny as you think you are.

Sitting now on the deck and watching Brooke swim toward their group, Love wondered if it might have been better keeping such lines to himself. When she climbed out of the water and onto the dock, water dripping from the yellow bikini and the flaxen hair that she was shaking out in a relaxed manner, unaware seemingly of the eyes on the boat observing her, the eyes from the deck of the cabin, Love thought silence would have been golden indeed when it came to the Dixie Chicks.

Beside him Snort snorted. Or whinnied. Maybe it was a moo. He and Woody exchanged a quick glance, and Love knew that only divine intervention would prevent his upcoming dismemberment and disposal if it meant the Fairview Boys could be alone with the two young ladies of Love's acquaintance.

This should be fun, said Julie, looking at Love.

Brooke was moving gingerly on tiptoes across the rocky lawn, the little pearly nails on her tan hands and feet catching the sun's rays and flashing in all directions at once. In response, Love fidgeted and tried to align his face in some fashion not completely ridiculous. He devoutly wished he'd been able to answer Question #8. It would have been over in a minute, the pain, the humiliation, the look of patient understanding and pity from Joel, the fresh bread maker in the group, regardless how he'd responded. The other guy in the group, the owner of the oft-used fondue pot, might have even offered a chocolate skewered morsel in a show of brotherly support.

Oh, said Brooke as she glanced toward their deck seemingly for the first time, I'm at the wrong cabin.

Her smile as she said this was disarming, ingenuous, and completely effective. Of course it was an act. But who cared? Seriously, who would care?

In response to the dripping lake maiden, the knights of the rustic roundtable began talking all at once, inviting her to join them for a drink—soda, water, beer, anything, by god, anything.

Meanwhile Love felt his face growing ever more ridiculous. What he wouldn't give now for a wad of gum to chomp in an open-mouthed fashion. He'd never felt less casual or relaxed. Maybe Pete Carroll and others of the Open Air Method were on to something.

Oh, hi Raymond, said Brooke.

Love said hi or hey or hello in response. No one was listening, least of all himself. He felt Julie looking at him in an amused way and wished she'd stop. Wry smiles in the peripheral vision were not the key to regaining one's composure. He pondered briefly and nostalgically humankind's prelapsarian state.

My cabin's right over there, said Brooke. Let me run get a towel
and dry off and I'll be right back.

It was apparent that Woody and Snort didn't favor this plan;
they'd obviously hit flirtation pay dirt and hated to waste even a
minute of courtly behavior. Nonetheless, they chose the better part
of valor and gave verbal acquiescence to the request.

Retaking their seats, they looked upon Love.

You mean to tell me you know Julie here, said Snort, and also
that gal there? You know both of them?

Love said that he did.

You talk to them and things like that?

Yes.

Well, when I walked in ole Woody here was talking about your
lack of gumption. I don't know how Woody describes gumption, but
if I was you, I'd be asking him if he'd like to shake your hand or kiss
your ass right about now.

Love laughed and so did Julie and then a voice cried out two
doors down:

I think I'm locked out. Raymond, do you mind seeing if you can
get in this window?

A Mixed Bag

Love stood in the kitchen of the cabin, his knee bleeding from some sharp object, a nail or jagged piece of wood, he'd passed over in his Herculean effort to get to—and through—the window of the locked cabin. He'd executed an awkward stretch-and-pull maneuver from the deck to the window and an even more awkward belly shimmy through the small opening once he'd ratcheted himself upward, his T-shirt riding up and scraping painfully against the storm window frame. From there he'd employed the frontward crawdaddy move from the window, over the kitchen sink, and then head and hands first down to the floor, slightly spraining his wrist in the process. All of this had been done with a steady stream of wisecracks from the Fairview Boys, who'd walked down into the yard to observe the process and to offer suggestions about his best method of gaining entry. He'd not heard Julie during this enterprise and wondered if she'd observed with the others or just gone back to her own cabin.

He went to the door to let Brooke in, stopping once to dab at his bleeding knee with his golf shirt. Say what you would about college football, you never lacked for golf shirts. When Brooke entered, she looked at Love's bloody shirt first and asked if he'd injured himself.

Love answered bravely that the wound was minor.

Well, I appreciate you helping me out.

Love said, no problem, glad to do it.

Who's that girl over there?

Love explained the graduate school connection and the fact that she worked in the athletic department office.

She's really pretty.

Love made no reply to this. They were standing in the den of an unchaperoned cabin. Save for a missing pair of useless glasses, and perhaps high heels, this situation was about as he'd have drawn it up if he were the type to indulge in fantasy. The fact that he was still sweat-stenchy from his round of golf and wearing a blood-soaked garment was frankly an irrelevant detail. Now was the time for gumption. Now was the time to earn his bon bon.

You didn't tell me you were the athletic director's daughter, he said.

He knew as soon as he said it that the line betrayed not the slightest hint of gumption.

Brooke smiled. I didn't?

No, you didn't.

Does it matter?

Love thought about it. Before him was a pretty, smart girl in a yellow bikini and wet hair. He judged the question ridiculous and replied in kind.

No. It's just an interesting fact, considering I work for the coaching staff of the football team and your dad is in charge of athletics.

Football is so stupid, Brooke said smiling. You've got to admit that.

Love returned the smile. Unless it was about books or movies or any other art form, he kind of enjoyed it when Brooke picked fights.

The game's not stupid, he said. It's a good game. A lot of the stuff around it is stupid, I'll admit that.

Like this Cavalcade?

Yeah, like this Cavalcade. So why are you here anyway? As I recall, you suggested rodeo attire would be appropriate, so I'll be expecting boots and a big belt buckle tonight at dinner.

Oh, I've got my hoop skirt ironed, Brooke said laughing. And yes, I come every year. My dad thinks it looks good if the athletic director and his family embrace the whole booster culture. Plus, I think he wants people to think of him as a regular guy and not just the person who raises prices on tickets and parking every year. Anyway, I used to fuss and moan about it when I was younger, but then I realized it was just easier to suck it up for a day or two. Plus it makes Daddy so happy to have us here with him. If you'd come to the book club like you were supposed to, I was going to tell you.

As Brooke talked, she'd moved down the hall toward the bedroom. Love assumed she was going to get a towel or dry clothes and stayed where he was in the den. He considered sitting down on the couch, but thought that might be presumptuous. The conversation had been to his liking, kidding and casual, up until the subject of the book club. Brooke was now talking to him through a closed bedroom door.

Joel answered your question for you, she said.

Love found this subject unpromising and kept his peace. To be honest, he had a hard time thinking about anything else but the state of dress/undress on the other side of the door. He felt unsettled and dissatisfied, but hell's minions couldn't have rooted him from his present perch.

What kind of bread did Joel bring to the meeting? Love asked, hoping to move the conversation toward more neutral territory. He wouldn't have admitted it in mixed company, but he actually thought bread was about the most boring food item on the planet. In his heart of hearts, he felt a well-buttered slice of Wonder Bread was as good as any other. Did this stop him from complimenting Joel's Russian pumpkin pumpernickel with the raisins and the cranberries, and just the hint, the smidgiest of smidges, of sassafras sorghum?

Of course it didn't.

Oh, don't you remember? said Brooke. We all decided it would be fun if everyone brought a bon bon or some other sweet snack to the meeting, one that summarized in some way your current dating interest.

Love squirmed a bit and took a sniff in the near vicinity of his underarm. Boiled peanuts? No. More like a wet beach towel left to dry on the railing, one with a few shells on top containing recently dead sea creatures. He knew he should have showered right after golf.

Oh yeah. I remember now.

Yeah. Guess what I took to symbolize my current interest?

What?

A Ding Dong.

Love laughed. Is that so?

It is.

Brooke was laughing lightly behind the door and Love thought his luck had taken a turn for the better. He couldn't help wondering if this pleasant development had anything—perhaps everything—to do with Julie's presence on the deck. And what if Julie were still over at his cabin? She'd be fine with Woody and Snort, but shouldn't he be getting back? It occurred to him that she was the only good friend he'd made in a year's time at the university.

Joel's answer was really quite good, said Brooke.

What? Were they back on book club questions again? He thought that subject was safely behind them.

Did you hear me?

Yes.

He didn't find the question embarrassing at all and gave a really good answer. I felt like I learned a lot about him.

That was just the point. Love didn't necessarily want people to learn a lot about him, at least not relative strangers in a book club. And what was possibly left to know about Joel? Not a meeting had gone by where he'd failed to update his love life, the status of his salary negotiation, or, most importantly, the changes he was planning for his kitchen. What Joel was after was space and lots of it. It was coming down to the hanging racks or the movable island. This much you could count on: the Formica counter would be hitting the road.

Joel's good at answering those questions, said Love.

So would you be if you'd try. Honestly, Raymond, it wasn't like I was asking to read your diary. It was just a silly question for our little book club. I don't know why you had to get yourself into such a state about it.

Maybe Brooke was right. Maybe he was unduly private. Maybe he should be better about expressing his feelings, even in front of people he didn't know very well or have much in common with. Wasn't it Henri in *Feast, Travel, Meditate* who said that every single thing uttered by humankind was ultimately carried off by the winds of time?

When Brooke came out of the bathroom wearing only a towel, Love's interest in the philosophy of Henri began to wane.

For the record, Brooke said, I know you're being sarcastic about Joel. And I know you didn't like a single book we read for book club.

Love wasn't sure where his eyes were supposed to go during a moment like this. Actually, he'd never had a moment like this. His first instinct for a safe landing spot was Brooke's feet, but one glance at those little tan numbers, all pearly with polish, and he knew this was the move of a rank amateur.

I didn't hate all the books, Love managed to say at last. I kind of liked the one-eyed cat named Sue. She was a good character. I liked the way she would follow the kids around the yard when they played hide-and-seek, almost like she was playing with them. That was a good touch. And it was funny that right before Aunt Gertrude burned down the Piggly Wiggly she checked her shopping list to make sure she hadn't forgotten the sweet potatoes for her casserole.

You're still being sarcastic.

Love actually wasn't, or not completely, but the jerky shaking of his head he'd employed to convey sincerity had likely been lost in translation. His eyes kept wanting to take a walkabout, but he knew that would be blatantly sexist. He wondered what sort of magical gravity was keeping that small bathroom towel in place. Or was it some intricate sailor's knot tied in back? Perhaps little birds like those that attended Snow White. Whatever the case, Love hoped the towel would stay firmly in place. In the few seconds he'd been standing there, he'd given up all notion of possessing gumption. Were there men out there who knew how to act or what to say in a situation like this? Other than European chefs and philosophers and yoga teachers in novels read for book clubs?

The one-eyed cat was realistic, said Love.

Are you implying that the other characters weren't?

No.

I think you are.

With this she turned into the bathroom. Love wasn't sure if he was supposed to stay or go. If Brooke meant to continue this discussion, he'd just as soon leave, current clothing situation or no. They'd never really had any major arguments in the time they'd been seeing each other. The closest they'd come was once when they'd been watching some celebrity reality show and one of the quasi stars had said: *between you and I*. Brooke claimed this as her number one pet peeve and went on to explain the irony inherent in the phrase, namely that by attempting to sound smart, i.e. using *I* instead of *me*, the person ended up sounding the opposite. When she'd asked if this phenomenon didn't drive him crazy, Love had to admit that it did not.

During the argument Brooke had accused Love of being intentionally middlebrow when the mood hit him. Standing here now he
wondered if the charge had merit. He wondered as well if *bookgeoisie*
was a word.

I'd like to know something, said Brooke, speaking again from
behind the bathroom door.

Love walked a little farther down the hall and said, okay.

If this trip hadn't come up and you'd been able to make our last
book club meeting, what bon bon or treat were you going to bring?

Love was stumped. He'd forgotten all about the assignment to
bring treats, so distracted had he been by Question #8 and the really
nasty girl-talk among the protagonists of *The Bon Bon Girls*.

I hadn't decided yet, he said.

I bet.

There was a pause here, long enough for Love to speculate what
the other members of the book club had brought for their treat.
For instance, had Joel brought bread as representative of his current
interest in bread?

Inside the bathroom no water ran or toilet flushed. The goings-
on in there were as foreign to Love as what happened behind Coach
Woody's mystery water closet.

I left my bag in my room, Brooke said. Do you mind getting it
for me? It's the blue make-up bag on the bed.

This request made Love's blood course a little faster. He hoped
this trip to the bedroom would prove a harbinger of trips to come.
Where were Brooke's parents though? Maybe they were hiking. Or
shopping. Or who really gave a shit as long as they were gone and
stayed gone?

Love grabbed the cosmetics case and headed back toward the
bathroom. When he announced his presence, Brooke reached a
hand out from around the bathroom door and took the bag. Love
much preferred this exchange to the earlier unpleasantries with

Woody and the toilet paper and pondered for a moment the wide tableaux of intrigue offered to the human condition.

I just realized, said Brooke, that the baby oil's not in here. I like to put some on right after I've been in the sun. Would you mind getting it off the dresser for me?

Would Love mind? No Love would not. He fairly sprinted down the hall for the bottle of liquid slippery.

Unfortunately, for he was in quite a hurry, quite a state, to deliver this and then to see how providence would have this episode play out, the bottle was not where it was supposed to be. He stood by the dresser and looked delicately around the room. To go rummaging would be the act of a pervert, a foot fetishist, one desperate for sandals to sniff and bobby socks to rifle. Love was just an all-American boy looking for baby oil, nothing more, nothing less.

Said Brooke from the bathroom: you know what bon bon I was going to bring to represent my current interest *before* you bailed out of the meeting?

Love did not, he surely did not. He did know this was yet another curveball. One minute he was baby oil errand boy, the next he was being book-clubbed to death. Only Coach Driver could find more ways to surprise and discomfit him. Frankly, he'd thought the Ding Dongs would have been funny and appropriate whether he'd shown up or not.

No, said Love, I don't.

Would you like to know?

Love wasn't sure. He could think of no food item that would well represent him to anyone, bon bon or no. He wasn't even sure he knew what a bon bon was. The whole food/sex thing continued to confound him. But there, alas, was the baby oil. He went to the nightstand and procured it post haste.

Before he could rush like a madman down the hall to deliver the bounty, Brooke came out of the bathroom. To make room for her,

Love moved a little down the hall in the direction of her bedroom. As he was doing this, the sound of the front door to the cabin being opened could be noticeably heard, followed by a hearty masculine voice saying: Brooke, we're home. Are you here?

Such was his surprise that Love barely had time to register—and very much approve—the ponytail and lip gloss touches that Brooke had recently added to the ensemble.

Simultaneously, Love comprehended that:

1. he was trapped between toweled Brooke and door/father.
2. ponytail + lip gloss = cowgirl at the mall and/or Rebecca of Suburbanite Farm.

As her father—and mother, it turned out—rounded the corner, still shouting *Brooke, Brooke*, in a kind of silly sing-song voice that parents use with very small children, she gave Love a smile that seemed to say, *you're busted but I'm not.*

No time like the present, and fortune favoring the bold, and all those other exhortations to action seemed completely absent from Love's mind, so much so that when the parent aggregate, athletic director and wife, stopped at the end of the hall and took in the order of things before them—betowelled daughter, strange sweaty golfer, bedroom door ajar—Love offered nothing in his defense but an open-mouthed look of terror and a bottle of liquid slippery.

What? said her father, the athletic director in tennis shorts.

Who? said her mother, a formidable matron also garbed for tennis.

Brooke stood there smiling, offering no rationale for Love's presence or the situation in total. She reached for the baby oil and Love dumbly handed it over.

Cavalry Charge

They'd been standing there for what seemed like a really long time, Brooke with her energetic smile looking at Love to see how he would react, the parents going back and forth from their daughter to the sweaty hotel groundskeeper next to her. No one spoke. Love was wondering about back exits and hoping against hope that Brooke would explain about the locked door and his heroic actions on her behalf, their prior friendship/relationship/teaseship, and the fact that he was, in fact, something of a gentleman, excluding of course all the smutty thoughts that had gone through his mind in the last ten minutes.

There came a knock at the door. Was it a knock? Four heads cocked, waited. Yes, it was a knock. Love assumed the police had been summoned telepathically and welcomed the cool comforts of the local penitentiary with open arms. He wondered what had taken them so long.

The athletic director looked at Love and said: I'll get the door.

Love nodded. He assumed he wouldn't get first dibs at answering.

Love and the athletic director's wife and her nude-save-for-a-towel daughter remained in the hallway. Brooke's mother was shaking her head in a distracted manner. It seemed clear that things like this—unexpected things—didn't often occur in her world. Brooke began to rub her arms and legs with baby oil. Love sweated. At the door a conversation had begun.

THE AD (gruffly): Yes?

WOMAN: Is Raymond here?

AD (gruffly, querulously, tanly): Who?

WOMAN: Raymond. Raymond Love. Your daughter was locked out of the cabin and he helped her get in. Coach Woody's looking for him. He doesn't know how to work the remote control.

Love felt a momentary thrill of victory. He knew that voice. He knew that faux sincerity when the situation called for it. The cavalry, in the form of Julie, had arrived, and just in the nick of time.

AD: Coach Woody, the football coach?

For a moment, Julie seemed stumped by this question. Love hoped she was now scouring the bushes for a large stick of some sort. The man was in need of a rejuvenating biff to the head.

Choosing pacific tones in lieu of the firmer treatment that Love preferred, Julie said: yes, the football coach. Raymond is on the staff too. He's a graduate assistant and he's here for the Cavalcade. Your daughter was locked out of the cabin. Raymond is staying two doors down with Coach Woody. He climbed in the window and opened the door. This happened just a minute ago.

Love realized he was smiling now and that neither of the women in the hall seemed to appreciate it. Julie had obviously been paying attention during Situational Psychology during grad school. Her docile approach, short, clear sentences, and swinging pocket watch were just what the situation called for.

Brooke huffed a bit, then went quickly into her bedroom and shut the door.

Love and her mother shared a moment in the hall.

The thought occurred to him that he could, if he wanted, just walk out the door right now. But would that be rude? Would it jeopardize his chances, nonexistent as they were, for the coaching position? Did he owe it to the parents to give an honorable account for his presence among the daughter, the towel, the natural oils?

Raymond!

It was a minute before Love grasped that he was being summoned. And then with a quick nod to Brooke's mother, he joined Julie and the athletic director in the foyer.

Apparently Coach Woody needs you, said the athletic director, tan and brooding in his snug tennis shorts.

Okay, said Love, trying not to look at Julie. She'd done a little number with her eyebrows as soon as the AD's head was turned and he didn't want to risk a second glance. His escape seemed all but inevitable now, and he began walking out the door.

So you helped my daughter get in the cabin? said the AD, following closely behind. His proximity and general body language indicated his goals were two-fold: removing the undesirable from the interior while maintaining a captor/captive relationship in the great outdoors.

Yes sir, said Love, stopping on the front stoop.

The athletic director nodded, but wasn't fully appeased. His sense of violation seemed profound. Sweaty strangers in the cabin was one thing. Sweaty graduate assistants was quite another.

And you're on Coach Driver's staff?

Yes sir.

The head of athletics was stumped by this response, or at the least unmollified. He adjusted his tennis shorts. Perhaps his sweatbands were cutting off circulation to the lower regions. Love glanced toward Julie, who was standing in the small patch of lawn between the two cabins. He tried to give her a look that said, *snap your fingers to break the hypnotic spell,* but she only made the get-it-moving hand motion, followed by the hasty thumb thrown over the shoulder.

And then you decided to just hang around while my daughter got in the shower, is that correct?

Love declined to answer this question, opting instead to scratch his head and blink spasmodically several times.

Do you know my daughter or something?

We're in the same book club, said Love.

What? The same book club?

Yes sir.

Behind him, Love could hear Julie walking away.

I thought it was all women.

No sir, there are a couple of guys in it.

Oh right, are you that fellow who makes the wonderful bread? Brooke brought home one of those loaves last month. It was really delicious.

No, said Love, that's Joel.

Right, right. The gourmand? Or is it *foodie* these days?

Love winced. This was truly below the belt. Totally bush league.

Some people use that term, he said.

Right, right, Joel's got the food blog, is that correct?

Yes sir, I think so.

My wife got a fantastic raspberry vinaigrette dressing from his blog a few days ago. Tart but sweet. But not too tart and not too sweet, if you know what I mean.

Love discerned that he was now being viewed through a different lens. He was a man in a book club. What harm could he do? For all Brooke's father knew they might have been discussing coffee blends while alone in the cabin.

And you really are on the football staff?

Yes sir.

It's kind of amazing, isn't it?

Love found the question unanswerable and said nothing.

So tell me what your name is, young man, said the athletic director, creasing his tan into a thin smile and sticking out a sweatband to shake.

Raymond Love.

Coach Love from the book club, said the AD with a wink and a smile.

Here Love offered a mirthless chuckle. His strategy now was to chuckle his way to freedom. What he really wanted was to be back on the deck, drinking beer and looking out over the lake. In retrospect that time on the waterfront had been a true respite from the many booby traps the Cavalcade had set up for him. Even with the Kenny Chesney and the girl-freedom anthems that had been their soundtrack for the afternoon, Love felt positively nostalgic about his time on the deck.

Brooke made us dinner for our anniversary, said the athletic director, shaking his head fondly at the memory. And every recipe was one she'd gotten from a novel. I'd never heard of such a thing. Which book had all the recipes?

All the books had recipes, said Love, nodding in a matter-of-fact way

Really? All the novels had recipes in them? That's amazing. It really is. Well, all of the food for our anniversary was Italian, I do remember that. What book might that have been?

That was probably *Gondola Summer*.

And what was that novel about?

I don't really remember it that well, said Love. It was one of the first books we read.

What was the basic premise then? If the story's half as good as the recipes, I might want to read it.

Love paused here, sizing up the scene before him. According to legend, most fathers would have just rolled up the sleeves for a little of the rough stuff after walking into a compromising situation involving their daughter. But not this sly dog, this Chillingworth of the rubico. Nothing but death by book club would satisfy his bloodlust.

I believe, said Love, that *Gondola Summer* was about a middle-aged woman whose husband has just left her for a younger woman. She decides to quit her job and head to Europe.

Just like that?

Yes. Her daughter had recently graduated from college and was backpacking Europe. The mother joined the daughter for awhile and did some backpacking but eventually they started cramping each other's styles. Plus, the daughter didn't like her mother's new dating self, her European self. Understandable, I guess. The mother and daughter were close, I don't mean to say they weren't. But staying in cramped hostel rooms and both of them wanting to date and have adventures, it just didn't work out. So the mother took off for Italy.

Right, right. So where does the cooking come in?

I'm afraid I don't understand the question.

All the Italian recipes. What plot device allowed for their inclusion in the book?

I don't think there was a plot device. Maybe the strategy was just to make the readers hungry. The main character just rode around on a gondola a lot and this one gondolier, this old guy who knew the ways of the world, would direct her to a different restaurant each day. Whatever she ate for that meal was included in the book, the recipe for the main dish. Though sometimes you got the recipe for the dessert or the salad.

So was it just an epicurean adventure?

No, there was a love story too. A couple of them actually. But in the end, she falls in love with the old gondolier's grandson.

How old was he?

I don't know. A lot younger than the main character though. He owned a restaurant. Actually it was the last restaurant the old gondolier suggested before he died.

A bittersweet ending then?

I guess so.

A bit like the raspberry vinaigrette.

Love couldn't muscle up a reply to this, but did grimace in a friendly manner. They were standing thus, grappling with sweat-bands and scratching new mosquito bites, when Woody and Julie came out of the cabin.

Hey there, Jerry, said Coach Woody, smiling and waving the remote control. My graduate assistant giving you any trouble over there? He's had a bout of kidney stones lately and is prone to making odd grimacing faces at times.

The athletic director laughed tanly, shaking his head in the neg-ative. All was well if you could trust that satisfied shake of the head.

I'm just meeting this interesting young man, he said. Did you know that Raymond here is in a book club with my daughter?

I did know that, said Coach Woody, meeting the AD's smile with a crinkly one of his own. He was telling me about a book they read about women who eat some kind of chocolate treat, then get together and talk about it.

This looked to go on indefinitely, but for once fate interceded on Love's behalf. Fate, in this instance, took the shirtless form of a volunteer firefighter who answered to the name of Snort.

The AD shied like a pony at his appearance and was whinny-ing lightly through his nose when Snort waved and shouted: *Howdy buddy!*

The athletic director had no response for this. He seemed to be wondering why the television repairman was taking such friendly liberties. Love observed his uncertainty and took a few sly steps off the stoop and toward his own cabin.

This here's my good friend Snort, said Woody. I've known him since I was knee high to a grasshopper. And Snort, this here's our athletic director.

Howdy buddy, said Snort again.

The head of athletics offered a mumbled greeting, glancing briefly in Snort's direction, then fixing his gaze somewhere along the roof above his head.

Jerry, tell this here fellow that it's okay if he goes to our little banquet tonight. He thinks it's some kind of formal affair and is worried his tuxedo's not pressed.

Yes, yes, of course. Any friend of Coach Woody's is always welcome. Now if you gentlemen will excuse me, I need to be getting myself ready for dinner.

And with that he was gone. Love looked around briefly, as if expecting sentries to rush from the woods, but none did. So with a lively step and a bound from the stoop, he hightailed it back to his own cabin, wondering what the night might bring.

Sundresses

ove was in the lodge thirty minutes before dinner was to start, checking his emails on the communal computer, reading a few sports pages, and generally just gathering himself for the event to come. On a whim he decided to give a quick glance to the Gridiron Gurus chat room to see what those anonymous critics might have to offer on this day. The first three topic headers that greeted the forum visitor were these:

> **Which play in the last decade made you throw up in your mouth the most?**

And

> **Anyone else refuse to settle for mediocrity?**

Also

> **Not trying to be negative about next year but . . .**

Love considered the opening topics, but none caught his Hobbesian fancy. Life might be solitary, poor, nasty, brutish, and short, but he'd prefer not to dwell on the thought, especially as it related to football. Thankfully, the next few headers were not so philosophically weighty, touching on a wide assortment of multiculturalism, religion, and current events. These included:

Just passed Spanish! Now I drink muchas cervezas!!

And

Where do most of the assistants currently worship (just curious).

And

Obamacare and our bowl game performance: a comparison.

Of these, it was the bilingual entry that most tempted Love. Something in its whimsical tone struck him as familiar. Before he could check out the triumphant Spanish student's online celebration, however, his eyes settled on this:

Plan to confront source on false rumor re: Anthony Scott as starting qb.

Moth to the flame, Love clicked on this last one and read the following:

Gridiron Wizard (Ninja Master of Gridiron Gurus): Hope to post findings later tonight after Cavalcade dinner in Fairview. Have feeling information was intentionally false. Can't say more at this point but hearing rumblings about a bad apple on the staff.

BallstotheWall: Hate to be that apple when the Wiz gets through with him! Get em GW!

Gridiron Wizard (Ninja Master of Gridiron Gurus): I should have said peripheral member of the staff. Don't want to give the impression there was an actual coach involved.

Ballstud: Wow, that's hard to believe Wizard. Are you inferring that the source has a grudge against the program?

KidGenius: Hola Ballstud. Cómo estás? I think you meant implying, not inferring. Easily confused word. Just an FYI.

Ballstud: Whatever Kid. Keep forgetting my Thesoraus.

KidGenius: Mi amigo, come drink muchas cervezas with me.

BallstotheWall: Kid, are you drunk already? It's not even noon yet.

KidGenius: Sí señor.

Gridiron Wizard (Ninja Master of Gridiron Gurus): I'm not saying for sure that the person in question is trying to sabotage the program, our forum, or anything else. He may just be a sore loser. Can't go into more detail now but should have something to report tonight or tomorrow. Trust me when I say that no one @#^* with my forum.

KidGenius: Wizard, mi amigo, chill. We all knew Anthony Scott sucked. Can't believe you fell for the disinformation, but no worries. Nothing that a few cervezas and a spliff won't cure. Comprende?

Ballstud: As I recall Scott's body percentage and 40 dash time were off the charts. You can't deny he had talent, Kid.

KidGenius: He was loco, amigo. El señor Scott drank muchas cervezas. And smoked mucho spliffs.

Gridiron Wizard (Ninja Master of Gridiron Gurus): As I said, I'll get to the bottom of this. I know not everyone on this forum takes our team—our program—emphasis on *our*—as seriously as I do (not mentioning any names), but one thing you don't do is give the GW intentionally false information. I take this forum very very seriously. And I take our program very seriously. There's nothing more important in my life. Or more sacred.

Ballstud: Well stated Wiz. I know you speak for many of us. Jesus is more sacred, of course. But I know what you mean. I am very very serious about the program as well.

KidGenius: Speaking of Wiz. All these cervezas are making me have to take one.

Ballstud: Moderator?

Gridiron Wizard (Ninja Master of Gridiron Gurus): One week probation KidGenius. You've been warned before. I'm not in the mood today.

KidGenius: To the penalty box? Seriously? Come on Señor Wizard. Have a heart.

Ballstud: God bless you Kid, but sometimes you are a blowheart. See you in a week. Maybe you can add some words to you vocabulary. The morale to the story is this: mess with a bull and you gonna get a horn. And that goes for that bad apple Wiz is gonna whup tonight too.

BallstotheWall: Sober up Kid and we'll see you in a week.

KidGenius: Adios Amigos. Volveré!

Ballstud: Almost forgot. If anybody's interested the Bible study group is defianatly players only. This summer and forward going to. I basically got kicked out yesterday when I tried to set at the next table and just listen which I thought was ok. Just a FIY.

Love finished his reading and pondered for a moment at the computer. Ballstud worried him. He seemed more than a little lonely. Somewhere a restraining order was being notarized in his honor. And what of KidGenius? The ruling from Gridiron Wizard struck him as capricious and high-handed. Power was surely going to the head of the forum's Ninja Master. The Kid would be back though. You could count on that. There was no stopping the Kid when it came to kickass online discussion.

Bad apple, though? Sore loser?

Love sensed the Gridiron Wizard had taken his little joke about Anthony Scott too much to heart. Then again, the forum in general seemed pretty easily agitated. Emotions flowed freely, and the passion would not be tamed when it came to football postings.

He was sitting thus, contemplating the social and emotional intimacies provided to the men of the football chat room, when he was hailed from behind by Julie.

She walked toward him looking even cheekier than usual, smiling in her wry way. He noted the pale pink sundress she wore, especially as it related to the healthy glow of the skin and the whiteness of that Cheshire grin. He made a sound, part throat-clear, part yodel, then swung round in his chair to face her.

You look sharp, she said.

He looked down at his only-slightly wrinkled slacks, checked out the miraculously lint-free sleeve of his sports coat, the freshly polished shoes. He was glad he'd taken the time to shine his shoes. It would not do to look slovenly in the presence of sundresses.

Thanks, said Love. I like your dress.

This was gross understatement, obviously so, and Love felt ridiculous for having uttered it. In his opinion the sundress was the apex of human achievement. Seriously, he liked them a lot.

Julie was looking around the lobby in a curious way, smiling and swiveling her head as if searching for someone or something.

Who're you looking for?

Anyone, said Julie, laughing. Snort's coming and you just know something has to happen when there's a Snort around. And your bookey girlfriend will be here. And her parents. And of course your pal Sparkman. You've got to admit that's a pretty solid line-up.

Other than Snort, Love found the line-up lacking. There was the Brooke angle, yes, but he found his thoughts on this front muddled, slippery even, and ventured no comment.

Seriously, that's a pretty sweet witch's brew, said Julie. You're not worried you're going to get mixed up in anything, are you?

Love made no response to this, other than to stand up and stretch his legs. He was suddenly fidgety.

I mean it's unlikely you'll be sitting next to the athletic director and his wife, isn't it?

Love smiled here.

I mean what's there to be nervous about? I see no possible scenario tonight in which you might feel the least bit awkward.

Love grinned wider.

She tousled his hair in an ironic manner, saying, you can handle it, Love, my boy. I've got faith in you. And if things get too dicey, I'll dive right in there. I won't leave your side no matter what.

Love was unconvinced.

I helped you with the athletic director, didn't I?

This was true and Love gave a grudging nod of assent. As he did so, something caught his eye at the entrance to the lodge, namely a stout and strutting detonation device, one who looked about halfway through his lecture on the advantages of the spread offense.

His companion? A tiny, frowning extra from the latest Harry Potter movie, wizardry personified.

Well, if you were excited about my night before, said Love, you'll definitely like this development.

What?

The guy I played golf with yesterday, the young booster, he just walked in. And so did the fellow who runs the football forum.

Julie's eyes widened at the prospect. You mean that TNT guy who cheated at golf and the Gridiron Wizard himself?

Love had not skimped on the details and was glad he'd included that about the golf cheating. Bogey his ass.

Yep. Don't look.

But it was too late. Julie's head had yanked around immediately.

Meanwhile, Love was subtly, smoothly—obviously—maneuvering

so that his back was now to the devoted fans. Yes, his flank was momentarily vulnerable, but he thought misdirection his only hope.

They won't try and talk to you, will they? asked Julie.

I don't know. I hope not.

Oh you're screwed. Here they come.

Love had been looking intently at Julie in hopes that he might go unnoticed by staying completely immobile. He'd also been talking through clenched teeth and in a whisper. All to no avail. The boosters were en route. And if the night was starting like this, what more could lie ahead? A special guest appearance by Bon Jovi? A reading by a local author?

Love's mind boggled at the possibilities.

He slowly, ever so slowly, turned toward the door to encounter his malevolent fate like something of a man. Even as he did so, Julie began to laugh.

I'm just messing with you, she said.

It was true. TNT and the Gridiron Wizard, seeing no people of interest, no coaches or sportswriters or other local celebrities, were heading toward the banquet room to try their luck.

You're shooting fish in a barrel tonight if you want to mess with me, said Love. There's about fifty people I'm trying to dodge.

Aw, come on. I told you, I'm with you through thick and thin. You can count on me. Let's man-touch to seal my commitment to the cause.

Saying this, she stuck out a fist.

Can't do it.

To seal the bond, said Julie, giving her fist a few enticing pumps in his direction. Sports management sticks together.

Love found the attempt at ironic dudeness, at wingmanness, hampered considerably by the fact of the sundress, but played along by offering a hand to shake.

Got to be a bump, said Julie.

It's not going to happen.

They stood there, hands extended, in a classic duel between old and new, Love's palm open in traditional and seemly fashion, Julie's fist knotted in dipshittery and juvenilia.

You're stubborn, said Julie, pumping her fist toward his hand.

If we were at a skateboard park, I might consider it.

What if we'd just rappelled down a really high cliff?

Maybe. I'd be more inclined if we'd just shot some rapids in a kayak.

Your girlfriend just walked in.

Love's back was to the door again and he wasn't going to fall for the same trick twice.

Wave at her for me.

Julie waved.

She's heading over here.

Love was temped to look behind him but resisted. He jiggled his open hand a bit, trying to wrangle a shake from Julie.

Some things don't go out of fashion, he said.

Julie was smiling and looking as if she was about to laugh.

We're wearing the same dress. That's pretty funny.

This seemed the kind of detail that sprang from real life, not tomfoolery, and it occurred to Love that Brooke was in fact heading their way. Instantaneously he recorded the possibility that there might be two pretty girls of his acquaintance in sundresses. Had a fist bump been offered now, Love would have been sorely tempted.

I'll see you later, said Julie.

Don't run off.

We didn't seal the deal. No man-touch, no deal. I'm a free agent.

Love nodded. He'd had his chance.

I'll talk to you later, said Julie.

She was grinning as she headed toward the banquet room, as if she found his predicament funny.

He turned around to find Brooke standing there.

And Seersucker Suits

I texted you, said Brooke. Why didn't you respond?

You did? I must not have had my phone turned on.

That's no surprise. You never do.

Love didn't reply. The fact that he got few calls or texts didn't seem germane to the conversation. Better to be a man of intrigue when confronted with the sundress + unnecessary glasses combination, as he was now. Brooke was dressed either as a scientist who modeled or a Playmate poet. Sometimes the glasses looked more scientific, other times more artistic, depending on the light. In the end, he decided that both a Bunsen burner and a dog-eared copy of *Leaves of Grass* would be proper accoutrements.

It was an awesome look.

Anyway, said Brooke, I was just wondering how it all went down with my dad. He came in looking a little flummoxed. Not sure if he felt better or worse after I explained you were my boyfriend.

Boyfriend?

Who? What? When? Where? Why?

If only CVD were here right now. Love needed answers and needed them fast. Of course none would be forthcoming from Brooke. She was like a crafty veteran pitcher, always one step ahead of the overmatched batter. Luckily, the bantering session with Julie had settled his nerves.

It was fine, said Love. No big deal.

What in the world did you talk about? He was out there forever.

Chitchat mainly. I spent a lot of time explaining what I did and why I was with Coach Woody on this trip. Seriously, it was no problem.

Can you believe he walked in right then? Brooke said, smiling and adjusting a strap on the dress to match the tan line of her bikini.

Right then? Right when? What? What? What?

Only ironclad discipline kept Love from giving voice to these questions.

You were white as a ghost, said Brooke laughing. I thought you were just going to sprint out the door.

Love grinned at the memory of his spectral self. Then from the corner of his eye he saw Julie come out of the banquet room and head toward the water fountain. She noticed him looking and offered a distant fist to bump. An ironic *you're the man* offering. He wondered if she'd already taken a seat and if she'd saved one for him as well. He hoped so. His chances of beating back what the banquet room had to offer were better with that smart-aleck by his side.

Who are you looking at?

Huh?

You just looked over there and smiled.

Oh. My friend Julie just made a face.

A face? What kind of face?

Actually she gave me a fake fist bump motion.

What?

It's an old joke we have from some of our classes. We're making fun of guys who man-touch.

What?

Guys who fist bump. I call it a man-touch.

That's kind of gross.

It sure is.

Brooke turned toward the water fountain, but Julie was now heading back into The Great Hall. That the banquet room was called The Great Hall had just become apparent to Love when he spotted the wooden sign above the entry recognizing it as such. Ye Olde Mead Hall. Home of ringing good cheer and warrior thanes, poor Grendel watching from the cold.

You seem to have a lot in common, said Brooke.

Love was still enjoying his recall of *Beowulf* and wasn't prepared for the statement. What's that?

You and your friend seem to have a lot in common.

Love now got the gist and said, yeah, I guess so. We take a lot of classes together, so we end up kind of laughing about the same things.

You know we're wearing the same dress.

Yeah, but who cares? You both look great.

We both look great? Thanks a lot.

Love's newfound status as boyfriend seemed in doubt. Fleeting were the winds of time. He couldn't decide whether to go back to the topic of the dress or his conversation with Brooke's father. Both were laden with pitfalls. Better to head into neutral waters:

How were your grades, by the way?

Brooke gave him a look. Fine, she said.

Straight A's as usual?

Yes, whatever. Listen, you're sitting with me inside aren't you? I told my parents you were.

He'd not prepared for this possibility, not in the slightest.

Well you obviously don't want to, so just forget it. Just go sit with your grad school friend.

As Love was trying to think of something to say that would both mollify Brooke and insure he was nowhere in the vicinity of her parents while the image of liquid slippery was fresh on everyone's mind, in came Sparkman. Instantly any doubts about seersucker and white bucks were abated. He was fully clad.

In a vicious retaliatory move for his nonexclusive sundress compliment and his reluctance to sup with her family, Brooke beckoned the latest addition to the planter class with an enthusiastic wave and toothy smile. Sparkman offered his teeth in return and headed over in a near sprint.

Giving Love a wink, he stuck out a fist to bump and said: What's up, Lovie boy?

Not a lot, said Love, extending his hand with fingers out and palm exposed to show, again, that he was unarmed and disinclined, at least at this moment, to attack.

Sparkman was in the process of fist bumping with a giggling Brooke. As their fists met in ridiculous public display, she gave Love a bit of a look, peppery and full of sauce. The finish was a little tart for his taste as well.

See Love, said Sparkman, it's just a man-touch, no big deal.

Brooke laughed and said: is it a man-touch if one of the people is a woman? I don't think it is.

Love refused to quibble on gender issues, or semantics either. He knew every English professor he'd had in college would be chomping at the bit for a weighty issue like this, but he was in no frame of mind and frankly lacked the training.

No, he said, it's a man-touch no matter who does it.

Sparkman looked at Brooke and laughed. Then he took a step back in open appraisal. Damn, he said, that dress is hot.

Brooke smiled at this in a way that implied if there had been a boyfriend around before, there wasn't one now. During the discussion above, Love had somehow been edged out of the conversational lanes. These maneuverings had been subtle but efficient. That is, what had once been a triangular formation was strictly linear now. He might as well have been over by the water fountain.

Thanks, said Brooke, I just got it. I love your suit by the way. You look like you're going to the Derby or something.

As they discussed spring fashion, Love wondered if his presence was required further here in the Turf Club. The mint juleps would be arriving shortly and then, of course, the singing of *My Old Kentucky Home*. He'd best be off to the grandstand where he belonged.

He looked about the lobby, filling up now with smiling boosters anxious for their time with the coaches. The colors of the university were in full bloom, and seeing them in such profusion Love realized, belatedly, that Sparkman's bow tie was of distinct university hue. A color-coded expression of team spirit. Kith and kin with the good folks—home folks all—who came to be a part of the Pigskin Cavalcade. He already looked like one of the staff.

Brooke slapped Sparkman's arm and said: I did no such thing.

Love had missed part of the conversation, stationed as he was outside the lanes of communication. The arm slap and mock protest were signs, however, that Sparkman was charming another.

Coach Love! came a shout from the entrance to The Great Hall. It was Coach Woody and he was gesturing in a fervent way. Love started to lean in and say his goodbyes, but Sparkman had him nicely boxed out and was either reading Brooke's palm or fitting her for a ring and he hated to interrupt. Instead he slipped into the crowd and was gone.

Love sat with Coach Woody in Ye Olde Taverne, the resort's bar, with frosty Budweisers in pint glasses before them. The furtive and anxious gestures from Woody had been translated as follows: *Meet me in bar. Too many jacklegs about. Afraid will harm stocky booster involuntarily if asked again about specific plays from last season.*

The old coach was taking no chances on sneak attacks and had chosen the seat farthest from the door, one that left his back to the wall and afforded a view of all who entered the premises. Apparently he'd innocently poked his head into the banquet room just to get the lay of the land and had been rushed by TNT and the Gridiron Wizard. They'd insisted on reciting CVD's Game Day Axioms in unison, as the team did every Saturday before a game. This recitation was a focusing device for the team, highlighting CVD's philosophies and points of emphasis. If the team followed the axioms to a tee, then chances for victory were exponentially increased.

An example of a Game Day Axiom was:

Handle the pressure and the pressure won't handle you.

Another was:

The enthused team efforts for sixty minutes!

Coach Woody sighed into his beer. He was efforting to get through the night's festivities. He was not enthused. The recitation of game axioms by the earnest boosters had taken its toll. Behind the bar, on the television, a basketball coach was lecturing a player who'd just committed a turnover. The announcer said: *he's coaching him up!*

What does *up* have to do with it? said Coach Woody. They're not coaching up, down, sideways, or loop-t-loop. They're just coaching.

My dad noticed that one, said Love. The *coaching em up* thing.

They just got to talk sometimes, don't they? Invent buzzwords. By god Ray Scott didn't need any buzz words: *Starr hands to Hornung. Sweep left. Touchdown Packers.*

Love took a long gander at the coach. His night on the lam had robbed him of precious energy. He was getting too old to burn the candle at both ends and still deal with the travails of modern football. Love decided to put his own minor situations on the back burner and stick close to the old coach for the rest of the night.

You all right, Coach Woody?

It's crazy as hell out there.

Love didn't know if Woody meant the sports world in particular or the whole of the technologically weird society. Either way, sports or Kardashian, it was a shitload of words and imagery coming right at people. The twenty-first century was efforting, you couldn't deny that.

Love looked for an agreeable topic. Where's Snort by the way?

Taking a nap.

Love decided to throw all his chips in. If this didn't break the malaise nothing would.

What kind of team did yall have in high school?

Woody smiled. Then laughed.

We had the craziest coach in the history of football. You ever hear of twenty-two men on the pile?

No sir.

Back in the fifties and early sixties you had a lot of these coaches who'd fought in World War II. Tough as hell, every one of em. Some of them got the notion that the best way to build toughness was to scrimmage and have every player on the field, offense and defense, dive on the pile after the play was stopped. It was kind of a fad there for awhile. You'd have offensive linemen jumping on top of their own tailback. The whole damn team was supposed to just hop right on. The whistle would blow and old Dog Williams would be hollering, *twenty-two men on the pile, twenty-two men on the pile*. It was the goddamnedest thing. Guys getting speared in the back left and right. And I'll tell you another thing, Dog Williams put *irregardless* in the dictionary.

Love laughed.

Irregardless where you are on the field, I want you sprinting for the pile. I don't care if we score a touchdown, I want a twenty-two-man pile in the end zone irregardless.

Old Dog loved that word.

Woody was laughing about his old coach and Love joined in.

They called him Dog, said Woody, because he had this kind of leathery, wrinkly face. Even when he was a young man, he looked like a dog. And I've thought about this a lot since then, but we played like he looked. Ugly but tough. Nobody wanted to play us. And then I started studying it some, and it came to me that teams play like their head coach looks.

Love was dubious and said so.

Look at Lombardi. He looked tough, but also smart with those glasses. A little cocky too when he grinned. His teams played smart and tough and they always had that hint of arrogance that all winners have. Tom Landry? Stone-faced. Unyielding, disciplined. His teams were fundamentally sound, robotic almost. Jimmy Johnson? Cocky looking like a golf hustler. He's a little pudgy but not the kind you'd want to tangle with. How'd his teams play? Loose, free-wheeling, always letting it all hang out. Spurrier? Smug and arrogant, kind of like the coach's son who's a pain in the ass but also the best guy on the team. Or the choir boy with a flask in his pocket. His teams never lacked confidence and there was always something tricky about em, something about em you just couldn't read all the way. And they used to talk about Bobby Dodd's luck when he was at Georgia Tech, and they *were* lucky. Lucky as hell. But look at Dodd. You never saw a more optimistic man. He'd smile on game day, which you didn't see much back then, like he was having a good time and expected good things to happen. His teams always thought they'd get lucky and they'd just hang around and hang around until they got the break they were looking for.

Coach Woody was laughing a little now, laughing at his theory.

You wait, he said, and see if you don't end up with some crackpot ideas about things after studying them a bit. Anyway, you're tall and handsome right now. Maybe when you're the head man, if you can hold on to your looks, like I did, your teams will play like those old Bill Walsh 49ers. I always thought they played handsome. Not soft and not pretty. Handsome is the word. It's a funny way to phrase it, a funny way to talk about a football team, but I don't know how else to say it.

Love smiled but didn't respond. He was imagining himself on an NFL sideline, how he'd carry himself, what his demeanor would be, and didn't want to spoil it with words.

But the moment was spoiled soon enough anyway. Sammy Dutch, the red-faced booster, had just entered the room. He hallooed Coach Woody with about twice the volume necessary, then joined them at the bar, sitting next to Love without a word of greeting.

Return on Investment

I'm not just spending my money for the hell of it, said Sammy Dutch, sipping on his highball and scratching a flaky, sunburned ear. I'm a businessman. Every now and then you'd like to see a return on your investment.

Here he laughed and slapped Love in a business-friendly way on the back. He'd yet to talk to him, or look at him, but he did seem to enjoy his back. Love wondered if this rough kind of Rotarian foreplay worked with the more eager members of Junior Achievement. He usually preferred to be friends before dishing out the benefits.

Don't you agree, Coach Woody?

Love looked at Woody, who'd done his best to keep his mouth shut during this odd session of braggadocio, name-dropping, insincere homilies, and none-too-veiled threats. What Sammy wanted was results. And he wanted them now, by god.

You know, Sammy, I think a man ought to spend his money the way he wants to spend it.

I'm asking about return on investment, said Sammy Dutch, firmly and with a false smile.

Woody looked the big booster in the eye now. He seemed to be weighing his words, deciding if he was going to say what he wanted to say or just hold his tongue.

Hell, I don't know. I'm just an old defensive line coach.

Sammy Dutch took the last big swig from his Makers and Coke, and hollered at the bartender's back for another. The flaky ear continued to bedevil him and he clawed away at it. Love wished he'd stop. Wayward epidermis was flying all about the bar. What Sammy needed was a touch of the liquid s.

Well, what do you think, young fella?

Love's shoulder was punched, his neck squeezed, his thigh goosed before he realized he was actually meant to answer the question.

He looked toward Woody, who smiled sheepishly into his beer. The smile seemed to say: *welcome to college football.*

There was no answer he could give. To agree with Sammy was to question the stewardship of the program under his head coach. To disagree would put him on the outs with the most influential person at the university.

I'm afraid I don't know much about how things work with the administration and donations and things like that, said Love.

You better learn, son. You damn well better learn. You won't last long in this business if you don't understand that it is a business.

Love gave an indefinite shake of his head. He was completely out of his depth.

Sammy took another large gulp of his drink and spilled a bit down his chin and shirt as he did so.

Love realized the booster was drunker than he'd first imagined and remembered that he'd spent a long day on the boat already, drinking beer and rocking out to Kenny Chesney. Today he could have sworn he'd heard a song called *Tailgating Boogie.* Then again it might have been *Mai Tai Dixie Mornin'.* Regardless what good-timing song it had been, the booster appeared to have taken its lyrics to heart.

Sammy, said Coach Woody, I've been thinking about taking a vacation somewhere in the next month or so. I was wondering what you might recommend.

Love found this a tactful question, and a savvy one, veering away from the prior dangerous topic. What rich man wasn't a vacation braggart, after all?

Sammy hesitated for a moment, but the question had been liberally sprinkled with rich boy catnip. When Sammy began to wax poetic about the beaches of Aruba and the rugged countryside of Peru, Love breathed a sigh of relief. The danger seemed to have passed. Feeling safe that the time was right, he excused himself and made a dash for the rest room.

Love was in the bathroom, minding his own business, when someone approached the urinal next to his. There ensued a number of grunts and moans, a fair bit of shoe squeaking, not a little jostling and harrumphing, and then a prolonged moan of satisfaction. In other words, it was a middle-aged man next to him who had just successfully unzipped his fly, extracted and pointed his pointer, and induced, after an awkward dry spell of shaking, gasping, and coaxing, liquid flow.

To celebrate his accomplishment, he had quiffed a minuscule and reluctant fart. The fart made Love sad. He found himself again lamenting the inevitable decline into middle age and beyond. It looked a humbling affair.

How's it going, Raymond, said the voice beside him.

Love's eyes were fixed, as appropriate and traditional, straight ahead, yet from the volume and clarity of the urinating stranger beside him, he could tell that the speaker had his head turned, was indeed looking directly at him. For a paranoid moment, Love was sure the speaker was offering a hand to shake as well.

Love's philosophy was to ignore all inquires while about his business, be that from friend, relative, or man of the cloth. Short of fire in the bathroom or a murderer on the loose behind him, it could wait. Truly, silence was golden in Love's book.

He glanced quickly, peripherally, to see who this chamber pot conversationalist could be. He sighted a shortish man with sandy red hair and moustache to match. Then his eyes were facing straight ahead again, as was natural and right. His friend of the latrine, how-ever, would be governed by no rules of etiquette. He continued to face Love, continued to talk and make other sounds, huffing mostly. Love wished he would labor a bit less strenuously. It was disturbing his own performance, which was usually so joyous and carefree.

You enjoying the Cavalcade? said the man beside him, and again Love feared a hand was being offered to shake.

Yes sir, Love said, refusing to turn and make eye contact with the sportswriter.

Playing a little golf, I guess?

Yes sir.

Love's mission here was finished and he went without further adieu to the sink to wash his hands. In the mirror he could see the sportswriter rocking from foot to foot at the urinal and gyrating more than seemed normal. The fact that he was humming what sounded like *Rock-a-Bye Baby* would have surprised Love at another time. Now, it seemed apt and fitting.

Finishing up the last bars of the song, he turned abruptly and joined Love at the next sink.

Listen, he said, I was thinking about doing a feature on coaches' wives. I understand your father's a high school coach and I was won-dering if you might be willing to answer a few questions about what you witnessed from your mother. How she approached the season and going to games and dealing with the pressures of being married to a coach.

Love reached for a paper towel to dry his hands. How did the sportswriter know about his parents? There had been the occasional article written about him when he was in college, but finding those would require an Internet search. Out of the corner of his eye, he could see Clay Dibble casually handcombing his hair in the mirror. Despite his apparent ease, he was studying Love's reflection closely.

I don't think I'd have much of interest to say, said Love. My mom didn't seem to feel a lot of pressure. She taught at the same school and knew everyone in town. I think she liked it.

Oh, it's not going to be a really in-depth piece. It's going to focus primarily on Mrs. Driver. How she deals with being in the public eye. What hobbies she has to help relieve tension. That sort of thing. I've always maintained that the family of the coach has it tougher than the coach. Wouldn't you agree, at least at the college level?

Yes, I'd agree.

And Mrs. Driver is an interesting character, wouldn't you say?

Clay Dibble offered a sly grin here, smiling with just the corners of his lips. In response, Love crumpled his paper towel into a tight ball and fired it, using the wall as a backboard, into the wastebasket behind him.

I don't know Mrs. Driver, said Love. Other than sitting with her at dinner last night, then giving her a lift to the hotel, I've never talked to her.

Oh, I'm just talking generalities. I wasn't implying that you were close with Mrs. Driver.

Love knew what was being implied and said nothing.

Might not hurt to get your name in the paper either. A young coach needs to get his name out there as much as possible. You've always got to be thinking about career advancement.

I'm pretty boring. I wouldn't make good copy.

Oh, I disagree. You strike me as a very interesting young coach.

Enigmatic even. You seem like a man who knows more than he lets on. Yes, I'd wager you don't miss much. Am I right?

I have no idea.

Dibble was drying his hands now.

For the record, I don't miss much either.

Love turned to leave. It was unusual for him to be unmannerly and not say goodbye, but it gave him no qualms now.

In the hallway, heading into the Ye Olde Taverne, Love was met by the only Snort of his acquaintance.

How's it going, Book Club?

Love smiled at Coach Woody's old friend, as much for the sobriquet as for his current appearance, which brought to mind a hard nap in a tornado followed by a gentle awakening by cartoon animals. He looked roguish and beatific, his uncombed hair askew, his volunteer fire department shirt tucked crookedly into his wrinkled pants. Atop this was a grin for the good time this afternoon, the excellent if turbulent nap, and the promise of the night ahead. In Love's opinion, Bobby Dodd had nothing on Snort when it came to an optimistic look.

Where's my partner in crime?

This way, said Love, heading toward the bar.

And where's that gal Julie?

I'm not sure. In the banquet room, I guess.

So you know where all the old farts are but not the pretty gals? Gumption, boy, gumption.

They entered Ye Olde Taverne to find Sammy Dutch sitting in Love's former seat next to Coach Woody. He was leaning forward and talking in an animated way, as if unsatisfied with the drift of the conversation. Woody glanced up when they walked in and gave a tired smile to his old friend.

This bistro open for business or are we just having tea and crumpets? said Snort.

The cause of Snort's consternation was the unmanned bar. Love assumed the Taverne keeper had gone out for fresh supplies, or was perhaps helping out in the kitchen for the dinner rush. Other than the four of them, the room was empty.

Where are all the women? said Snort.

You scared em all off, said Coach Woody.

Then will someone be so kind as to fetch me a clean young fat boy?

Love had never heard this one before and laughed out loud.

I'm not particular about looks, said Snort. But he must be clean and he must be fat.

Coach Woody only smiled. An old routine apparently. But Sammy Dutch, who previously had his back to them, turned full around in his seat to glare unequivocally at the pride of Fairview. He seemed to feel an important conversation was being interrupted. Love's one and only beer of the night was sitting half full in front of this same booster, but he made no move for it. He'd picked up on a vibe and remained standing where he was.

Coach, said Sammy Dutch, I want to finish this conversation. Your buddies will just have to hold their horses. I'm simply asking your opinion on what my reasonable expectations should be. I'm not giving five million dollars to the athletic department for a new weight room so we can go to the goddam Capital One Bowl every year.

Capital One is a New Year's Day game, said Woody. A lot of folks would be glad to get there. And with the injuries we had last year and our inexperience at the quarterback position, I thought it was a pretty fair performance.

Goddammit Woody. You ain't going anywhere, and I ain't going anywhere, and both of us is older than dirt. All I'm asking you is if you think I'm getting a good return on my investment. I'm just making conversation. I'm not asking for a referendum on Coach Driver. I just want your opinion, nothing more, nothing less.

Woody looked at Snort and Love and smiled, shaking his head as if to say, *well, you heard him, he wants my opinion.* The old coach's blue eyes were clear and sharp as he appraised Sammy Dutch, the man with the gold who made the university rules.

Well, Sammy, he said, I guess I'm confused. Sometimes you say you give money to the university. And sometimes you say you want a return on your investment. If the university and the football team are a business to be bought and sold like a stock, then I'd say you have a right to expect some kind of return for your money. But if it's a gift—a donation—then that's another thing. I always thought a gift should come with no strings attached. It's just something you do out of the goodness of your heart. That's just my opinion of course.

Sammy Dutch pushed away from his seat and stood up, his face no longer a mask of joviality.

Oh don't be naïve, Woody, he said, pointing at the coach, his voice rising. Don't give me any of that innocent bullshit.

I'm not naïve. Let's just call a spade a spade. You're not giving gifts. You're not making donations. You're paying money so you can tell the university what to do.

Is that right?

Of course it is.

Why don't you stand up and say that?

Love considered this an unwise request by the large but softish booster. A night of bourbon was overweighing that little voice in his head that spoke of self-preservation.

Woody didn't reply but could be seen tapping his forefinger against the bar in a methodical way, a man trying to keep his temper in check.

But Snort was already moving toward the confrontation zone.

He eased behind Sammy Dutch until he was essentially between the two men, careful not to squeeze in too close as if physically interfering. His manner was breezy and his smile genuine. Love surmised he'd been in these types of situations before.

Woody, why don't you and me go find our seat inside?

Mind your own business, hayseed, said Sammy Dutch, without bothering to look in his direction.

Snort laughed.

But Woody did not. He stood up and faced the booster, saying: what did you call my friend?

He called me a hayseed, said Snort. And you don't hear me arguing. I am a hayseed. In fact, I kind of like being a hayseed. It ain't a bad life. Now let's go inside. I'm ready to eat.

Coach Woody was not so easily placated. He stared at Sammy Dutch with a hard look on his face and for a moment Love thought he was going to strike the booster. Then a moment's hesitation crossed his brow and Love could see his better instincts taking over. He looked at Love and nearly smiled. Unfortunately, this was when Sammy Dutch decided to shove him with all his might. The blow to the chest sent the old coach reeling into bar stools and nearly to the ground. Surprised, but unhurt, Coach Woody paused at the bar, taking stock. He shook his head and smiled. Then with one quick hop-step for momentum, he cracked the puffed-up booster a square one upon the nose. Thereafter, the proverbial sack of potatoes made its drop.

Love's first reaction was clinical. He'd never seen such a hard and efficient strike and found it a neat piece of work. His second reaction was to be pleasantly surprised by the swiftness and righteousness of Justice's sword. Had anyone ever so had it coming? He thought not. His moment of universal harmony was short-lived, however. Almost immediately he recognized that Coach Woody would be in deep trouble, possibly out of a job.

Snort looked down at Sammy Dutch, moaning slightly with his hand over his gushing nose.

Somebody get that fella a drink, he said.

Woody smiled but didn't reply. Reaching over the bar, he grabbed a clean towel and tossed it on the heap that was Sammy Dutch. The addled booster took the towel without comment and placed it over his face.

I best make a strategic withdrawal, said Woody, stepping crisply over the pile of boosterism at his feet. Let's go, Snort.

Love was bringing up the rear when Coach Woody stopped him.

I need you to stay here, he said. Once the banquet's over, tell Coach Driver he can find me at my cabin if wants me. Or he can call.

This was an assignment without appeal for Love and his face must have shown it.

I'm sorry, partner, said Coach Woody. But if I go in, there's liable to be a scene that will embarrass the coach. Best to let him find out later when there aren't so many people around.

I'd just as soon go with you, if it's okay, said Love. Coach Driver told me to stick with you.

I know, I know. But listen here, son. I'm all done at the university now. That right there is all she wrote. But don't worry about it. It's no big deal. I been wanting to do that for forty years to one of these fatcats. But you're still on the staff and you need to look out for yourself.

Love nodded his assent and they shook hands quickly. Then Woody and Snort were out the door, well-wishers in the hall hallooing the old coach as he passed.

At the moment, only he and Sammy Dutch occupied Ye Olde Taverne. Love went to the bar and finished off the last half of his beer. He figured the bartender must be helping in the kitchen and wasn't coming back anytime soon, so he went behind the counter, found a plastic bag, and filled it with ice.

Mr. Dutch, he said, leaning down. Why don't you put this ice on your nose?

The booster hadn't cleared enough cobwebs to sit up, or even to fully open his eyes. But he was able to speak.

Kiss my ass son.

Love declined the offer but left the ice. Then he headed for The Great Hall and whatever lay within.

Coveralls and Cocktails

A sizable crowd milled at the entrance to the banquet room, awaiting their turn at the check-in for table assignments. Julie was taking photos of everyone who entered for the alumni magazine and Love couldn't get her attention. He stood within the pack of fans, struck by their eagerness to mingle with the head man. It dawned on him that many—perhaps most—in the crowd weren't well-to-do boosters or donors, but regular people, for whom the fifty-dollar ticket was pretty dear. Looking around, he realized that for every Sammy Dutch, every TNT and Gridiron Wizard, there were ten like the middle-aged woman beside him, who, screwing up her courage and adjusting a university-colored blouse, had finally asked if he were one of the coaches.

I'm a graduate assistant, Love replied.

Well, that is just so exciting, the woman said, patting his arm in a supportive way. You're doing your part for our team.

They talked for a minute about the coming season, and the one just past, Love answering her questions as best he could about players and the schedule and the breaks, both good and bad, the team had recently experienced. After the briefest of exchanges, the woman seemed to feel she had taken enough of Love's valuable time.

Well, I'm just talking your head off.

No, not at all. I've enjoyed talking to you.

But the woman would hear nothing of it. Her internal clock had gone off. She'd not be too familiar.

It was a real pleasure to meet you, the woman said, offering a hand to shake. And I wish you all the best with your coaching career.

Saying this, she turned with a tight smile toward the check-in table, anticipating the night to come.

Love found himself oddly moved by the encounter, though he wasn't sure why. Maybe he'd just needed a reminder that there were a lot of nice people out there who cheered for the team. He'd wanted a quick word with Julie before the banquet started, to tell her about Coach Woody's situation and his assignment with CVD, but that seemed unlikely now. He waved once, high over the heads in the crowd, and caught her attention, but smiling and pointing at the waiting people, she made it clear she couldn't talk now.

Brooke, sitting at a table near the front with her parents and Sparkman, saw him as well and offered a grim appraisal of his right to enter The Great Hall. At the same table, Brooke's mother was shaking her head in fond remembrance at one of Sparkman's humble offerings and tittering in a manner that made Love question the notion of a benevolent God and an orderly universe. He felt sure he'd never be able to erase the tableau of *Matron Tittering* from his memory, no matter how hard he tried.

The athletic director, meanwhile, seemed content to jot notes from Sparkman's talk and consider his prospects as a future doubles partner.

Only Brooke, if her body language and steely silence were any indication, was immune to the anecdotist's charms. Wait. Was Sparkman being painted—*The Asskisser's Reward*—as the parents' favorite? That was the death knell of lust, even Love knew that, especially with a girl like Brooke. And if this were the case, did that make him the bad boy alternative? He tried to flash her a sympathetic smile, one to say, *I too have been Sparkmanned.*

In response, Brooke put her arm around the back of the surfer/linebacker/aristocrat's chair and smiled in an encouraging way to her mother.

Titter more, Mother, the look seemed to say. *Titter ever and anon.*

Love decided a breath of fresh air might be just what the doctor ordered. There seemed no real reason to hurry his arrival, no real clamor from the assembled for his immediate or prolonged presence in The Great Hall.

He stood just beyond the entrance to the lodge, under a streetlamp, on a pleasant spring night, nodding to the late arrivals who came hurrying up from the parking lot. He was going over the episode in the Ye Olde Taverne. The more he thought about it, the surer he was that Coach Woody was jumping the gun about his future with Coach Driver and the program. Woody's reaction, the punch to the nose, was a matter of instinct and had come after being prodded, provoked, and forcefully shoved. If Sammy Dutch was any kind of man, he'd just take his well-earned medicine and let bygones be bygones. All he had to do was slink back to his cabin after the crowd had entered the banquet and no one would be the wiser. Only three people had witnessed his comeuppance and none of the three was the sort to talk. The booster had to know that.

Love felt sure the athletic director hadn't heard of the dust-up in the bar yet. Otherwise, he'd have been a little less attentive to Sparkman. Maybe Coach Driver hadn't heard either. But did that even matter? Well, not for his own position, it didn't. It had been his job to keep Coach Woody out of trouble and he'd failed at that. The coaching position he'd hoped for was now off the table. There was even a chance he'd lose his graduate assistantship altogether. Contract renewals didn't go out until July.

Okay. Fine. The chips would fall where they may. The thing to do was to bum-rush CVD immediately after his speech. Getting to him before Sammy Dutch did would allow Love to give his version of things before the booster muddied the waters. Maybe Love could help the old coach keep his job. What happened to his own position was of secondary concern.

Oh there you are, said a voice approaching from the parking lot.

It was Mrs. Driver. She approached with a smile indicative of joint conspiracy. Love was unsure how exactly they were birds of a feather, but thought he'd take his allies as they came. Smoothing her black dress and giving one quick tug on some hosiery Love was afraid to look at, she said: I've been in and out of there twice, but never did see you or Coach Woody. If I have to go to these things, Coach Woody's usually my man. He's a hoot, you know.

Love agreed he was a hoot. As he did so, a spunky heavy-set couple in matching university-colored coveralls walked past, nudging each other in the ribs and nodding at Mrs. Driver.

Hello there, said Mrs. Driver with a charming smile.

Can't wait for tonight, said the man. Can't wait to hear the coach.

Oh, me neither, said Mrs. Driver.

I guess you're excited they got that quarterback from Texas, said the woman.

I certainly am. It was touch and go there for awhile.

I know, said the woman, stepping closer to Mrs. Driver. I thought for sure Southern Cal was going to snag him away from us. We sure need us a good quarterback.

It's an important position. It certainly is.

The couple stood there for a moment, in their bold coveralls, deciding whether to dive into a full-fledged attempt at a conversation with the coach's wife. But something in Mrs. Driver's smile, while friendly, didn't invite the taking of liberties. It was a trait Love both admired and knew he'd never possess. There had never been a time in his life when the lost old lady at the mall didn't pick him out of the crowd to ask for directions. Actually, that was a good thing. He liked helping little old ladies. But at other times, as when faced with a TNT or a Gridiron Wizard, he wished for a more inscrutable look.

There was an awkward moment after the couple went inside when Love was brooding on the friendliness and approachability of his face and Mrs. Driver was equally lost in thought. She pulled a cigarette from her purse and lit it. She waited another moment, drawing and exhaling at her leisure.

I feel like I should make some comment on the coveralls. But I find I don't quite have the energy.

Love laughed. He couldn't tell if she was trying to be humorous or not, but it was plain she was impressed by her own restraint.

Perhaps it was a lark. They likely have friends in there from town who will hoot and holler at their arrival. The coveralls as an ironic fashion statement.

Probably so, said Love.

One would like to think it was a costume, you know. And not actual daily wear.

Yes. Maybe that's the case.

What do you think?

Love gave the matter some thought. Mrs. Driver took her second drag of the cigarette, then went to the standing ashtray nearby and stubbed it out.

My guess is they weren't being ironic.

Oh no, of course not. Why would they be? Who would get it? *Who* is there to be ironic to?

Love smiled.

One can hope though, said Mrs. Driver. One must never lose hope. But more importantly, is Coach Woody here? Is he in the bar? He's usually the gentleman to bring me a vodka tonic when the situation calls for it. And if those coveralls are an indication of what lies ahead of me, he will need to make it a double.

Love nodded in an ambiguous way, unsure of the best way to proceed.

Well, is Coach Woody in the bar? Is he on the premises?

I think he's back in the cabin, said Love.

Mrs. Driver eyed him suspiciously. He wasn't sure what kind of lawyer she was, but wouldn't want to see that look from the witness box.

Is he not feeling well?

I don't know.

Mrs. Driver paused, giving him another look. It was not the invasive and discomforting bug eye of her husband, just a shrewd once-over that made the recipient want to come clean and reveal, in a squeaky voice, that which the gazer seemed already to know.

In that case, she said, turning and heading into the lodge, you'll just have to take Coach Woody's part for another night.

Love followed her into the lobby and down the nearly empty hall. Only three or four people were waiting to be seated, so the banquet would be starting any minute now. Mrs. Driver stopped at Ye Olde Taverne and pulled a twenty from her purse.

Vodka tonic, she said. Go cup. No garnish. And get something for yourself. A strong one. For all I know, we'll be singing patriotic songs in there. Yes, on second thought make mine a double. I was once at an event where Lee Greenwood sang his *God Bless the USA* and thought he'd fomented a yeoman revolt right then and there. You should have seen the tears on their homespun faces.

Love stood where he was, not taking the proffered twenty. The chance that an angry bigwig still roamed the premises loomed too large. He needed to avoid Sammy Dutch until he'd passed along Woody's message to CVD.

Well, said Mrs. Driver. You'd best get going. I just heard the opening trills of the jug band. Or would you prefer I ordered? I don't mind in the least.

Love took a meager step toward the entrance and craned his head as little as possible while still giving the impression of peering.

I don't think the bar's open, he said.

Nonsense, said Mrs. Driver, striding into Ye Olde Taverne as if she were the proprietor of the place. Love was slinking in behind her when she suddenly stopped. They were at the top of three steps leading into the tavern. The first thing Mrs. Driver seemed to notice was the absence of a barkeep. The second was a large man holding a towel to his nose. This man was talking vehemently into a cell phone. Mrs. Driver shot Love a look, then turned deftly and exited the room. They had not been sighted.

I'm not going to ask you about that, said Mrs. Driver when they were back in the hall.

Thank you.

Anything I need to hear I ought to hear from Von. It's cleaner that way. And it makes it easier if there's someone I might want to help.

Love nodded in appreciation. How Coach Driver had managed to cajole/bribe/hypnotize Mrs. Driver into becoming his spouse however many years ago was a mystery for the ages.

Inside The Great Hall the evening's emcee was giving his opening Tarzanian throat-clear into the microphone. The banquet was starting.

Shall we go in? said Mrs. Driver, smiling in a sympathetic way.

All right, said Love. Let's go on in.

Envoy

ove lingered near his table at the back of The Great Hall, waiting for the hordes of well-wishers around Coach Driver to thin out a bit. The banquet itself had proceeded smoothly. It had opened with a firmly denominational prayer, then the Pledge of Allegiance, and finally a rousing sing-along of the university fight song. Love had been prepared for the Nicene Creed, but that had been mysteriously left off of the docket. At some point, he guessed, you just had to trust that most of the treasonous non-Christians had fled the room and it was safe to talk a little football.

Coach Driver had done so with gusto and relish. Love had never heard him quite so vociferous as he enumerated the points of his *Isosceles Triangle of Success*, especially when working up to the climax, which was broken down thusly:

1. The TEAM BASE which supported the whole of the triangle
2. The EFFORTING LEG and the ENTHUSING LEG which strove tirelessly
3. The APEX where SUCCESS patiently waited

The aphorisms had come fast and furious after that and not just the standard fare of Coach Driver's Game Day Maxims. Love had never previously heard that:

The greatest ability is coachability.

Or that

Loyalty is a two-way street that always circles back to Respect.

Or even that

The IN in W-I-N is in you.

Coach Driver finished his talk to the same standing ovation offered up at the Goshen Country Club, this one led by none other than TNT himself, who, exhorting his fellow Cavalcade attendees with raise-the-roof hand gestures and a flurry of machine-gun fist pumps, was not to be denied. He was *en fuego* when it came to *manning up*.

The Gridiron Wizard, meanwhile, proponent of the thinking man's school of football, could be seen studiously—furiously—jotting in his notepad. The scowl of determination across his wizened brow showed that devotees of football man-chat would get the details of tonight's banquet down to the au gratin potatoes.

Love was deciding where to position himself for earliest contact with Coach Driver, and also scoping out possible angles of interception should CVD make a sudden dash for the door, when he turned around to see the Gridiron Wizard staring at him. When Love met his gaze, the Gridiron Wizard made a point of flipping several pages backwards in his musings, writing aggressively for a moment, then making several stabbing-type punctuation motions with his pen.

Love took this as an ill omen for his future standing in the man-chat, but that was water under the bridge anyway. The press, avatar-enhanced or no, would have its say.

He felt someone pinch his arm from behind. Then a voice was whispering in his ear: *the IN in W-I-N is in you.*

He turned and found Julie smiling.

It really is, you know.

Love thanked her and offered a weak smile in return.

Did you see who I was sitting next to?

I did, said Love. Your man Clay Dibble.

I mean, what are the odds? I wanted so bad to ask him if he got paid for each and every period.

Did you tell him you were a fan of his work?

I just looked at him and said:

Saturday was a cold day. A perfect day for football. Maybe the punter didn't notice. He sat at his locker. His head hung low.

Love smiled.

He pointed over to your table one time when you and Mrs. Driver were laughing about something and made a comment about how you two sure seemed to hit it off.

He knows that Mrs. Driver doesn't like him, Love said. You know how sportswriters are. They're sensitive as hell.

Julie looked at him as if he were being less than forthcoming, but didn't press the matter.

By the way, she said, where's Coach Woody?

Back at the cabin I think.

Is he sick or just Snorting it up? I noticed he skipped dinner.

Coach Woody might be in a little trouble, said Love.

Really? I hate to hear that. What happened? I mean if you're allowed to say.

In a few quick sentences Love laid out the situation as it now stood.

That sounds pretty bad, Julie said. I mean for Coach Woody.

Love agreed that it did.

You're not going to get mixed up in this, are you? I mean other than having to pass along the word to Coach Driver? You didn't do anything.

I was supposed to keep Coach Woody out of trouble.

That's ridiculous. You're a graduate assistant. Nobody listens to you. Even the managers don't listen to a GA.

You can tell that to Coach Driver.

Maybe I will.

Just then Love spotted Brooke walking from the front of the room toward them.

Don't run off, he said, for Julie had noticed her approach as well.

I think I will. That's a gal with some things on her mind.

Well, I could probably go for a beer after this is over. You want to join me?

Sure. Just stop by the cabin. I want to hear how it all shakes out with Coach Woody.

I'll definitely stop by, said Love.

All right, good. And listen, don't put up with a lot of shit from CVD. He's not in your league.

Love gave her a curious look.

I'm a grad assistant, he said. He's the head coach.

I'm not talking about coaching.

And smiling once at Brooke, who had just arrived, she was gone.

Brooke watched as Julie walked away but said nothing. She then adjusted her glasses which hadn't been crooked before and flipped her hair behind her ears in a casual way that Love found winning.

Do you know that Sparkman guy very well?

Not really, said Love. Just around the football team.

Well he's an idiot. I was talking about books and I mentioned that he should consider coming to one of our book club meetings. Do you know what that meathead said?

Love tried to fight off the smile that was making its way to his lips, then gave it up as a lost cause. No, what did he say?

He said he didn't read books. That he hadn't read a book since college. Can you believe that?

Actually Love could. None of his guy friends read books. Did anyone even expect them to?

I guess I can believe it, he said.

I could never go out with someone who didn't read.

As Brooke said this, she placed a hand on Love's arm and gave him a friendly smile.

Love was confused. Hadn't she been irritated with him earlier that day, both for his lack of book club vim, and for his refusal to sit with her parents? Now he was back in her good graces? Perhaps it was his nervousness about the upcoming meeting with Coach Driver, or maybe just a sense of general fatigue, but for the first time it occurred to him that Brooke, for all of her good traits, might not be someone he wanted to spend a lot more time with, as a friend or otherwise. It was just too tiring and unpredictable.

They've got some pretty good coffee in the restaurant, she said. Some interesting blends, which is kind of surprising for a place like this. You want to join me for a quick cup?

I don't think so. I've got to do something here in a minute.

What's that?

I can't really say.

Is it with that girl you've been talking to all night?

No, not at all.

Yeah right.

Listen, she's engaged. We're just friends from sports management like I told you.

Okay, fine. I believe you. Well, do you want to meet up after you do whatever mysterious thing you have to do? I thought I might swing by your cabin later on. Unless, of course, you'd like come to our place and hang out some more with my dad. He said you were an interesting and unusual fellow.

Brooke smiled in a way that Love was quite fond of, casual and playful. He wished he'd seen more of this side of her all along.

She said: well, what do you think? Are you free later?

I don't think so.

Really?

Well, technically I'm free. And listen, I appreciate you inviting me to the book club and all. It was good to do something away from football. But I think maybe we ought to just go our separate ways. This feels like it's run its course.

Run its course?

We just don't have that much in common.

I think we have a lot in common.

Okay, maybe we do. I just think you probably need someone who's more sophisticated than I am. Someone who's more into food and coffee and things like that.

At that moment Brooke's father walked into The Great Hall with a cell phone to his ear and a pained expression on his face. He observed the crowd around Coach Driver and seemed to weigh his next move.

What does food and coffee have to do with anything?

Nothing. I'm just distracted. But listen, I really do have to go now. Take care. I'll see you around.

Excuse me, Coach Driver, said Love, talking over the head of TNT and ten or so others crowded around the coach.

The head coach gazed at him without comprehension, his eyes straining against the confinement of their own sockets, his eyebrows bristling as if subject to a high and confounding wind. Was someone really shouting him down? And was that someone a vaguely recognizable graduate assistant?

I'm sorry to bother you, said Love, who was being nudged off of his spot by TNT with a hockey-style hip check.

Coach Driver continued to stare at him, and now those who had just been talking to the coach and those whose turn was upcoming turned to stare as well.

Coach Driver, shouted TNT, taking advantage of the stoppage in play to skip around Love and several others. What's the chances of us getting a home and home with Penn State? Cause that would be awesome.

Coach Driver, back in familiar territory, acknowledged TNT with a practiced smile.

That's a question for the athletic director, he said. He's the one in charge of making my life miserable by scheduling all these tough non-conference games. If I had my druthers we'd be scheduling Oglethorpe and nothing but Oglethorpe.

With a quick drop step as most often performed by NBA centers, Love moved ahead of TNT and boxed him out. He then maneuvered, *jitterbugging through the hole* as Brent Musburger would say, until he was face to face with CVD.

Coach Driver, I need to talk to you alone for just a moment. It's important.

CVD stood rooted in place, befuddled. Graduate assistants didn't interrupt head coaches.

Love leaned into a hairy ear and said in a low voice: Coach Woody said if you need to see him, he'll be in his cabin.

A look of alarm came to the coach's face, signified primarily by a crossing and uncrossing of eyes and a high bristle alert for the brows.

Yes, Coach Lowe. Of course. I'll be right with you.

This is one of our fine young graduate coaches, said CVD to the people assembled around him. He needs to talk to me for just one minute. I'll be right back, so you folks don't run off. I'm anxious to talk to each and every one of you.

With a smiling nod to the crowd and an indelicate eye probe

for Love, he stalked toward the lobby with a stride usually reserved for players who jumped offside on fourth and one. Love followed in his wake.

Coach Driver, shouted the AD, moving his tan at rapid speed toward them. I need to talk to you please.

The head coach stopped without warning in the hall and Love nearly smashed into him, avoiding collision by a deft pirouette that left him facing toward the coach, the banquet room, and the approaching athletic director.

Watch where the hell you're going, Lowe.

Yes sir. Sorry about that.

They stood in front of an empty anteroom, and it was into this that the athletic director walked, motioning with a jerk of his head for Coach Driver to follow.

Don't move, said CVD. Stay right where you are.

Yes sir, said Love.

The Bugler's Call

Love had been out in the hall for perhaps ten minutes when he was called into the room. Coach Driver met him at the door and pointed toward a seat at a long rectangular table. There were four such tables in the room and they would be conferring at the one farthest from the door. The walls were blank, other than three prints of noblemen at the hunt. No fox could be seen, but from the expectant look on the faces of the horsemen his musk was thick in the air. A bugler was just putting horn to lips. It was obvious that fox stew with tarragon was on everyone's mind. Perhaps with risotto. Perhaps with couscous.

The chair reserved for Love left him with his back to the door. CVD took his seat across the table from him, next to the tan smile of the athletic director. Whatever doubts Brooke's father once had of Love were assuaged now. He smiled warmly, his tan warming his face, warming and tanning the room. The whole place seemed suddenly soaked in cocoa butter. He had the look of someone about to bestow a wonderful prize.

Come in, Raymond, he said. Yes, sit right there. Make yourself comfortable.

Love did as instructed.

You've enjoyed the Cavalcade so far?

Yes sir.

This answer pleased the athletic director, for he turned to Coach Driver and nodded in a way that seemed to say: *I like this fellow. I like the cut of his jib.*

In response, CVD glanced once at Love in a forlorn way, then stared down at the table in front of him. He rubbed his hand back and forth across the surface and would look nowhere else in the room. The athletic director turned back to Love, shaking out a gold bracelet in the process.

It really was quite an honor for Coach Driver to ask you along, he said. You're getting a firsthand look at another part of the coaching life. A very valuable look for someone who wants to make a career in the profession. You do hope to stay in coaching? This is something you'd like to spend your life doing?

Yes sir.

Good, good. I think you'd do well. And the position you have now with a high-visibility program looks really strong on a resume. Many—if not most—of our graduate assistants land a job with some program or another. It might not be Notre Dame or Michigan. More often than not it's someplace like Eastern Kentucky. But many a coach has started where you are and ended where *he* is.

Saying this, he pointed at Coach Driver, who gave a curt acknowledging nod, before resuming his staring contest with the table.

We understand there was a dispute in the bar tonight, said the athletic director.

This wasn't posed as a question so Love didn't answer. His father had told him to be careful of answering a question that hadn't been asked. He'd also taught him just to sit tight during a pregnant pause, for a pregnant pause was just what the athletic director was now offering up. The AD looked at Love and waited and Love looked at the AD and said nothing.

Is that right?

Yes sir.

And you were there when it happened, weren't you?

Yes sir.

The athletic director nodded, no longer smiling. He seemed less tan when not smiling. Beside him, Coach Driver cleared his throat.

I understand that Coach Woody and Mr. Dutch were talking and Mr. Dutch said something that upset him. Then Coach Woody stood up suddenly and knocked into Mr. Dutch.

No. That's not right.

If you'll just let me finish, said the athletic director, holding up a silencing finger. We're here to assess what happened. So, after Coach Woody knocked into Mr. Dutch, Mr. Dutch pushed Coach Woody away. That was when Coach Woody threw a punch that hit the most generous booster this university has. The most generous booster this university has ever had.

Love was trying to control his thoughts. He didn't want to sound rash or emotional.

You'd like to say something?

Yes sir. That's not what happened. What you just described. Coach Woody was provoked. And it was Mr. Dutch who pushed him first. Coach Woody didn't knock into Mr. Dutch at all. That's incorrect. That's wrong.

Maybe you didn't have a good angle on what happened. Mr. Dutch very strenuously holds that Coach Woody bumped into him first. He said this startled him and he just acted instinctively by pushing Coach Woody away. It sounds like it happened so fast and was so chaotic that what did or didn't happen will be hard to determine. At the end of the day one of our coaches committed an act of violence in a public place. That won't fly. We can't have that.

Love said nothing. Why were they even talking to him if they'd already made up their minds? Who cared what a grad assistant had to say when his word disputed the bigwig donor?

Coach Woody will be relieved of his duties tomorrow, said the athletic director.

When he said this, Love looked over at his head coach. He kept looking at him until CVD managed to raise his head from the table and meet his gaze. Though the gel in his hair still glistened like stars in the night sky, the intimidating eyes were nowhere to be found.

The athletic director was smiling again now and the shine of his white teeth illuminated the room, bouncing off the stardust in CVD's hair, and the fluorescent light above, and even off his own glittering gold bracelet.

Here's where you come in. Coach Woody is gone no matter what. That decision has been made and is irrevocable. But Coach Driver, understandably, is a little concerned about fan reaction to this decision. As you know, Coach Woody is a popular figure among the fans and has a long history with the university. It would be a lot easier on Coach Driver and the school, and even on Coach Woody himself in the long run, if the reason for his dismissal was so cut and dried that it was beyond question. If he provoked Mr. Dutch and then punched him, no one could argue that he shouldn't be fired. If, on the other hand, your version of the story was to get out, that might not go over as well. And the team would suffer. And the head coach would suffer. And the fans would suffer as well. It would be very messy for everyone. You don't want that.

Love didn't say what he did or didn't want, but waited for the other shoe to drop.

We'd like you to talk to a sportswriter who's here tonight. Clay Dibble, you've probably heard of him. Mr. Dutch is talking to Clay right now. He's telling him about the episode in the bar. All in all, Clay is a friend of the university and he'll want what's best for everyone involved. We're not asking you to confirm Mr. Dutch's version of things. All you have to say is that you were there when a disagreement broke out. Say things happened so fast you're not sure what you saw. That's the truth.

No, that's not the truth.

One man says one thing, another man says something else. Who's to know?

Coach Woody knows. And so does his friend Snort.

Who?

His friend who was there in the bar too. His name is Snort. You met him this afternoon.

We feel safe that this Snort fellow won't go to the media. And you know as well as I do that Coach Woody won't. He's never been one to lobby his cause. And he's a team player. He wouldn't want this to cause any turmoil with the players or with Coach Driver. He's loyal to a fault, surely you know that.

Yes, I know that.

It's cleaner this way. Simpler and neater.

It's just not the truth.

I've had about enough out of you, young man, said the athletic director, shaking a finger in Love's face. We're not asking you to lie. Clay Dibble will just need someone for his *witnesses-say-a-dispute-broke-out* lead-in. That sort of thing. After that I'm sure he'll write an elegiac piece about Coach Woody the man, the coach, and the icon. It'll be tastefully done. Everyone loves Coach Woody, but everyone also knows he's a bit of a wild card. Always has been, always will be. People will be saddened, but not surprised, that he lost his temper in a moment of passion.

It was amazing, thought Love, how quickly this had all been thought out. You had to be smart and fast to be in the upper echelon of athletics. And slick. Slick as hell.

I'll talk to Clay and tell him not to ask a lot of follow-up questions, said the AD. Again, no one is asking you to lie. You can just say something like: *an argument broke out and then things got physical. It was an unfortunate event.* That's it. Okay?

No. It's not okay.

The athletic director offered a smile now, one of faux surprise.

You understand that you're on a one-year contract, right? All graduate assistants are. We can let people go anytime we want. Some folks are better fits than others. It happens all the time.

Love didn't respond to this. He didn't have any words for the rush of thoughts going through his head.

But now the AD changed tones yet again. His strategy seemed to be the giving and taking away of his tan affection. Love wondered whom this would actually work on.

Coach Driver says he's got a position open for a graduate assistant. One who's actually on the field coaching. That's what a head coach really wants to see when he's hiring. Who's been down on the field getting their hands dirty with the players. A recommendation from Coach Driver will virtually guarantee a job at a Division I school for any young coach fortunate enough to get one. You understand that, don't you?

Yes, I understand that.

Do you have any other connections?

Not really.

We're just asking you to be a team player. We're not asking you to lie. An argument did break out. Things did get physical.

Love had often marveled at the non-apology apologies that athletes and coaches offered when they were in trouble and how they always managed to avoid taking responsibility or placing direct blame. Nopologies. Mea sortas.

I am deeply sorry if anyone was offended by my comments . . . it was not our intent to circumvent the rules . . . the panties in question were not on my head.

Anything and everything but the unvarnished truth, the direct distributing of blame or absolution.

Not telling exactly what happened is telling a lie, said Love.

No, it's not.

Love didn't counter this. It would do no good.

Are you a team player or not?

Yes, said Love. I'm a team player.

Good good.

Just not this team.

He knew what he was doing. Even as he was pushing his chair under the table—even now a formality—he had the image of himself on a high school field. It wasn't what he wanted. Or not what he wanted without at least seeing how he'd do at the college level. But at least it was coaching. Maybe things worked out for a reason.

You're making a huge mistake, said the AD. Coach Woody would tell you that himself.

This isn't just about Coach Woody, said Love.

Coach Driver looked up now as he was about to leave, his eyes dull and unanimated, his gelled hair glimmering in the light. He looked like a man who wouldn't mind trading places right now with Love.

Coach Driver, said Love, I appreciate the opportunity. I learned a lot this year.

CVD winced a bit at this, then nodded.

Love thought he'd never seen a more miserable-looking man.

Meet the Press

Love opened the door to find that most of the crowd who had been waiting for Coach Driver in The Great Hall was now assembled in the lobby. He was no longer a member in good standing of the Pigskin Cavalcade, and its bonhomie made the finality of his recent meeting all the more real. He was out of a job and so was Coach Woody. One minute they're riding smoothly along two-way Loyalty Street, the one that always circles back to Respect, the next they're being run over by a party boat cranking the Dixie Chicks. He'd known all along he was a long shot to get the coaching position, but he'd counted on that second year of the assistantship. Had taken it for granted, in fact.

He walked down the hall, trying to recall the terms of his apartment lease and whether he could get his deposit back. In the lobby, he made his way through the lively and affable crowd, toward the parking lot and his cabin. He had his mind on a cold beer—several in fact now that he was no longer a university representative—and hanging out with Julie by the lake after he'd checked in with Woody.

About halfway through the lobby, however, he found his path obstructed by a monochromatic roadblock, the same large couple in matching coveralls who'd so unmoored Mrs. Driver earlier in the evening. They were stuck in place trying to decide whether to break out into an impromptu version of the school fight song or the familiar strains of the alma mater.

Love thought either choice would be appropriate and wished they'd just go ahead and choose. As he looked for ways around the human blockade, snippets of an impassioned dialogue came into his ear. On the other side of the coverall wall, two young men were arguing about the hand size of a recent commitment to the football program. One was adamant that the star quarterback signee had a ten-and-a-quarter-inch hand. He'd read it in several magazines and knew, personally, a friend of the recruit's cousin who would vouch-safe the same. The other begged to differ. It had come in at ten and seven/eighths at last measuring. On this he was willing to bet hard American cash. The recruiting website he belonged to had shown a photo of the mitt in question next to a ruler. Every bit of ten and seven/eighths. And mind you, the kid was still growing! Come this fall, he'd be gripping that leather with eleven inches of manpower!

The conversationalists paused for a moment to take in the image, lost in man-inch reverie. Who knew? Maybe next year's starting quarterback dilemma was solved after all.

This reverie came to an abrupt end with the sighting of Love, who had just squeezed through an opening in the roadblock when the woman—the larger section of the barrier—had reached into her duffle bag for a can of Pringles.

Look who we have here, said TNT, who took a step in front of Love as if to block his path yet again.

Love had not properly steeled himself for a Bataan Death March to the parking lot, but he did so now. He looked down at the squatty keg of explosives and considered what he'd do if this aggressive-looking fellow continued to bar his exit. He wasn't exactly waiting to be called Hondo in a roadhouse bar in Wyoming, but did feel his patience for chat room disputes was at its lowest ebb.

So Anthony Scott's going to be the starting QB in the fall? said TNT. Yeah right.

The Gridiron Wizard, as befit his title and station in the virtual world of sports knowledge, stepped in front of his pink-hued friend and said: I'll handle this if you don't mind.

He now looked up at Love, his wizardly face scowling beneath a university-themed baseball cap. It was apparent he was fond of the hat because he'd worn it throughout the duration of dinner. He took a moment to compose himself.

Listen man, I'm not going to stand here all night, said Love.

I trusted you to be a reliable source, said the Gridiron Wizard.

A source for what?

My forum.

I thought it was a chat room.

It's a forum.

I thought it was basically just a place for guys to whine when the team lost and to talk about what player or coach they'd seen at lunch that day.

You have no idea what we're about. We traffic in information. Pure and simple.

Okay, said Love. I understand now.

So what do you expect me to do? I put it out there that Anthony Scott might be the starting quarterback next fall and the next day he's gone? Do you know how that made me look to the other guys in the forum?

I guess not.

The Wizard was breathing hard now and some near-color had come into his pale cheeks. To the other members of the forum he was simply the Wizard, with the Merlin hat avatar to prove it. But Love was seeing the real thing, live and in person. It occurred to him that the poor fellow was unused to face-to-face confrontation, as mild and non-confrontational as this now was.

Listen, said Love. I'm sorry I said that about Anthony Scott. I didn't mean to cause anyone any trouble. I was just screwing around.

The Wizard blinked approximately three hundred times but said nothing. Love wondered if he'd gone suddenly comatose and wished for some instrumentation to check his current brain-wave pattern.

I wish I hadn't done it, said Love.

Here the Gridiron Wizard put out his small pale hand. It couldn't have measured more than four and seven/eighths inches.

Forget it, he said.

Love took the hand and shook it. He felt worse now than when he'd been in there with Coach Driver and the athletic director.

Thanks, said Love, moving subtly past, moving ever so slowly, toward the door and away from the virtual dust presently being kicked up by the Cavalcade.

TNT had come up now and placed a comradely and comforting hand on the thin shoulder of the Gridiron Wizard. And as Love passed by, he gave a quick dude-to-dude nod of *it's cool*. In doing so, he offered up a fist to bump, the twenty-first-century peace pipe.

And then the Gridiron Wizard, his eyes watery from the ordeal but now brave with forgiveness, added his small fist to the assembly.

Love hesitated for a moment, then man-touched them one by one. It seemed the only thing to do.

The next moment he was outside and walking the short paved path through the woods to his cabin, hearing the tree frogs, the cicadas, a fish breaking the surface out on the lake and landing with a decisive plop. Nature was good, he was telling himself. One only had to stop for a moment and breathe in the clean spring air, see the bats flitting and barrel-rolling like barnstorming stunt pilots, to know that life did not begin and end with SEC football. He took another deep breath, feeling that if nothing else, he was free of the nonsense of the last few days. All things Cavalcade were permanently in the rearview.

Hey Raymond, called a wheezy voice from the nearby woods. Then this same forest dweller was bustling through the underbrush in Love's direction. Next came a watery clearing of throat, as if perhaps a small insect had been swallowed with the suddenness of the decision to move. A few hacking gags ensued. Then spitting was worked into the equation, quite a lot of it actually.

Love thought it was time to face facts. The bug had flown in at a high rate of speed, enabling it to make unusually deep penetration into the windpipe. Quick or easy dislodgement was unlikely.

Coming to the same realization, the man in the woods approached, navigating his way by the light from a cell phone, his loafers tentative, his reddish brown moustache moist from recent trials.

So, said Clay Dibble, arriving on the walk beside Love, it sounds like you've had an interesting night, all in all.

The sportswriter had kept his cell phone open and now held it up to better gauge Love's reaction to this statement.

Looks like you have too, said Love.

I don't know what you mean.

Love smiled. He thought that people who observed and wrote about others for a living probably disliked being observed more than most. The shoe on the other foot fitting a little more snugly than was comfortable.

Didn't you just swallow a bug?

No. Just a little trouble with allergies. But enough about me. I was just on the phone with the athletic director. And I talked to Mr. Dutch earlier. Seems like there was a little problem between him and Coach Woody in the hotel bar. Was wondering what you have to say about it.

Not a thing.

Listen, I'm going to write an article about Coach Woody that will run in tomorrow's paper, one way or another. I just thought you might want to add your two cents.

I thought you were writing an article on Mrs. Driver and the role of the coach's wife.

Oh, that can wait. Plenty of time for an article like that. That's one of those pieces for a slow Sunday in the summer. Plus I'm still gathering information.

Well, she should be back at the hotel soon, so you might want to hurry over and get your spot behind the Coke machine before someone else snags it.

I got off on the wrong floor the other night. That's all it was.

Just took you awhile to figure that out, I guess.

Listen, did Coach Woody start the fight or not?

No. But you won't put that in your article.

You have no idea what I'll write.

I've a good idea you don't want to make Sammy Dutch mad. I'm betting he's got quite a few little goodies for journalists who are for and against the same people he is.

The sportswriter smiled at this.

You have no idea what you're getting into, said the sportswriter. That is, if you even stay in college coaching.

For the second time in ten minutes, it had been brought to Love's attention how little he knew about college football and the ancillary things that attend it. Love thought that was likely so. He knew football and how to coach it but not much about the rest. He did, however, have a good feel for the man standing in front of him.

Do you even like sports? Love asked.

As he said this, he removed his cell phone and shined the light on the sportswriter's face.

Clay Dibble stood blinking for a few seconds under the glare of the light, but gave no answer to the question. Then he turned and started walking back to the main lodge. He had a story to file, after all, and couldn't waste time on triviality.

About thirty yards from the cabin, Love began to hear music of the operatic variety. The stereo was being run at full bore and the windows of the cabin were shaking with the stress of those decibels. The tenor presently singing sounded fairly full of himself. It wouldn't be accurate to say that the song was triumphant, as it might have been after a great victory on the battlefield or when first in love or even after offering the Whammo-Bammo! to Landry Burns. But the man singing seemed satisfied with the day at hand, jaunty even. He was making no apologies.

Love approached the front window and peered in. Coach Woody stood in front of one speaker, his friend Snort in front of the other. They were singing for all they were worth.

Anything Love needed to say could wait till later. The Fairview tenors looked to be just rounding into form and Love didn't have the heart to intrude.

Gumption Man

ove and Julie were out on the dock in front of Julie's cabin, sitting on chairs they'd moved down from the house and drinking canned beer. The music coming from next door was not nearly so loud as it had been earlier, and the genre had switched without segue from opera to outlaw country. Waylon, Johnny, Willie, Merle. Earthy names from another era. Woody and Snort were sitting out on the deck now, listening to the music that drifted out through the sliding glass door. Love couldn't see the old crooners from his vantage point on the lake and they couldn't see him, but he could hear their soft singing and the occasional murmur of conversation between tunes.

So you're definitely out? You're sure about that?

Yeah, I'm pretty sure, said Love. The AD said I wasn't a team player.

Team player? That's funny. The only team he cares about is the booster team. And the public relations team. And maybe the team down at the tanning salon.

Love laughed.

When he's down at the tanning booth, said Julie, do you think he leaves his sweatbands and tennis socks on? Or does he go for the full body tan, front and back?

I refuse to entertain the thought.

It's too late if you say something like that. You've already pictured it. So what was it? Front or back? Bracelet and socks or au naturel?

It's not going to work.

I think it did.

It didn't.

What about a thong then and socks but no bracelet? And he's reading a novel.

Moving on, said Love.

Julie smiled slyly, shaking her beer to see how much was left. Her attempts to take his mind off his uncertain future were transparent, but Love appreciated them nonetheless.

What about his daughter then?

Love wasn't sure if they were still playing the imagine-the-tanning-booth game, but thought he might have an easier time this go-round if that were the case.

What about her?

Are you guys still book club dating?

No, said Love. That's over.

That's too bad. You're going to miss the fresh bread and fondue.

I wish you'd gone with me at least one time.

It did always make me hungry when you talked about it.

Yeah, said Love, the food was pretty good.

They each took a sip of beer. There was a beer apiece in the fridge and after that they'd have to start in on Coach Woody's stash. Love planned on doing just that. He no longer had to be up and at em in the morning and thought he wouldn't mind sitting out by the lake until the sun came up.

Julie finished the last of her beer and set the can down beside her.

Any idea what Coach Woody is going to do now? she asked.

No.

He's kind of old to change jobs, isn't he?

Love started to mention how Coach Woody was still a vibrant presence on the field and a great teacher, but checked himself. It usually didn't end prettily for old coaches.

Well, maybe a job will turn up, said Julie. You never can tell.

That's true, said Love.

What about you? Do you have any plans yet?

His own unemployment was a topic he felt little interest in. What was the point of sitting on a dock and drinking beer if you had to consider unpleasant things?

No plans, he said. I'll probably just head to my folks' house and try to figure out my options. My dad needs an offensive coordinator, so I could do that if nothing else turns up.

You could try again next year to get on with a college team.

I guess so. We'll see.

I'm not really sure what I'm going to do either.

This caught Love by surprise. He said, really?

Yeah, I waited too late to start looking for teaching jobs. And I'm not completely sure I want to teach anyway. I guess I could stay on at the football office for another year, but there's no guarantee the position would be full-time. I'm thinking about maybe just picking a cool place to live and moving there. Waiting tables or doing some odd job just to make ends meet until I decide for sure what I want to do. You know, it's starting to dawn on me that this sports management degree might not be the fast track to success I thought it was.

Love smiled at this last comment, as was expected whenever they made fun of their graduate program. But his mind was on other things. One important word had been left out of Julie's discussion of future plans. That word was *fiancé*.

I thought you were going to head back to D.C. after you graduated. To be with your fiancé while he finished up law school.

No, said Julie. I'm not moving to D.C.

It was now or never for the question he'd been wanting to ask.

And while it wasn't exactly the epitome of gumption as defined by Coach Woody, it was a move in that direction for a fellow like Love.

How are you guys doing by the way?

We're not, said Julie.

Really? Since when?

Well, officially about two weeks ago, but it's been moving in that direction for quite awhile now.

Love nodded, trying to keep his face in something of a neutral expression, a look meant to convey support or compassion or some other emotion he didn't actually feel. His eyes faced the lake, but he could sense Julie beside him, still in the pale pink sundress, long legs stretched out before her and less than a foot from his own. Such a short distance. Not much farther than the length of a high school quarterback's hand. He realized that several seconds had passed since Julie's revelation and that as yet he'd made no reply.

I guess long distance relationships are pretty tough, he said.

Yeah, they are. But that wasn't the main problem. We just didn't have that much in common. We realized that by Sunday morning after a weekend together, we'd run out of things to say. He's a nice guy, but I don't believe it would have worked out long term.

For a brief spell as Julie talked Love's mind had raced with possibility. Ever since he'd known her, he'd liked her. But the leap from goofing-around pals to something more substantial was a long one, and one that felt beyond him at this juncture. Anyway, they'd soon be going their separate ways. He hadn't the money to stay in town and he'd have to get going on some kind of job as soon as possible. If he were to say anything of the romantic variety, it would just be awkward.

It was then that he felt a leg brush against his. Before he could give this much thought, a hand was on his knee and Julie was leaning over to kiss him on the cheek.

After she'd settled back in her chair, Love gave her a quizzical but not displeased look, as if to say, *what was that for?*

You just looked like you needed a kiss, said Julie.

Love nodding, smiling. He had needed a kiss and hadn't even known it. But here was the question. Was it simply a friendly kiss, a sympathy kiss? A kiss on the cheek could mean anything or nothing at all.

Julie was now leaning back in her own chair, her leg no longer against his. He thought of the word *gumption* as it applied to situations like this. He turned in his chair to face Julie, aware of the idiot's grin on his face that he couldn't suppress. Then he placed one hand on a bare shoulder and the other on a knee and offered an unapologetic kiss, the sort not commonly shared by mere friends and acquaintances.

This went on for quite awhile, the two of them configuring their chairs to make the arrangement more comfortable without bothering to stop the kiss, scooting a bit here and there. Had this been a scene from one of the book club books, the smell of olive oil and sun-dried tomatoes would be gently wafting in the air, the aroma from the kitchen amplifying the moment, food and romance in perfect union. Here on the dock, there was only the faint smell of honeysuckle drifting in on the breeze, but Love wasn't one to complain.

They were taking a break from the proceedings, Julie now sitting on Love's lap with her arm draped around his shoulder. Love was looking out over the lake, trying to fathom—to put in perspective— this wonderful reversal of luck. He felt he had gumption in spades now. He was Gumption Man. Or Mr. Gumption, if you preferred. He'd answer to either. At one point during the smooching, he'd considered offering the very practical suggestion that they might be more comfortable inside, but had decided against it. He wasn't convinced his current—if still embryonic—stint of awesome smoothness would hold if they moved from this dock. The dock, in fact, might be the one place in the world where he could work his special magic. Better not risk it.

I guess now you can tell me what that question was from your book club, said Julie. The one you didn't want to answer.

Love cleared his throat several times in response to this. Nothing could have been further from his mind than the book club, its members, or supplementary reading guides in general. He was outside on a beautiful night with a girl in a sundress sitting on his lap. A very nice girl. How many nights like this did a person get?

What's that? said Love.

I asked if you were going to tell me what the book club question was.

It was Question #8.

Oh, come on.

No chance.

It can't be that bad.

Buy a copy and see for yourself.

Okay, what would it take for you to tell me?

I don't know. Something big. Something really good.

Our first kiss doesn't count as something really good?

Love smiled. He liked the sound of that word, *first*. There was implication in a word like that.

Something momentous, I mean.

What was the book called again? Julie asked.

The Bon Bon Girls.

Julie smiled at this.

Wait, said Love. You remembered the title, didn't you? You just like getting me to say it out loud.

Julie smiled, then she laughed.

Then Love was laughing too.

The Lake Calls

Love walked quietly up the back steps of the deck, not wanting to wake Coach Woody and Snort if they'd already hit the sack. The sliding glass door was open but music no longer played on the stereo. It was just after one when Love entered the cabin to find Coach Woody sitting on the couch reading. All the lights were off but for the lamp on the table behind him. The book looked to be a biography of Francis Marion, the famed Swamp Fox of the Revolutionary War. Love thought he'd come in without being heard, but after finishing up a page and marking his spot, Coach Woody looked up and said: well look what the cat drug in.

Love felt like a teenager trying to sneak in past curfew, only to find his father up waiting.

Hope you didn't wait up, he said. I know I'm supposed to be the responsible one on this trip.

Coach Woody smiled at this. In the dim light from the lamp, he looked older than Love remembered, the lines on his face deeper, his hair more subdued than usual. Love went to the refrigerator and got a beer. He'd only had the two at Julie's and though he'd not minded the interruption in his drinking plans, he did think he might have a couple more before bed.

Do you mind if I get a beer? Love asked.

Lord no. Help yourself.

You want one?

I'll drink one with you.

Love procured the beverages, handed one to Coach Woody, and sat down in the chair nearest the sliding glass door. He popped his beer and drank with a long, satisfying gulp.

I believe you were thirsty, said Woody.

Yes sir.

Beer tastes better in warm weather.

I think it does. Where did Snort get to?

He's got some animals he needed to feed, so he hit the road. I thought we might swing by his place tomorrow if you're not in a hurry to get back. He's got a neat little cabin out in the woods.

I'd like to see it.

Hey, you ever read anything about the Swamp Fox? He was a sly dog, I tell you that much. Those Redcoats never knew which way he was coming at em.

I'm pretty good on European history and not bad on the Civil War, but I need to read up on the Revolution.

Oh, that's my favorite. I don't care what anybody says, George Washington is the greatest president we've ever had. He defined the job, you know.

I always thought Washington was a little overrated, said Love smiling.

Shit you do.

Love grinned and took another sip of his beer.

I got books stacked to the ceiling I've been waiting to read, said Woody. Looks like I might finally have a little time to read em. I'm looking forward to it.

Love nodded. He couldn't tell if Coach Woody was whistling by the graveyard or if he meant what he said. The thought of the old coach reading in his den next fall and not on a football field was odd to consider. It also brought home the finality of his own situation with a clarity that had been lacking out on the dock with Julie. He'd never don the fashion-statement visor. He'd never chomp gum with his mouth agape for the viewing audience at home.

You ever been hungry and had a peanut butter cracker and been surprised how good it tasted, how satisfying it was?

Love thought about it. He had, in fact, experienced that sensation.

Yes sir, he said, I've noticed that before.

Well, if I'm eating peanut butter crackers next fall, that'll be fine. Nobody needs to worry about me.

All right, said Love. Fair enough.

I'd have liked to coach with you for another fall. See what you've got. See if any of those plays you've got diagrammed in your notebooks will fly.

I won't be on the staff next year either.

What? asked Coach Woody, sitting up straight on the couch, then standing up completely. What are you talking about?

Love quickly related how things had gone in his meeting with the athletic director and Coach Driver. For reasons he couldn't quite explain, he left out the part about the request to talk to Clay Dibble and give a less than truthful account of what had transpired in the bar.

Hold on, said Coach Woody. So you gave my message to Coach Driver and then they wanted to talk to you alone? Both of them, Coach Driver and the AD?

Yes sir.

None of this should affect you. You didn't do anything.

Love got up and went to the refrigerator for another beer, hoping the discussion would soon be over.

Coach Woody followed him to the kitchen.

They asked you to play ball on something, didn't they?

Love lingered about the open refrigerator, not responding.

They wanted you to help get them and old Sammy off the hook? Help with the PR a bit? I tell you one damn thing, every athletic director in the country is just alike. Sometimes I think there's a factory up in Flint, Michigan that just pops em off of a conveyor belt knowing how to cover their own asses.

Probably so, said Love.

Come on, son, you can tell me. It doesn't matter now. I can't blame them for letting me go. I had that coming. I knew better than to hit a man like Sammy Dutch. The smart thing to do was just to let him yap, then head on out the door. But they're sorry as hell if they took it out on a young fellow just minding his own business.

Love turned now and faced the old coach, handing him a fresh beer in the process.

It doesn't matter, he said. I always kind of thought it was a long shot I'd have a college coaching career. It was a good experience being on Coach Driver's staff. And I think I've got a job lined up already if I want it.

Who with?

On my dad's staff.

Do you want to coach high school?

It'll be all right.

I didn't ask you if it would do. I asked if that's what you want to do. Is that your goal, to be a high school coach?

No sir.

I didn't think so.

Woody took a sip from his beer, then sat down at the small counter that divided the kitchen and den.

Listen, he said. Connections and self-promoting can help you get a first job, maybe even a couple of jobs. But you can't connect your way to being a great coach. At some point, you've just got to have what it takes. You aren't much of a self-promoter, are you?

I guess not, said Love.

All right, that's fine. But let me ask you this. Do you want a career as a coach or do you want to be a great coach?

I wouldn't really want to be a coach if I didn't think I had a chance to be a really good one.

Great, you mean. You can say great.

Okay, great.

All right then, you can stop worrying. The great coaches trust their ability and they trust their luck. If you're made of the right stuff, you'll get where you want to go. If you're not, you won't. Either way the pressure to politic or do things you're not comfortable with is off. I'm assuming you're not afraid to work hard, of course.

No, I'm not afraid to work hard.

I didn't think so, said Woody. But I tell you what. Let's forget these peckerwoods that just let two good coaches go because they didn't want to hurt some rich boy's feelings and sit out on the deck and talk a little football. With all this Cavalcade bullshit, we hadn't had much of a chance to talk about our game.

I'd like that, said Love.

But first things first. There's a lake out there that's been calling my name since I got here. I'm heading in. Right now. I'll be diving off that dock in sixty seconds.

Love smiled.

You coming?

Oh hell yes, said Love.

Mea Sortas

Love checked the time. It was not quite eight a.m. He thought his chances of wooing Julie were probably minimal at this hour, so he decided to head up to the main lodge for a bite to eat. Julie and Coach Woody likely wouldn't be up for awhile and he was too hungry to wait.

After he finished breakfast, he still had time to kill and went to the computer in the lobby. Without quite knowing why—perverse curiosity or a stubborn masochistic streak—he went first to the *Bugle Register* website and Clay Dibble's column, where he found the following:

> Coltrane's last notes were always sad. Is that what we remember? Or do we remember the performance? All of it? From beginning to end? To many he was a legend. A throwback to a bygone era. But even legends make mistakes. Bill Woody made one last night. A big one. One that cost him his job. Circumstances are cloudy. But some facts are known. A punch was thrown. Coach Woody threw it. In a public place no less. Leaving the university with no choice. Coach Bill Woody had to go.

The article went on like this for quite awhile but Love had stopped paying attention about halfway through. As he'd read the eulogy for Coach Woody's coaching career, however, a whimsical thought had come to mind. What if he could get the old coach to offer a nopology? Love thought something along these lines would be perfect, should the subject of Sammy Dutch come up in the next few days:

I'm sorry if anyone was offended by my actions. I regret if anyone, anyone at all, perceived my actions in a way that upset them. It was not my intent to be perceived in an upsetting fashion.

It could be better, but he and Coach Woody could work on it in the car, craft the perfect non-statement, a mea sorta for the ages. But would the old coach play along? Surely he would. What did he have to lose now? What did either of them?

I promise from this day forward to be diligent in trying to be perceived as others would like to perceive me, no matter what I might do . . .

Love knew he could go on like this forever, but thought he'd save some of it for the long ride home. He was about to head back to the cabin when he remembered another member of the media who might have something to say about the events of last night. Yes, there was no way around it, it was Gridiron Guru time.

Upon entering the land of football man-chat, he was greeted by these topic headers:

Anybody know where I can get a v-neck like CVD wears on the sidelines?
Wondering about coaches who hunt and fish
A Weird Feeling About Next Year (and not in a good way)
Why does ESPN hate us so bad?

Although Love found each of these promising in its own way, his eyes soon settled on the following:

Anthony Scott Issue Cleared Up.

Yes, that was the one he was looking for:

Gridiron Wizard (Ninja Master of Gridiron Gurus): Good Morning Gurus. Just a quick follow-up on the misinformation I received about Anthony Scott this week. It turns out that the staff member who told me that was trying to pull some kind of (lame) gag. He apologized profusely and I accepted the apology. While I don't like the idea of someone goofing around when it comes to our program, the staff member is a young fellow and I truly believe he meant no harm. I'm sure he'll learn from this experience. So as far as I'm concerned, the matter is closed. And good riddance to Anthony Scott.

TNT: I agree with the Wizard on this one. The source in question is just young and has not yet learned how to conduct himself as a member of the program. Not a bad guy at all. Just a little immature. If it makes anybody feel better, I did kick his ass in golf.

Ballstud: Glad to put this behind us, GW. Like you, I value good information and reliable sourses. Thanks for all you do to keep us informed on all matters relating to the program. It means a lot.

KidGenius: I have a couple of *sourses* on my feet today from breaking in a new pair of shoes. I don't value them that much, but I do value Ballstud! Rock on Stud!

Ballstud: Sources, I mean. Hey, I thought Kid-diapers was on probation.

Gridiron Wizard (Ninja Master of Gridiron Gurus): I gave the Kid a shorter sentence. Figured he was over-excited about being done with school for the semester and just got a little carried away.

KidGenius: You da man, Gridiron Wizard!

Ballstud: That's ok by me. Hate to admit it, but it does get a little dull around here without the Genius. On another topic, I am trying to complete a scrapbook of last year's season and was wondering if anyone has a photo from the Blue Angle flyover opening game.

KidGenius. Re: the photo. Do you care what *angel* it was taken from?

Love flipped back to the main page where this topic header had just appeared:

Coach Woody fired? WTF?

But he decided he'd spent enough time in the chat room. He had to admit he was proud of Gridiron Wizard for revising his draconian stance on KidGenius. It was the right call for everyone involved and now the Kid could get back to doing what he did best, kicking all kinds of Internet ass. As for the comments about his maturity and golf game, Love thought them a small price to pay for harmony in the man-chat.

He was heading back to the cabin, wondering if Julie were up and if she might want to head out to Love's magic dock for a spell. He felt rife with gumption. When his cell phone rang, he was wondering how to disassemble a dock and whether the boards would fit in Coach Woody's trunk.

The number was unfamiliar, but the novelty of getting a phone call was too much to resist. He answered with a saucy *hullo.*

Coach Love? said a feminine voice on the other end.

This is he.

This is Barbara Driver. How are you?

I'm fine, Mrs. Driver, how are you?

Mad as hell. But that's what I'm calling about. I've talked to Von and we've agreed that yesterday's conference with the athletic director was mishandled. So the job is yours if you want it.

I can keep my assistantship?

Yes, of course. And Von wants you to have the on-field coaching position as well.

I'm not quite sure what to say. This is all a big surprise.

Why don't you just say yes? I've let Von know what an asset you'd be to the staff. You can never have enough of the right sorts of people, and I think you're the right sort.

Love managed to mumble some words of thanks, but his mind was reeling.

So, said Mrs. Driver, can I tell my husband you've agreed to the position? And for the record, you don't have to worry about anyone in the administration. Von's making this call.

Hearing Coach Driver referred to again and again as Von disconcerted Love nearly as much as this recent development. He sounded so much smaller and less scary without the full three parts of the CVD moniker. Love pictured a small boy running around in short pants, face sticky with peanut butter, little bug eyes yearning for a ride in his big brother's wagon. Von? It didn't sound right.

Would it be all right if I got back to you or Coach Driver in a little while? I didn't see this coming.

Yes, of course, take all the time you need. And you can call me, not Von. It might be easier that way.

Love said he'd call back shortly, then hung up the phone and stared in a dazed fashion around him. A hundred yards away the athletic director was loading his car in front of their cabin. He thought of Brooke briefly and abstractedly, a person from his distant past. How his luck had changed since he'd walked out of the meeting with Coach Driver and the AD.

But thinking of that meeting reminded him of what they'd wanted him to do and how they'd treated Coach Woody. Did he need the position badly enough to work with those sorts of people? And did he want a position that he'd gotten only because of the intervention of the head coach's spouse?

He called Mrs. Driver. When she answered, he said: Mrs. Driver, I appreciate the offer and I appreciate you going to bat for me. But I believe I'm going to pass and just take my chances elsewhere.

You're sure about that?

Yes maam.

I can't say I blame you. It's a shoddy, shameful business sometimes. I'm still beside myself about Coach Woody. Well, good luck to you. I think you'll do fine wherever you end up.

And then the line was dead and Love was walking toward his cabin, feeling no qualms at all about his decision. If high school coaching it was, so be it.

The Worm Turns

He was on the front stoop of the cabin when someone shouted his name. He turned and saw Sparkman coming his way, wearing university-themed shorts and golf shirt and donning for the first time a Tampa Straw, the very model recently seen on Coach Driver's well-gelled head. Was it actually CVD's hat? Or did Sparkman simply share a haberdasher with the head man? Perhaps Coach Driver had dictated that all members of the staff were to wear these hats until Labor Day and the formal opening of baseball cap season.

Who knew? Who cared?

Love smiled and called hello and Sparkman soon joined him on the stoop. He was shaking the Tampa Straw in a discouraged fashion, saying, man, it's a bummer about the Wood Man.

Love agreed that it was.

Just knocked the shit out of Sammy Dutch, huh?

Yep. But for the record, Sammy Dutch was showing his ass the whole night. And he's the one who got physical first.

Not surprising, said Sparkman. He was pretty lit up.

Love nodded, then couldn't help but smile. Sparkman in a CVD hat? Soon he'd be driving a Lincoln Town Car and pining for the next Larry McMurtry novel.

You laughing about the hat?

Not at all.

Hey, if it's good enough for Driver, it's good enough for me.

There were several comments Love could make here but the time wasn't right. He and Sparkman would soon be heading separate ways. No need to get smart.

Well, said Sparkman, with Woody gone, I guess me and you'll just have to work double time.

I won't be here next year either, said Love.

What? Why not?

Love explained that it was a long story, but ultimately it was a mutual parting of ways.

Sparkman shook his hat in a sincere fashion. Love wasn't sure earnestness was his strong suit, but he admired the attempt.

Man, that sucks, he said. I was looking forward to me and you being the elder statesmen and making the new grad dickheads do all the shit we had to.

Yeah, that would have been fun, Love agreed.

As they were talking, a door slammed at the athletic director's house and Brooke came out.

I'm going to go holler at the babe, Sparkman said. You don't care, do you? You guys don't have anything going, right?

Not at all. Just book club pals.

That still cracks me up.

As well it should.

All right, said Sparkman, I'll see you later then.

He smiled and stuck out a fist to bump. As Love had been man-touching like crazy since the night before, he saw no reason to stop now. It was the Cavalcade way.

At the last minute, however, Sparkman changed his offering from a fist to an extended hand.

Got to go traditional with Coach Love. A man-touch won't do.

Love shook the hand and said, good luck next year.

You too, douche boy.

Then Sparkman was on his way to visit with Brooke, who was now leaning against her parents' car, reading. Love offered her a small, friendly wave, but she was too engrossed in her literature to respond.

Coach Woody wasn't in the cabin when Love walked in, so Love went to his room and packed up his belongings. He carried these and both sets of golf clubs to the car. When he came back in, Coach Woody was walking through the sliding glass door from the deck. He was saying into the phone: all right. I'll find out. Good talking to you too, partner. I'll be in touch.

He closed his phone and glanced for the first time at Love.

You eat breakfast already?

Yes sir, said Love. I'm packed too and ready to go whenever you are.

How was the breakfast up at the dining room?

It was good. Really good.

Oh yeah? What did you have?

Bacon, eggs, hash browns, and a couple of pancakes.

That it?

I was pretty hungry I guess.

Coach Woody smiled at Love's appetite and walked into the kitchen for a drink of water. His back was to Love when he said: you ever been to Boulder, Colorado?

No sir.

You want to?

You mean right now?

No. In about a month, I'd say. I got you a position out there if you're interested.

Love had been caught by surprise for the second time in less than ten minutes.

You got me a spot as a graduate assistant?

No, I didn't think of that. Maybe I should have. I thought you'd rather coach tight ends. That's the position they had. You know anything about tight ends? They're going to be passing the hell out of it, so I doubt you'll need to know a lot about blocking schemes right out of the chute.

Love couldn't comprehend what he'd just heard. A lot of words had come out of Coach Woody's mouth but they seemed tonally and topically inconsistent with Love's career to date in coaching. The old coach came around and patted him on the shoulder. Perhaps it was a pre-Heimlich maneuver. He was smiling at Love's discombobulated status.

They offered forty-five thousand, said Coach Woody. But I said you were a young man with an eye for the ladies and would need more cash. I said if they'd bush it five grand, we might have a deal. So it's fifty thousand and you're a full-time assistant coach. What do you say to that?

Love said nothing. He'd obviously been slipped an excellent hallucinogenic at breakfast.

If you like, said Coach Woody, I could call back and ask about the graduate coach position. Or do you want to hold out for offensive coordinator?

Love smiled. He was too shocked to be happy.

I know blocking schemes, he said. I know line calls.

Good, good. I didn't think you were just another lemonade boy. You'll probably want to teach my linemen a few of your swim moves too.

Love nodded, only half hearing what was being said. Finally he managed to ask how Woody had swung this sweetest of deals.

Well, the head man is an old buddy of mine, said Woody. He's been after me for awhile to come work on his staff so I gave him a call this morning. He made an offer and I told him it sounded good, but I was part of a package deal.

You didn't need to do that, said Love. In fact, you shouldn't have.

Hey man, I wouldn't have done it if I didn't think you could coach a little. I told my buddy you were a hard worker and loyal as they come. Told him you were a coach's son and ought to know a little about the game. And I told him you were the all-time leading passer at Woodford College.

Love smiled. How'd you know that?

I looked you up on the Internet.

Love paced around the room a bit.

Fifty thousand dollars? A year?

Yep.

Love was rich. He'd buy a sports car. He'd buy a sports jacket. He'd buy a set of golf clubs not endorsed by a caddie from the 1950s.

So you're agreed? said Coach Woody, wild-haired and grinning.

Yes sir. Absolutely. I don't know how to thank you.

No need for thanks, my friend. When you're my age, you can help out some talented young buck like yourself who doesn't have connections. I had a little help along the way myself.

Love had just knocked on Julie's door, been greeted with a small kiss—not the full dock session he'd hoped for, but still—and now stood in the den of her cabin, looking apparently a bit worked up.

Are you okay? said Julie. You look kind of weird.

Love's brain was moving quite fast. Julie was still in her pajamas, cute little light flannel numbers, and this had distracted him more than a bit. He found himself thinking about women's outfits and how he liked so many of them.

Do you need some water or something? Are you choking on your tongue? Should I get a spoon?

Love thought it best to handle one thing at a time.

I like those pajamas.

Thank you.

He came over and gave her another kiss, a better one, better than a peck. It was impossible not to. This didn't compose him as much as he'd hoped, but he soldiered on nonetheless.

What do you think about Boulder? he asked.

Colorado?

No, Iowa.

I haven't had my coffee, smartass.

Yes, Colorado.

Never been there, said Julie. I heard it's cool though. I like skiing.

Love agreed that it was cool, or that at least he'd heard so as well. He followed this up with a fairly unintelligible recounting of his last fifteen minutes, emphasizing primarily his job—with its king's ransom of a salary—and the coolness of Boulder. When he'd finished, he said, I think you should move there too.

Just like that?

Yes.

She smiled. He'd thrown a lot at her in a very short time.

I don't know, she said. I'll have to think about it.

Fine. Of course. Just think about it.

Julie smiled and Love wondered if he'd been panting a little as he spoke. His mouth felt pretty dry.

It was Julie who walked over this time. She gave Love a kiss, a good one, which left him wondering why flannel always felt so much softer on women than it did on him.

This job thing is pretty big, said Julie.

Oh hell yes.

Really big.

Julie was smiling when she said this in her cheeky way, and Love sensed something was afoot.

Really big, he agreed.

Momentous, even.

Oh, I don't know about that.

You just landed a job as an actual assistant coach at a Division I school. Yesterday, you were hoping to be a fancy graduate assistant. That's not momentous?

You want Question #8?

Yes. Yes I do.

Seriously?

Yes, seriously.

Love thought about his last seventy-two hours, the movement from book club meetings and general university bootlick to his current position in the universe. There seemed nothing else to do but to move in close to that girl in the soft flannel pajamas and tell her what she wanted to know.

Questions for Discussion

1. This book doesn't talk much about relationships. Despite that fact, did it make you think of a first love? If so, do you think of this first love often? Is there anything you'd do differently if you were that age again? Tell the group how/why this relationship came to an end.

2. This book has no recipes or long descriptions of meals. Did the absence of these reader favorites make you think of books that did include lots of food descriptions? If so, what book made you the hungriest while reading? Did that same book make you want to take a cooking class or start a food blog? What is your favorite Italian recipe?

3. Reveal an intimate detail about yourself to the group, one you've never told anyone else before.

4. The locales in this book are not very exotic. How do you think Love would have performed in Prague or Paris under similar circumstances? Have you ever been to Europe or New York City? If so, describe your perfect night out on the town and whom you'd like to spend it with. Also what you might wear.

5. Coach Woody and Julie tease Love about his lack of gumption? Do you agree with them that he is not as proactive as he could be? What kind of personality do you have? Are you more glass half-full, or glass half-empty? Talk about yourself for awhile and what you like and don't like.

5. Brooke loves good food, good books, and good coffee. Knowing that, do you think she would prefer an intimate lunch in a Parisian bistro with a friend or just curling up on the bench of an Italian piazza with a good book? What about yourself? What is your favorite place to go and why? Alone or with a special someone? What does the way you answer this question say about you? Talk some more about yourself.

6. At one point Love calls his mother. Though we don't really learn much about the nature of this relationship, did it make you think of a time when you have reached out to a parent or vice versa? Do you like your mother? Why or why not?

7. Why do you think it took Love so long to show Julie how he felt about her? Have you ever been slow to share your feelings or an opinion you have?

8. Brook's book club has both a fresh bread maker and a fondue aficionado in it. What about your own? Is it more of an hors d'oeuvres/desserts type get-together or full sit-down meal? Wine or Appletini? Cappuccino or espresso? What foods do you think go best with reading? What coffee blends? Think of the old chicken/egg riddle. Now apply it to food and books. Which do you think comes first? And why? Is there even any way to separate the two? Share your opinion (and a side dish!).

9. Life is difficult. Why do you think that is?

Acknowledgments

No book of mine would be written without my wife, Christy. Her optimism and steady demeanor, especially during the dog days of composition, are what keep the train on the tracks. And no writer could ask for a better muse.

Thanks to Tessa Rane and Maxwell, my sweet children. Comedic writing comes easier with these little jokers flying around the house.

I owe a large debt of gratitude to my primary cadre of early draft editors: Frank Majors, Allen McDuffie, and Chris Vescovo, who have taken time from their busy lives to help me with this book and with the others. Their input on issues of plot, character, and just whether something was funny or not was invaluable and greatly appreciated. Deserving a special mention is Reid Oechslin, who read the manuscript three times before it was sent to the publisher. I am especially grateful for his willingness to read a chapter on short notice and get back to me almost instantaneously with answers to questions I had.

I feel grateful to be working with one of the great editors in the business, Star Lawrence. His excellent feel for language improved this book dramatically, and his grace of manner throughout the process reminded me, yet again, that this was not his first rodeo. I am also appreciative of his advocacy of my work, which has meant so much to me, my family and my career.

Assisting Star on this book was the fantastic Melody Conroy, who proved a stalwart at every turn and who helped shepherd this book from beginning to end, and always with the same style and good humor. Her advocacy of the book bears mentioning as well. It was noted and appreciated. India Cooper, my copy editor, was a joy to work with as well.

Thanks to my agent, David McCormick, and also Bridget McCarthy of the McCormick & Williams literary agency.

Stuart Bloodworth and Howard Bahr said funny lines many years ago that made their way onto these pages. And Leslie Stevens, that expert on airplanes and pepper sandwiches, deserves special thanks for her help with this book and the last one. Barry Paige and Tom Doyle read early versions of the manuscript and offered encouraging words when things were bogging down a bit.

As always I'm appreciative of Mark Parker and David Jeffrey, my department head and dean, whose support has been constant and unwavering. And thanks to Rose Gray, my good friend at JMU, for all that she does. This book was also supported by the James Madison University Program of Grants for Faculty Educational Leaves.

Thanks to Stan Braun for sticking with me through thick and thin.

Finally, thanks to Uncle John, Uncle Larry, and Uncle Tommy for sharing so many wonderful football stories down through the years. And also my father, who participated in the twenty-two-men-in-a-pile drill under Coach Ears Whitworth at the University of Alabama, and lived to tell the tale.